The
Protector

Patricia Bandurka

TRAVELOGUE 219

TL219-208 Edition 1.3 January 2016
Published by: Travelogue 219
                Toronto, Canada
                www.tl219.com

ISBN 978-1-927679-39-5

Editors: Laura Sliz and Jody Aberdeen

Other novels by Travelogue 219:

`In Search of Time Lost' by Barry Schultz
`Nowhere to Run' by John Sliz
`The Code of History' by John Sliz
www.tl219.com

Contents

Mom, this one's for you. Thanks for always telling me to take a chance and for being the first person to read this book. There is no doubt in my mind that you will always be the first person to read my stories and give me feedback. Good and bad. You have no idea how much your input really means to me. Trust me, the story has only just begun. Thanks for always being there for me no matter what.

To Babcia & Didi and Bacha & Dido - I miss you and wish you could have been around to read this. I think you would have enjoyed it and I know that a piece of each of you can be found in this book.

Chapter 1:

The Protector and The Ward

"Death, or a second chance?"

Jesse Knight stared down at his lifeless body. "Damn it!" Clearly, he was dead. It didn't take him long to realize that he'd messed up and that was just not the way he thought he should go.

And what was he doing driving his Porsche when he was so hung over he could barely see straight? What an idiot. The car of his dreams pancaked into a dump truck and then... blinding light.

This must be what people were talking about when they described their near-death experiences. He could feel his body being pulled apart in every direction. It was like being on a never-ending roller coaster ride. Jesse was grateful when he slammed into the ground.

"This must be what hell feels like."

Jesse brushed himself off and got up slowly. The blinding light was now gone and he found himself standing in a narrow tunnel where before him stood a woman in white.

"Excuse me?" she asked.

"I'm sorry. I don't understand," he said as he stared into the angel's blue eyes.

"It's simple. Death, or a second chance?"

Simple? He just crashed his car. He was dead. Wasn't he?

"Aren't I dead?"

"Not yet. The deal is death or a second chance. You're wasting time."

Jesse took a good look at the woman before him. To him, she made Grecian goddesses he'd read about look sub par. Her dirty blonde hair was swept up in a bun with loose tendrils framing her heart shaped face. He didn't believe in perfect but, well, she came pretty close.

"Jesse?"

"Yes," he whispered.

"Death or a second chance?"

The deal was a no brainer. Death wasn't an option, not for Jesse Knight anyway. There was too much living he still had to do.

"Second chance. I definitely want a second chance."

The smile on her face seemed somewhat unsatisfied. It was almost as if she was disappointed by his answer.

"Very well then. Follow me."

The woman started walking and Jesse had no idea what just happened. Realizing that she had left him, Jesse ran after her.

"Hey! Wait up!"

The woman appeared to be gliding as she navigated her way through the grey corridors. There were several twists and turns along the way and Jesse was doing everything he could to keep pace with her.

"Can you clear something up for me?" asked Jesse. "At the moment, am I dead or alive?"

"You are neither," she replied in a soft spoken voice.

Neither. How could he be neither?

"Can you tell me anything?"

She turned to him. "We are almost there."

"Where is there?"

The woman stared at him with annoyance clearly written on her face.

"You will know soon enough."

"Who are you?" he asked.

"Isabella," she said.

"Okay, what are you?"

Isabella stopped and turned to stare at him. As she did, her head tilted to the side slightly and it was clear that she was appraising him. The unamused look on her face spoke volumes and he figured now was the time to shut up.

"I'm a Saviour and I have chosen to save you."

Jesse stood dumbly trying to process everything. This woman was trying to save him? Why?

"We're here," she said.

Jesse took in his surroundings. The room was covered in grey shadows with a steel door. The walls were bare and in the middle of the room sat a worn, wooden chair.

"Redmond, will be here soon," she nodded at him and left.

"Redmond?" Jesse repeated as he broke out of his stupor.

"Who the hell is Redmond?" Jesse regretted those words the minute he said them. He felt a rumbling of thunder beneath his feet and cold wind blowing around him.

"What did I do to deserve this?" he said as he sat in the chair, burying his head into his hands.

"You took life for granted," came a voice. "You must be Jesse Knight. Welcome to Purgatory."

Jesse's head snapped up as he heard the cold tone in the man's voice. He turned slowly. Standing in the shadows, he saw a tall figure with his arms folded standing before him. Jesse tried to look beyond the shadows to catch a glimpse of the man, but it was to no avail.

"Why am I here? I thought for sure I would be way down south burning to a crisp."

"You've been saved. Consider yourself a lucky man."

"I don't get it."

"Let me clear this up for you then. You are my new Protector."

For the second time in a matter of minutes, Jesse was speechless. Scratching the back of his head, he checked for signs of a concussion because there was no way this was happening.

"A what?"

"A Protector," he repeated, as he stepped out from the shadows to shake Jesse's hand. "Allow me to introduce myself. I am Redmond, Keeper of the Protectors."

Jesse stared at the hand before him and shook it. He appraised the so called Keeper very carefully and when Jesse's blue eyes locked onto Redmond's green ones, he knew that this man was not a man you wanted to mess with. His physique alone was intimidating and Jesse had a feeling that he used his build and stature to get what he wanted. Jesse easily compared him to Russell Crowe's portrayal as Maximus from the movie *Gladiator*.

"I think there's been some mistake," he said.

Redmond looked at him for a few moments and replied, "I don't make mistakes. You are here to help those who have been waiting for their day in court."

Jesse's eyes bulged out of his head as he heard Redmond's statement.

"Court? I am not a lawyer! I know nothing about the law-

"Believe me, you not being a lawyer has nothing to do with this. You wanted a second chance and by accepting Isabella's offer, you have become one of my Protectors. "

An uneasy feeling crept over him. Jesse could feel Redmond's gaze suffocating him beyond his control.

"I don't even know what a 'Protector' does" Jesse said as his voice raised a few notches above normal. "How can you ask me to be something I know nothing about?"

Redmond rubbed his beard and smiled, "You know, you are the seventh person who has asked me that question."

"Is that supposed to make me feel lucky?" Redmond's folded arms and stern posture told Jesse immediately that he was, in fact, not impressed with him.

"Mr. Knight, I am the Keeper of the Protectors and you are now a Protector, which means you listen and obey me and the Court of Angels."

"And if I don't?" he asked.

Redmond shrugged. "You die. Somehow though, I don't think you want that as an option."

"Why is that?"

"How did you put it? Ah yes, 'down south, burning to a crisp.' Trust me, you wouldn't survive Purgatory, much less hell. You are a man that thinks he knows everything and you thought that this would be an easy way out. Death, or a second chance. Those who choose a second chance are the ones that fear death. You think you can cheat death? No one can do that. Now, I believe you asked me a question."

Seconds passed and no words would come to Jesse's mind. He knew what he wanted to say, he just couldn't seem to say it.

Redmond laughed. "I never would have pictured you as someone who would be at a loss for words. Never mind, I remember. A Protector is an officer of the Holy Court. You defend those who want a second chance and should the Court grant them that opportunity, your role is to guide them."

Defend them? Guide them? Second chance? Wake up, Jesse he thought to himself. This cannot be real. No such world exists. Jesse closed his eyes and counted to three.

"I know what you're thinking and believe me Mr. Knight this world is real."

"You can't be serious? You are going to make me help

people I don't know and try to get them a second chance at life?" Jesse said in disbelief.

"This is not complicated, Jesse. You made a deal."

"Wait! I did make a deal and from what I know, deals can always be renegotiated."

Jesse saw the Keeper's jaw tighten considerably. For some reason, Jesse had the feeling that he had just poked the bear.

"So, you're choosing death?"

"No," he shouted. Crap. He was screwed. Pigeon holed into doing something he had no business doing.

"I want a second chance, just not like this."

The disapproving glare from Redmond made Jesse extremely nervous. Right now, the Keeper held all the cards and Jesse could only hope that there was some humanity in him.

"You want a way out of this. Well, you have just proven to me that you are a coward and afraid of this challenge."

Jesse hated being called a coward. He could take just about any insult, but coward was one label he couldn't handle.

"I am not a coward. I'm the guy you don't want for this job. I'm a royal screw up. There must be another way."

The look of hesitation on Redmond's face gave Jesse a glimmer of hope that this 'Protector' business would end and he could move on.

"You don't want to die, you don't want to do this. You want to feel. You want to live? Am I right?" he asked.

"Yes! I want to live! I want to go back to earth and just be me. I don't want to walk around like I'm half dead!"

"Seems to me you were half dead already."

Jesse eyes widened at him. Redmond had touched a nerve and at that moment, Jesse wasn't impressed at how personal things had just gotten between them with just one statement.

"Let's get one thing straight. Whatever you think you know, you're wrong. Never make assumptions about me or my life again. You don't know anything. Are we clear?"

Redmond started to pace back and forth across the small room. Jesse crossed his arms. "What do I have to do?" he asked.

"You have to help one person. A person who has waited a

long time to get her second chance. You help this person and I will restore your life as it was before your accident."

"There has to be a catch. It can't be that simple."

"I am a man of my word and up here that means something. Help one person and you will get your life back."

Jesse frowned. There had to be some kind of ulterior motive.

"What is your answer?"

Jesse contemplated this. It wasn't like picking out a car from the Porsche store, this was his life and if helping someone get her life back was part of the deal...then he would do it. There was no other choice. He had to say yes.

"Alright. I accept. I will help this one person in exchange for my life to return the way it was exactly before my accident."

"Very well then. You will meet your ward shortly. Remember, you are helping this person present their case. Hopefully, you will learn the value of life and that not just *anyone* can have a second chance at it."

Jesse unfolded his arms and waved them around.

"Whoa, when you say shortly, do you mean today? Look, I'll do the job. I'll help the person, just don't expect a miracle to happen. I don't know who was thinking that I could do this because I guarantee you they need their head examined. Then again, perhaps I need my head examined for agreeing to this."

"Go to Room 23, Jesse," said Redmond. "It's the fourth door on your right. There you will receive further instruction."

Within an instant of saying his final words, Redmond disappeared in a cloud of red smoke that smelled like cherries. "This can't be happening!" Jesse groaned.

***

On a maple wood bench sat a young, beautiful, successful, woman who once had it all. One minute she was staring at her bright, white dress and the next minute, she was staring into a bright, white light. Her memory was still a little vague, but from what she could recall, she had been walking to her limo, when out of nowhere, a car rammed right into her.

Natalie Parker's acceptance of her own death had been anything but easy. She was confused, scared, and alone. The anger she had felt as she entered Purgatory coursed through her veins. But it was Redmond, Keeper of the Protectors, who assured her that one day, everything would be okay. To this day she wondered what she had done to deserve such a fate and she was now on the precipice of learning the truth.

So here she was, sitting on a bench just as she had seven years ago. Only now she wasn't only waiting for her day in court. She was waiting for her Protector. The one who would help her get her life back. As the minutes continued to pass, she began to worry.

"Where is this Protector?" she said, and stood up. Natalie didn't want to get her hopes up because all of this seemed to be too good to be true. She had done her share of waiting, now she wanted her life back. The idea that someone had the power to help a person renew their life amazed her in ways she still couldn't fathom.

During her stay in Purgatory, she had met people just like her, waiting for their day to plead their case. Some of her friends were lucky. Others that she had met were not. One of them, Drew, had told her that the opportunity of getting a second chance solely relied on how good your Protector was, and she knew that whoever her Protector was would literally have the fate of her life in their hands.

Natalie began to pace the floor when she felt a tap on her shoulder. She turned around hoping to see her Protector. Instead she was greeted by the solemn eyes of Redmond, Keeper of the Protectors, and she immediately knew something wasn't right.

"Is something wrong?" she asked.

His hesitation to her question made her that much more anxious. For the past seven years, Redmond had been her mentor and friend and if there was one thing she knew about him, Redmond never minced words with her. He was honest and trustworthy. Looking at him now, she didn't see her friend. She saw a Keeper just doing his job.

"No, don't worry, Natalie. Your Protector is preparing. There is one thing though."

"Yes?"

"Natalie, your Protector is new to all this, so I ask that you be patient with him."

Patient. There it was. The reason why he seemed so flustered.

"What do you mean be patient?" she asked as she raised her fingers to her head to rub her temples. "He does know what he is doing, doesn't he?"

"I promise you, you will get your chance. You have waited long enough and you deserve it."

His promise was anything but reassuring. Natalie had trusted Redmond for the last seven years. He had told her that when her day came for her second chance that he would help and she was holding him to it. As she stared into the face of the angel, she couldn't help but wonder why she was getting someone who was inexperienced.

"He will be here shortly. I promise, Natalie. It will be okay."

For years, she believed that she could trust someone who would save her life. This news was making her question everything. As she continued to contemplate her situation more, her thoughts were interrupted by Redmond. "I'll be back. I will go see where your Protector is now."

***

Jesse ran his fingers through his hair in agitation. His current situation made him feel like a lion trapped in a cage. He was stuck and there was little he could do to get out of the mess he was in.

"Natalie Parker," he read aloud as he continued reading the document before him. Since Redmond had left him to his own devices, Jesse had no other choice. He had to read about the woman he was to 'help.'

The room he currently occupied was quite different than the other one. Room 23 in Purgatory reminded him of an interrogation room he had seen in the movies. Once again, he was surrounded by four grey walls, a steel table and matching chair rounded out the décor. Small and confining.

As he read more about Natalie Parker, he began to imagine what she would look like. Was she thin or fat? Tall or short? What colour was her hair or her eyes? His fascination with her was currently causing his distress. Was there a picture in the file? He hadn't seen one yet and not knowing what she looked like was weighing heavily on his mind. The last thing he needed was some beautiful woman distracting him from doing his job. 'Oh God', he thought. This wasn't a job. This was a means to an end and if she was the one he needed to help get out of this mess, then he sure as hell was going to do whatever he needed to. He flipped the page of the file and read about Natalie.

"Successful. Grew up in the Hamptons. Loving family," he muttered. As he read the pages, something new crept into Jesse's experience: disdain. Natalie Parker seemed to have had a perfect life, and some deep part of him resented her for that.

"Tell me there is some flaw." He flipped to the next page and frowned at his discovery. "Died the day she was to be married." Jesse didn't know why that piece of information irked him so much. He was currently trying to deal with his own demise. Daring not to compare his situation to hers, he focused on the task at hand and read more about the woman in question

"Reading anything interesting?"

Jesse jumped at the sound of Redmond's voice. Composing himself, Jesse faced his 'boss.'

"I'm just reading," he replied. "Question. What's the deal with Houses? There's three of them. Reminds me of boarding school. Which house will preside over the case?"

"That's a fair question. Given the circumstances, your Judge will come from the House of The Son. Sofia is a fair judge."

"I see," he said. "So I have to go up there, present Natalie's case, and argue against this Defender dude that she deserves a second chance?" Redmond nodded. "I hope she can appeal because my track record with the law isn't that great. The faster I get this done, the faster I can be me again."

Jesse winced at his own words. Why was he feeling remorseful about everything that flew out of his mouth? He never cared nor did he ever worry about what others thought. Jesse could see Redmond analyzing him carefully. The last thing he needed was someone judging him. Especially now.

"Will you be ready soon?" asked Redmond.

"Yeah, yeah. I'll be there."

The sound of the door shutting relieved him. Picking up the file, a page slipped out and fell to the floor. Bending down to pick up the paper, Jesse's eyes widened as a pair of warm brown eyes stared at him.

"Natalie Parker," he whispered at the photograph in his hands. He must have missed this page when he was looking through her file. His idea of what Natalie Parker looked like was no longer a mystery. She was beautiful. "Why do I get the feeling you are going to cause me nothing but trouble?" he said as he stuffed the photo into the folder and left the confining space of Room 23.

As Jesse made his way through the corridor out into the hallway he could hear the faint voice of a woman.

"Redmond, this man, he will help me, right?"

"Yes."

Jesse could hear the hesitation in his voice. "He was just reading up on a few things. Trust me when I say, I only choose the best." Jesse winced at Redmond's own words. Clearly he was saying whatever he could to ease her anxieties.

Peering his head around the corner, Jesse could see Natalie's back facing him. He could feel his palms sweating and his heart beat pick up its pace.

"You got this."

Jesse strolled out from his hiding spot and approached the unaware pair.

"I'll go and check on him again."

"No need. I'm here," he replied.

Hoping neither one would see through his false bravado, Jesse waited for Redmond to make the next move.

"Natalie Parker meet Jesse Knight, your Protector."

Chapter 2:

First Impressions

Jesse had seen his fair share of women on earth. As of right now, Purgatory was currently filled with beautiful women. The picture in her file did not do her justice. Her golden blonde locks reminded him of a lazy summer day in July. Her brown eyes were the colour of milk chocolate, and her skin looked soft and warm. How did someone like her end up here?

"Hello," Jesse waved nervously at her. His hands clammed up as he extended his right hand out to her. He watched as she appraised him and was relieved when she shook his hand.

"Redmond, I believe there is some kind of mistake," she said. "I know you said he's new, but I don't think he's ready for this. This is my life we're talking about."

Jesse dropped her hand and stared at her. She was beautiful alright, until she opened up her trap. He was going to help her. She may have been right about the fact this was new to him, but he was going to whatever he needed to in order to help her.

"Redmond?" she asked. "Can you please do something about this? Can you get another Protector?"

Jesse's eyes flared. Could she do that? Could she get someone else? Would his deal with Redmond be null and void? He needed to control the situation before she screwed up everything for him.

"Hey! Look, I didn't ask to be the one to help you. So you'll forgive me if I don't know the exact protocol here."

"And you need to understand that I have waited long enough for a chance," said Natalie, "I did not spend seven years in Purgatory waiting for this just to have it all go to waste by some guy who has randomly become a Protector. I want this more than anything and if that means waiting seven more years to have another chance, then I will wait."

Clenching his fists, Jesse stared hard at Natalie. The soft brown eyes in the photo he held in his hands moments ago didn't capture the fire and drive that he saw now.

"Please, Redmond." She turned to the Keeper "Say that there is someone else."

Her plea echoed in his Jesse's head. She saw him as a joke. A person who she couldn't trust.

"I understand how you feel, but Natalie, he is your Protector. There is nothing I can do about that." Jesse felt instant relief. One, he knew that Redmond would not go back on their deal and two, he needed to get Natalie to believe that he wasn't who she thought he was.

"You two must work together," continued Redmond. "Your date with the Holy Court is in one hour and by then I hope that you two can work something out. I am sorry, Natalie." There was a look of hesitation on Redmond's face and there was an air of guilt behind his green eyes. Jesse had a feeling that he had lied to her about not being able to get her a different Protector. The question on Jesse's mind was why he hadn't done so. Before Jesse could further ponder the situation, Redmond touched his shoulder. "You, come with me."

Jesse followed him around the corner where he'd been hiding earlier.

He was greeted to a threatening glare. "So help me, if you ruin this opportunity for her, I will ensure that you do end up in Hell."

Jesse knew he wasn't kidding. He noticed Redmond's jaw tightening.

"Whoa," Jesse said. "I was being cordial. She was the one who threw the first punch."

"Clearly, she can tell you don't want to be here. You read the report and you know everything there is to know. Now, you'd better talk to her and make some progress. You need her and she needs you. I don't care if she insults you." Jesse simply nodded and watched Redmond walk back toward Natalie.

"You're in good hands, Natalie." Turning to face Jesse, Redmond gave him sinister look. "Now Jesse, kindly escort Ms. Parker to Room 23," he added before he finally stalked away.

"Yes, sir!" he said, saluting Redmond.

Obliging Redmond's request, Jesse simply nodded and watched Redmond walk back toward Natalie.

Chapter 3:
Now or Never

As Jesse led her to Room 23, Natalie took a good look at the man who was to be her Protector. He was handsome alright, with dark blue eyes that looked like the ocean and short black hair matching the colour of a midnight sky. He was tall with an athletic build and Natalie pegged him to be the kind of guy who knew how attractive he was.

Silently, Natalie appraised him further and the more she did, the less appealing she found him. In the few minutes they had spent together, she found him checking her out in turn. No doubt, he was trying to see if she would cave to his unyielding glare. Fifteen minutes of grunts, rolling eyes, and annoying sighs by both sides had accomplished absolutely nothing.

The knock on the steel door had broken the tension in the room. A woman peeked her head into the room.

"Mr. Knight, Ms. Parker," she stated in a formal tone, "the Court will be ready for you soon. Please be ready,"

A few more moments passed until Natalie finally spoke.

"Look, I told you that I have been waiting a long time for this and I don't want any screw ups..."

Jesse closed his eyes and waved his hands around furiously.

"Whoa, whoa, whoa! Hold on one second, Nat. I have no intention of screwing this up."

"My name is Natalie."

"Alright, Natalie," he continued. "I have just as much invested in this as you. So, let's go over what has to be done."

Natalie looked at him and raised her eyebrows.

"You have something invested? A new haircut perhaps?"

"Really? That's the best you got?" Jesse smirked. "Let's just get this started."

Anger was evident in his tone and she could tell that he was trying to restrain himself from saying what was on his mind. "Finally. We can agree on something and for the record, I don't really care about what your intentions are."

The smirk on his face continued to grow and Natalie wanted nothing more than to wipe it off. She pulled out the chair and sat down facing him.

"Now, from what I can tell, all I have to do is explain what happened to me the day I died and why I want a second chance."

"Correction, 'Princess,'" Jesse said as he hopped on the table. "I have to tell the court what happened to you the day you died and why you should get a second chance. As far as I can tell, you were hit by a car on you wedding day." He paused. She could see the look of sympathy on his face. Natalie wasn't sure if Jesse was pitying her or unsure of what to say. Awkward silence passed between them and Natalie was grateful when Jesse spoke up.

"So tell me, why do you deserve it?"

"'It'?"

"Yes, 'it'. The second chance. The reason we're here. Please tell me you have some answer as to why you think you 'deserve' it. I mean you keep saying that you have been here for seven years. So, tell me why."

Natalie couldn't tell if Jesse really wanted to know or if he was just doing what he was being told to. She stared at her hands which were neatly folded in her lap.

"Do you really want to know? Or are you just doing your job?"

"Listen, Princess, I know you want out of here. I know that you were going to get married and that you died before that could happen. I know that you want to ask why you? I also know that for this to work you have to give me some answers." Jesse stopped, looked her straight in the eye. "So, do you want this second chance or not?"

Of course she wanted a second chance. She had thought of nothing else these past seven years. When her brown eyes locked on to his blue ones, she saw understanding.

"Why do you want a second chance?" he asked again.

She hesitated. The sudden sincerity in his voice surprised her.

"I want to know what my life would be like. I was going to get married and start my life with someone who I loved. Instead, I'm here with you because some idiot lost control of his car and hit me. I didn't deserve this fate. No one does." As

Natalie spoke, his eyes never left hers and it unnerved her. She could feel him in her answer across his features.

"You know, you really didn't answer the question."

"Oh really? You just become a Protector for what, like a minute, and you think my reasons are not good enough."

"Your reasons are selfish," he said. "You make it seem like you should get a second chance based on the fact that you weren't at fault for your death to begin with. You want to go back because you want to see what your life would be like. I have news for you: everyone would say that. What makes you any different?"

Natalie didn't know what to say. For so long she had tried to answer the question. She tried to come up with a decent reason as to why she should be given something so precious. A second chance was something one earned and to date, she couldn't offer a single reason as to why she should be given that chance. Standing up from the chair, Natalie folded her arms about her and glared.

"Look," he said. "I get that I'm Public Enemy Number One right now, but I think you know I'm right. And I think you hate that I'm right."

The only thing Natalie hated was the vulnerable position she was in. Turning away from him, Natalie stared at the grey walls that encased her.

"What if I told you that I don't really know?" she said, surprised that she didn't lose her voice during her admission.

"I would say that being honest is far better than giving an answer you don't fully believe in."

Jesse and Natalie whirled around as they saw Redmond casually leaning against the door frame.

"Are you checking up on me?" asked Jesse.

Composing herself, Natalie gave Redmond an appreciative smile.

"No, I came to see how you two were getting along. I can see that you two are still at each other's throats." Redmond closed the door behind him and continued speaking

"Natalie, the best answer you can give the Jury of Twelve is an honest one."

She stared at Redmond in disbelief. He was supposed to be on her side. He was supposed to say that she was right. Her answer was good. She would have a second chance. She would give anything to hear him say that Jesse was not her Protector and everything was a joke.

"Are you sure, Redmond?" she asked.

"Trust me. Jesse, I would like to talk to you."

Natalie noticed Jesse's reaction as he stiffened at Redmond's request. As they left, Natalie prayed that when the door opened once again, Jesse would not be there.

"What did I do now?" she heard Jesse say.

"I just want to say that the Defender will make the Jury aware that you are new to all of this. He will show you no mercy. So, don't lose your temper."

Eavesdropping wasn't something Natalie considered polite, but seeing as how they were talking about her life, she decided that now wasn't the time to be courteous. Secretly, Natalie was enjoying the fact that Redmond was treating him like a petulant child.

"I have never needed luck and I don't count crashing my Porsche into a dump truck."

Natalie backed away slightly from the door when she heard that. So that's how he died?

"I know what I have to do and I am going to do it. Not for you, not for her, but for me. Now if you will excuse me. I have to go to court."

The harshness of his words resonated. He was hurting and obviously bitter about his death and the fact that he had to help a total stranger. Natalie made her way back to the chair just as Jesse opened the door.

"Did you enjoy the show?" he said, the anger in his words masking the sadness evident upon his hard features.

Natalie decided to play dumb and not answer. Before he could pursue the conversation further, the woman from before came back out, "Mr. Knight, Ms. Parker, it's time."

Natalie looked at Jesse and stood up. No words needed to be exchanged. She knew that he was feeling just as nervous as she was. Natalie had waited for this moment for so long, why did she feel like crawling into a hole to hide?

She didn't know how she managed the walk from Room 23 to the Holy Court. Nevertheless, as she stood before the threshold of the doors, she turned to Jesse.

"Well Mr. Protector, it's now or never."

Jesse's eyes widened in horror and his mouth parted

slightly. Natalie rolled her eyes and left Jesse alone to ponder. With a deep breath, Natalie marched toward the doors of the courtroom. Her hand shook as it reached for the handle.

"Now or never indeed," she told herself.

Chapter 4:
Meeting The Defender

Jesse waited a few moments and followed Natalie into the court room and stopped dead in his tracks. This was the afterlife's version of a courtroom? He slowly walked forward with trepidation and became mesmerized by the courtroom's simplicity.

The walls were dominated with white and accented with shades of grey above the judge's desk. Hanging on the wall behind the desk was a portrait with what looked like several coats of arms. Jesse instantly recognized the red and blue shield of the Protector with two gold swords overlapping. White wings appeared to grow out of the shield and a halo rested above.

He took note of the others and safely made the assumption that they were the coat of arms for the other angels.

To his left, Jesse saw the jury box. It, too, was white with black wood on top. On Jesse's right, a similar box stood where he could see people filing in, taking their seats before the trial got underway.

Realizing that people were staring at him Jesse moved forward, bumping into a rectangular box where Natalie was sitting.

He grimaced as his knee made contact and silently cursed the pain away.

"What are you doing in there?" Jesse hissed as rubbed his knee.

"I am supposed to be in here," she stated.

Natalie was a lot of things, but a prisoner wasn't one of them. She didn't do anything wrong and he didn't see the need for her to sit in there with his back to her while he plead her case.

Boldly, he opened the door and signaled for her to come out.

"Get out of there."

Sensing her unwillingness to move, he gently touched her shoulder and looked at her.

Patricia Bandurka

"You're not a prisoner. You committed no crime."

Jesse saw Natalie recoil from his touch while carefully processing his words. Slowly she stood up and left the boundaries of the box.

Jesse watched as Natalie sat down beside him at the wooden desk. Over his chair, he found a royal blue robe with red trim laying there. He assumed that this was the robe he needed to don while he was in court. The colours weren't terrible, they just weren't exactly his style.

"I think you're supposed to put that on," Natalie whispered.

Sighing, Jesse picked up the robe and pulled it over his head. He couldn't tell what he looked like, but it had to be ridiculous. He brushed off the wrinkles and felt something on his chest. He looked down and saw the crest of the Protector right over his heart.

Tilting his head upwards in despair, he was taken by the design of the ceiling. Stained glass windows adorned with the image of the Garden of Eden, or what he believed to be the Garden of Eden, stared back at him. In a world that appeared to be dominated by black, white and grey, Jesse welcomed the colours.

"He doesn't look too happy," Natalie said as she broke Jesse from his gaze. He took a good look at his opponent as he watched the Defender take his seat.

The man donned a black robe with a gold trim and the crest of the Defenders. His brown eyes matched his hair, neatly coiffed over his pasty white skin.

"He probably doesn't like you moving from the penalty box," Jesse replied. "Can't say I blame him. I do think the extra attacker is warranted in this situation."

He watched her stare dumbly at him and sighed.

"It's a hockey metaphor," he offered.

"I know it's a hockey metaphor!" she said.

"You know, outbursts like that and you could be held in contempt of court Ms. Parker," the Defender said smoothly as he walked over to them. Jesse took a good look at his opposing counsel. He could clearly see the smugness on his face and arrogance in his eyes.

"I am Edward Mathison, The Defender and you Ms. Parker should be sitting in the prisoner's dock." He pointed to the box.

Jesse took a good look at Edward and sized up his would-be opponent.

"She's not a prisoner."

"It's the rules. All wards sit there."

"Well, today, she belongs here. Beside me. Got it?" said Jesse.

He watched as Edward's eyes widened in shock. Waiting for a comeback, Jesse was surprised when Edward focused his attention on Natalie.

"Ms. Parker. Good luck today. With him as your Protector, you're going to need it." He walked back to his desk.

Taking in a deep breath, Jesse sat down beside Natalie and massaged his temples.

"You just don't know when to shut up," she hissed.

"What? That? Oh come on, he was asking for it. You're not a prisoner here, Nat."

"It's Natalie," she said through clenched teeth. "Let me explain something to you, you idiot. He has done this before, you have not. I can't believe I let Redmond talk me into keeping you as my Protector."

Jesse looked at Natalie and saw that she was leaving to go back to the dock. He reached for her hand and tried not to get annoyed when she flinched at his touch.

"Hey," he said. "Trust me."

He felt like an idiot for asking her to do so. Letting go of her hand, he focused on his papers; desperately trying to forget the spark he felt when he touched her.

Sensing Natalie's desire to tell him off, a man announcing himself as an Advisor had entered the courtroom.

"Please rise. From The Domus Filius, Her Royal Honour, Sofia."

Jesse stared in awe at the woman standing before him. She was about as powerful as anyone could get and his fate, along with Natalie's, rested in her hands. In Jesse's eyes, Sofia was a vision. Her dark brown, wavy hair rested at her shoulders. Her eyes appeared aqua blue, but they seemed to change colour in the light. Her Honour wore a gold coloured robe that seemed to shine like the sun. It brought about a certain regal aura that made Jesse more nervous than he cared to admit. It was without any doubt that Sofia knew everything there was to know about him.

As his eyes stared into Sofia's, he couldn't help but feel like he was the one on trial. And yet, there she sat, engaging him in a staring contest. Jesse felt as though she was reading his mind, soul, and heart. In any other circumstance, Jesse would feel threatened and yet for some reason, he was calm and at peace. Snapping back to reality, Jesse remembered where he was and what he needed to do. Get the second chance and get the hell out of here.

"Would the Defender please present?"

Jesse breathed in relief as Her Honour diverted her attention off him. Now, he would have to see what he was up against.

"Your Honour, The Jury of Twelve, Ms. Parker is asking for a second chance. I feel that she should not be permitted a second chance based on the fact that she does not meet the criteria and has given the courts no reason as to why she should be given an opportunity to live again. As far as I am concerned, her death was legitimate. There are no facts in evidence to suggest otherwise. In my opinion, there is no benefit to her resuming her life as before. I appeal to the jury that she remains in Purgatory."

Criteria? This guy has definitely lost touch with reality. Jesse watched Natalie fume during Edward's little speech. He was grateful that the look wasn't directed toward him.

"Thank you, Mr. Mathison. Mr. Knight I understand you are new to all of this, I expect that you understand what you are being asked to do. You may proceed."

Jesse took a quick glance at Natalie and stood. He wanted to run out of the courtroom and vomit. When he saw Redmond staring at him; he took a deep breath and thought about the deal. Jesse stared back with conviction in his eyes. At that moment, it was almost as if Redmond were daring him to quit. Casting a glance at Edward, Jesse saw that he too was waiting for him to crash and burn. He had already done that. Now, he had something to prove. He took a look around the room and breathed.

"Your Honour, The Jury of Twelve," he stuttered. He closed his eyes and thought back to every law movie and television show he ever watched. He channeled his inner Matlock and let the words come to him. "The Defender says she does-n't 'meet the criteria' for a second chance." Pausing like the lawyers he'd seen on television, Jesse walked toward the Jury and continued. "Natalie Parker has been in Purgatory for seven years and I somehow doubt the Defender understands what it is like living in that world. I don't even know what it's like to live there and I can guarantee you, I hope I never do." Turning towards the bench he stared at the judge. "I certainly doubt he knows what being there is like and he alone is certainly not capable of deciding as to whether or not Natalie deserves to stay there for all eternity. To be quite honest, how can anyone make that decision?"

Jesse returned to his seat and looked back at Sofia.

"I may be new to this. I don't know the rules or the players. Do you need witnesses? Evidence? Facts? No disrespect to you, Ma'am, but if The Defender can win his cases simply because Natalie and others in Purgatory don't meet a certain criteria then why bother doing this? Why make her wait? Why make others wait?"

Jesse sat down and heard murmurs of shock float throughout the room. His eyes locked with Sofia's and then looked in the direction of where Redmond was sitting. Jesse couldn't tell if he was angry or stunned. He didn't even bother looking at Natalie. Turning his head toward the Defender, he saw him clench his fists. It was obvious to Jesse he had hit a nerve. Then again, everyone in the room seemed a little perturbed by his declaration.

"Well, Mr. Knight," said Sofia "You certainly know how to silence a room. Natalie? We have heard from the Defender and your Protector. I will go against protocol because your Protector is new and because I believe that you know why you want a second chance better than anyone."

Jesse's eyes bugged out of his head.

"That wasn't in the guidebook," Jesse whispered to Natalie.

"Neither was your speech," she spat.

Jesse watched skeptically as Natalie stood.

"Crap," he muttered. He could feel dozens of eyes staring at him and thought it best to shut up.

"Your Honour," Natalie stopped herself and Jesse anxiously stared at her as she thought about what she would say next. "The truth is," she said, nearly losing her voice, "I don't really know. I could give you a million reasons and there is no doubt you have probably heard them all before. The only answer I can give you is that I want to know why. I want to know why I died that day. Why out of the millions of people in New York City did that car hit me?" She stopped. "I think if I knew the answer, I could move on and accept that I am really dead and that there is no going back. At the very least, ma'am, I'd have closure."

After a few moments of silence, Sofia turned and spoke to the jury.

"I would like to speak with the Jury of Twelve in my chambers," she said.

Jesse sat there dumbfounded. What the hell was going on? The only thing he was sure of was that Edward was just as confused as him.

"Well," said Redmond. "You certainly know how to make things interesting."

Jesse wasn't sure if Redmond was praising him or humouring him. For Jesse's sake, he was hoping for praise.

"Is that good Redmond?" Natalie asked.

"I have been a Keeper for a long time and I have been a Protector long before that. It is rare when a Judge asks to speak with the Jury." He paused and turned to Jesse. "It's also rare for a new Protector to run his mouth off and tell a judge what is wrong with the Holy Courts Judicial System."

"Finally something we can agree on, Redmond."

They turned to see that Edward had approached their conversation. "Coming to see the disaster your Protector has already caused?"

"Edward, now is not the time," he replied. "If you will excuse me, I would like to talk to Jesse and Natalie, without interference from the opposition."

"As you wish." The Defender backed away from the trio shaking his head in disgust.

"Are you alright, Natalie?" Redmond asked.

Was she alright? Jesse rolled his eyes at Redmond's question and then actually thought about it. Did he just screw up royally by telling the judge to stick it?

"I don't know." She replied. "I just don't know."

"Natalie. It will be okay."

"How can you say that, Redmond?" said Natalie as she massaged her temples with her fingers. "Did you actually hear what Jesse said? You know, I don't know who is worse. Jesse or him."

"Hey! Do you honestly believe that what he said was true," Jesse asked. "Did you want to sit in that dock? Did you want to be told that you don't deserve the possibility of a second chance because you don't fit the bill? That's stupid."

"But it's the way it has always been done," Redmond stated.

"Then you're wrong."

Jesse surprised himself with his boldness.

"What could they be talking about in there Redmond?" Natalie questioned.

Grateful for the interruption, Jesse pondered that notion as well. He was still new to this and had no idea if this was standard protocol.

"I'm not certain, I imagine that they will be out soon."

As soon as he had said those words, the door opened and Sofia appeared without the Jury of Twelve with her, then took her seat and waited for silence.

"I have sat on numerous cases where a person has asked for a second chance," said Sofia. "And in this case, I do not think a jury would be needed."

"Your Honour," said Edward. "If I may, I don't quite understand?"

"There are a lot of things that are meant to be a mystery, Edward." She paused and then focused her attention on Natalie. "Natalie, I have heard many reasons over the years and yes, some have been the same. Each case is different. However one element stays the same for every person that walks through those doors. 'Why me?'" Jesse watched as Natalie edged her way to the bench.

"I have sought counsel from the Son and it is my ruling that Natalie Parker deserves to know what happened the day she died and why."

Jesse narrowed his eyes at Sofia in confusion. He honestly didn't know what warranted this result and he was scared out of his mind. When he turned to Natalie, he saw a similar expression of confusion and shock across her features. He could only imagine what she must be thinking.

"Therefore," continued Sofia, "I am granting Natalie Parker seven days. In those seven days Natalie, I hope you find the answers you're looking for. Now, gentlemen," Sofia looked at Jesse and Redmond. "If you don't mind, there is someone who wishes to speak to Natalie personally."

Sofia motioned for Natalie to follow her and led her through the court's chamber doors.

"Did she say what I think she just said?" Edward said to Redmond and Jesse once Natalie and Sofia had left the room.

"Don't look at me," Jesse replied as he raised his hands. "I'm just as stunned as you are."

"This doesn't make any sense. What did you do?" Edward pointed his finger to Redmond. "I get that he's new, but this was too simple."

"Edward," Redmond said.

"Tell me!" interrupted Edward. "I have argued for years on behalf of the court and now all of sudden simply wanting to know 'why' is a good enough reason. Damn it, Redmond! Everyone wants to know why they died and I don't blame them for that. But not everyone is ready to accept what really happened to them and I can assure you of one thing: neither Natalie or Jesse are ready for this."

He then turned toward Jesse. "You may have won this one, but I know people like you. You're going to abuse this chance and you're going to abuse the power that comes with it," he then turned to Redmond. "Redmond, your new Protector over here will crash and burn and the only one who will pay is that girl." Edward paused. "It's a shame you know."

"What is?" asked Jesse.

"She has no idea that a selfish person like you is going to ruin what's left of her life."

Chapter 5:
Second Chance

Jesse paced back and forth as he waited for Natalie to re-emerge from behind the closed doors. The Holy Court had emptied out as soon as Sofia granted Natalie the right to find out why she died. Though they had won, the victory felt hollow. What had Jesse really done? He hated to admit it, but Edward was right. It was simple, even for a rookie. He'd made a statement and questioned a system that had been in place long before he was born. The rest had been all Natalie.

"It can't be this easy," he muttered as he continued to watch the door. He could feel Redmond's gaze upon him. Deciding that he would do everything in his power to avoid Redmond's glare, Jesse studied the court room further. He went to the prisoner's dock and sat down.

"It was very bold of you to take Natalie out of the dock," Redmond said, following him. "However, to mock a system like ours, and in front of a Judge no less, was completely stupid. Rules are meant to be followed here. You should keep that in mind for later."

Calmly, Jesse stood and walked out of the claustrophobic cubicle.

"Well, in my world, rules are meant to be broken, challenged even. I don't understand why she was in that thing to begin with? She's not a prisoner. She didn't do anything wrong."

Redmond's raised eyebrow unsettled Jesse.

"You're right. She's not a prisoner. It's just the way things are done here."

Ignoring Redmond, Jesse focused his attentions once more on the door and the fact that Natalie was on the other side.

"What's taking so long?" he muttered.

"Patience, Jesse. Give her time."

Time? He didn't have time. He had no patience. He wanted out and he wanted out now. Before he could light into Redmond about his displeasure, the Keeper beat him to the punch. He fiddled with the hem of his robe and shuttered when he realized he was still wearing it.

"Jesse, we have to discuss something rather important."

"Now what?" he replied, locking his gaze off the door. "What could there possibly be left to discuss? I did my bit in the courtroom, now she has to do hers and I will get my life back."

"A watched pot never boils. Listen, Jesse. There's something you should know."

Jesse turned to Redmond, giving the Keeper his full attention.

"Jesse, Natalie's death occurred seven years ago."

Jesse raised his eyebrow in exasperation. He already knew that so why was Redmond telling him this?

"When you're down there," he continued, "you will feel drawn to finding the you that is still alive and that cannot happen. You can't change the course of history and tell yourself what happens to you in the future. If that were possible, then my job would be a lot easier. This also means that Natalie cannot tell herself anything about her death either. Both of you are merely observers, looking for answers."

"Redmond," said Jesse. "I've seen *Back to the Future* a few times. I know that you can't change history because it will mess everything up. Look, I won't screw this up. I don't cheat on bets. I will consider this a stipulation to our bet."

Jesse watched closely as Redmond smiled. Tons of questions about his new capabilities entered his mind. If he couldn't talk to his living form, what else couldn't he do? More importantly...what *could* he do?

"There's one more thing," Redmond said.

Of course there was, Jesse thought. He crossed his arms and sighed.

"Now what?"

Jesse observed Redmond closely. He was anxious about something and given the authoritative demeanor the Keeper had shown, he seemed concerned...and not about him and Natalie going back in time.

"The Sanctuary. I am assuming you read that part when you read over Natalie's file."

"Yes. What about it."

"I will make it clear to you," Redmond replied as he

cracked his knuckles. "You cannot tell Natalie that St. Patrick's Cathedral is where you will be staying for the next seven days."

Jesse furrowed his eyebrows in confusion.

"What I mean to say," Redmond added. "The Sanctuary is meant to be a safe place-"

"And to Natalie it wouldn't be?"

"It will be. Natalie..." Redmond hesitated.

"Was supposed to get married there."

The look of surprise on Redmond's face made Jesse smile. He could put two and two together and had a feeling that the Sanctuary would make Natalie very emotional. Jesse wasn't stupid. He understood that Natalie never made it there on her wedding day and would no doubt be a wreck.

"I did read that in her file. So my next question is how do I get her there and what happens after she realizes that we're staying in the place where she was supposed to get married?"

Before he could get a response, the doors opened and Natalie walked out.

"Finally!" Jesse declared.

"Sorry that took so long," she said. "I just didn't want the moment of peace to end."

"That's perfectly normal, Natalie," said Redmond. "Most people don't want to leave the presence of a judge."

"Sofia and the Son said that we could go to the Gate and that they would both like to speak with you afterward," she added.

"That doesn't surprise me. Very well then. Jesse, Natalie, follow me."

Jesse followed Redmond and Natalie out of the Holy Court down a narrow corridor, feeling a sudden jolt of déjà vu. Shades of grey walls once again surrounded him. Could they not pick another colour? He noticed that Natalie looked a lot calmer than she did before and that made him wonder what she, Sofia, and the Son were talking about. Then there was his unanswered question about The Sanctuary. What the hell was he going to do? Stall her?

"Alright, we are here." said Redmond, interrupting Jesse's thoughts.

Jesse followed Natalie and Redmond down the grey

walled corridors. The Gate stood before him and once they walked through, everything changed. It was unlike anything Jesse had ever seen before. It reminded him of the stained glass windows he saw on the ceiling of the court room. It was vibrant and colourful. Until now, Purgatory had been nothing but dull greys and now, this place looked like a Thomas Kinkade painting. Jesse made a 360-degree circle around the area and saw nothing but grass, trees, and clear blue skies. A warm glow radiated off the gates. To Jesse, it felt like being in a safe place where nothing and no one could ever hurt you.

"This part is easy," Redmond said as he pulled something from his robes. "You both know what you have to do and I hope that you both realize how important this is. All you have to do is jump over the edge."

Jesse looked around and for the life of him couldn't fathom what edge Redmond was talking about.

"Edge? What edge?" Jesse asked.

"Just wait."

The grass beneath their feet began to part and a porthole to the world down below appeared before them.

"Holy crap!" Jesse said as he stepped back.

"To reiterate, Jesse. All you have to do is jump over the edge. Grab Natalie's hand and jump. You will be transported back to the appropriate time."

Jesse raised his eyebrow at the Keeper.

"Anything else?"

"Before you two jump," Redmond said. "I have one more thing to say. You will be going back to the exact moment in time where Sofia and the Son felt you would best help start your journey. Remember, Sofia gave you seven days to find the answers to your questions. Here, put these on." He handed Jesse a gold medallion with a sword and shield on it and gave Natalie silver heart-shaped locket.

"If at any time you need to speak with me, hold the medallion in your hand and say *Fidelis Deus Quod Is Mos Servo Vos*. This will transport you back to where I am. If you are separated from each other, the locket and the medallion will lead you straight to each other, but you both must be wearing them in order for it to work. I wish you luck."

Jesse looked at the world below once more and felt his fear of heights increase. He read the inscription on the medallion and gripped it tightly. "Trust God and He will Protect You," he quickly looked back to Redmond. "Redmond, you never answered my question."

"You'll figure it out. I believe in you. All you have to do is trust each other. "Now, jump!"

This was insane. He didn't know what was down there. For all he knew there would be a devil down there welcoming him to hell.

"Isn't there another way down?"

"What's the matter Jesse? Scared of heights?"

Jesse wanted to say he was. The last thing he wanted was for Natalie to know that he was freaking out.

"No, let's...let's just do this." he glared at Redmond.

The Keeper's last words echoed. Figure it out? He was just supposed to figure it out? Before he could say anything else, Jesse felt Natalie grab his hand in hers. Before he could say anything else, he felt himself being pulled down into the tornado like portal.

"Redmond!" Jesse's body thrashed wildly around. He made sure that he didn't let go of Natalie's hand as they tumbled.

Images of Natalie's life flashed before him. There were typical milestone moments: he saw her blowing candles out on birthday cakes, dancing with a guy at prom, riding horses with her family. It was clear that she had a good life and that it was taken from her too soon. The images continued to flash on and Jesse looked at Natalie to see what her reactions were. There were tears in her eyes as she experienced an onslaught of emotions.

"Nick," he heard her whisper and watched closely as a man got down on one knee asking her to marry him. Jesse then saw her at a stable talking to a horse and he wished that there could have been some audio so he could hear her memories unfold as well.

Seconds later, Jesse felt his body land on cold concrete with a solid thud. He found it difficult to breathe and realized that Natalie was on top of him.

"Well, that could have been worse," Jesse groaned and touched the back of his head. "You could have at least told me you were going to jump."

Natalie rolled off him, and Jesse had to admit, the loss of her body heat disappointed him. He slowly got up and tried to fight off the wave of nausea. The urge to vomit overwhelmed him and he reached for the building for support. When he looked over at Natalie, he saw her fighting off the same disorientation he was feeling. He smiled at that. It felt good to know that he wasn't the only one in discomfort.

As a native New Yorker, Jesse knew every inch of Manhattan, but right now, he had no idea where he was. Taking in a deep breath, the foul scent of ink and paper entered his nostrils. He was so disgusted, he could taste it. The city didn't smell spectacular in general, but this was just bad.

Looking down, he spotted Natalie still on the ground, glaring at him.

"What?" Jesse asked as he crossed his arms.

Natalie simply shook her head and stood up. She brushed off some of the wet snow from her body and started to walk toward the street. Jesse followed her and heard the familiar sounds of car horns honking and the slush of dirty snow beneath the tires of the cars driving by. The darkness outside made it evident to Jesse that it was sometime after 6 pm.

Before he could tell Natalie about his theory, he saw that she was nowhere near him. He did a complete 360 degree turn and couldn't find her. Jesse saw a flash of blonde and ran up to the woman. "Natalie!" he said as he spun her around.

"Excuse me?" came a surprised reply. Jesse blushed when he realized he had just accosted a random stranger. "Sorry," he said and continued his search for her. "She couldn't have gotten far." He saw another blonde in the distance and he knew for certain that he had found her. Jesse chased after her and saw that she was looking everywhere but where she was actually going. It was also clear to him in that moment that she had no idea that there was a bus coming right at her.

"Watch out!" he yelled as he pulled her back from the oncoming bus. Natalie was clearly startled as Jesse pulled her against him. Once the bus was gone, Natalie pulled herself away from him at looked anywhere but at him. "Okay, let's try not to get ourselves killed before this little adventure of ours begins."

"I'm pretty sure we can't die twice Jesse," she replied.

"You're right. I just don't want to have to explain to Redmond why I couldn't protect you from a bus. So, can you just humour me and be careful?"

Natalie rolled her eyes at him in agreement and he smiled sheepishly at her.

"Okay, so according to my calculations I believe that we are in Herald Square. As for the time, I am guessing anywhere between 6pm and 6am."

Jesse's eyes locked on Natalie's and the look of discontent puzzled him. He was being helpful and insightful. Not to mention, he just prevented her from becoming a pancake on the side of the road...again.

"Jesse, now is not the time for guessing," she said. "It's the week before my wedding. I need to know and you're going to help me!" Jesse watched her closely as she walked away from him. He clenched his fists and sighed. "What did I get myself into?" he said aloud and followed Natalie once more.

***

Natalie was a woman on a mission and no one, not even Jesse Knight was going to get in her way. She started walking down the street, wishing she had a coat. She also wished Redmond had given her one. She vaguely remembered how cold that December had been and on more than one occasion questioned why she would get married during one of the coldest months of the year. The cashmere sweater and jeans weren't cutting it.

"Excuse me sir, could you tell me the date and time?" The man gave her a strange look and replied. Natalie hugged him happily and smiled. She turned around and spotted Jesse just a few paces behind her waiting obediently for her. It was then that she began to notice how handsome he really was. His black hair framed his face perfectly, his dark blue eyes were captivating. However, there was something troubling him and she could see that he was avoiding her gaze.

"So?" he asked, breaking her from her thoughts. "I am assuming by the smile on your face that today is a good day. Well, what is today's date?"

"Yes! It's 12:12 AM, December 10th 2005," she said. It dawned on Natalie then the significance of the date. Mortified at her realization, Natalie took off running. The sounds of her shoes made contact with the concrete of the wet streets. The cold air wasn't exactly inviting but it was refreshing, and the city lights of Midtown Manhattan were a welcome sight. When she reached her destination, she collapsed on the bench and sighed.

"Damn girl, you can run," said Jesse as he hunched over trying to catch his breath. "Now that the oxygen is actually getting to my lungs, would you mind telling me the significance of this date? More importantly, why you ran away like that. Last I checked, good news was a good thing."

Natalie knew she wasn't being fair to him. Yes, he may have read her file and knew things about her but at the end of the day, he didn't know everything. She turned to him slowly and sighed. She folded her hands on her crossed legs and avoided his penetrating gaze.

"If you must know, it is the week before my wedding."

"And?"

"And? Did you hear Redmond? He said that we were going back to the time that would best help me figure out why I died. I didn't think I would be sent to the time where the week before my wedding would become the week before my death."

Before he had the chance to say something, she stood up and started walking.

"Damn it! Natalie, wait!"

Natalie stopped and cringed at his touch. She shrugged his hands off her shoulders, turning away from him.

"Okay, I am sorry," said Jesse. "Look, I know we're not the best of friends, but somebody up there seems to think otherwise. If that means me helping you save your life, then I want you to know that you would be helping me save mine."

Natalie listened intently to his words and slowly turned to face him once more. For the first time, she saw that he was just as scared of what was going on.

He smiled at her and nodded.

"So, do you think we can work together on this?" he asked as he stretched his hand to hers.

Natalie hesitated, but she had no alternative. Grabbing his hand in turn, she nodded.

"Yes, I think we can."

Chapter 6:
The Life That Was

For the past hour, Jesse had been following Natalie across the darkened city. His jeans, T-shirt, and black leather jacket were giving him little warmth right now. It was December, it was freezing cold, and Redmond didn't exactly dress them for the frigid New York temperature. Natalie was a little better, but was only wearing a sweater and jeans. He too could see that the winter air was taking a toll on her body.

Despite the weather, Jesse was happy to be walking on the streets of Manhattan once more. Being dead for only 24 hours made him appreciate everything he'd taken for granted in life. At that moment he started to wonder more about Natalie and how she was able to live in Purgatory for seven years.

Jesse was letting her take control over where they were going because he had no idea how he was going to get her to St. Patrick's. Redmond had said that he would know what to do and while Jesse was pretty charming, he had a feeling she wasn't going to buy it. He needed time and unfortunately, they lacked that. Shoving his hands in pockets, he thought of ways he could break it to her and each result he had in mind ended badly.

Jesse snuck a quick glance at Natalie and grimaced. She was intriguing to say the least and he couldn't help but watch her. She had a habit of chewing her bottom lip when she became frustrated, her teeth clenched tightly when she was annoyed at him, and then there was his favourite, the eye roll she would give him when he said something she didn't particularly care for.

He did find her beautiful and not in a typical way. He was used to provocative women with dark hair and sultry eyes. They were the type of women who used their bodies to get what they wanted. Natalie, on the other hand, was the opposite. Her blonde hair and brown eyes gave her an air of innocence, but she possessed a quiet demeanor that he couldn't explain and a mysterious quality that drew him to her unlike anyone he'd ever met.

"Problem?" he asked as she let out a sigh.

"Why haven't we found anything yet?" she sighed. "I mean, what am I looking for?"

St. Patrick's Cathedral, he thought. This was killing him. They were wasting time and he was being a scared little chicken because he didn't know how she would react.

"We? Princess, for the past hour, we haven't done anything. You have been dragging me up and down Lower Manhattan and I have been following."

"What did I say about calling me Princess?"

"Well, considering that you've been treating me like I'm one of your subjects obliged to do as you say, then yes, that would constitute my right to address you as such."

Jesse needed time and stalling her seemed to be the only tactic he could come up with.

"Why don't you tell me about the Natalie from seven years ago."

"I'm lost," she replied. "Don't you already know? Didn't my file say something?"

Jesse winced. Yes, he knew quite a bit about her. However, there was no harm in trying to get her to tell him more.

"I know what I read. I know that you were going to get married and that you died on your wedding day. I know to a certain extent everything about you. That you were a children's book author. That you grew up in the Hamptons and that you have a younger sister and two parents who most likely took your death pretty hard. I only know what I read and that's the gist of it. I just don't really know you. Other than the fact that you are the most stubborn woman I have ever met."

Jesse's words were met with silence and he was worried that he may have said the wrong thing. He was cold. He was tired. He wanted to be some place warm and safe. Instead, he was acting like a scared puppy because he didn't want to deal with an emotional Natalie.

"Listen," he continued. "I don't mean to make you uncomfortable. We're still strangers and I know that I'm the last person who should be doing this with you. I just need you to know that I'm on your side and that if you let me in just a little bit, I may be able to help you get what you want."

Jesse stared at Natalie as she processed his words, rubbed his hands together in an effort to warm up and hoped that she would take them to heart.

"No, you're right," she replied. "You should know about my life from then. I mean we're here. Makes sense."

Jesse breathed a sigh of relief. Maybe she wasn't as difficult as he initially believed. Maybe she would be okay with where they were supposed to go. Perhaps, just like with the majority of women he has encountered, she just needed time.

"Why don't we sit on the bench over there?"

Natalie nodded in agreement and he led her to the bench.

"Well, what do you want to know?"

"Children's book author? Not quite what I imagined. Guess I never pegged you as a writer, much less that."

"Isn't that the point of this little Q & A? You ask and I tell."

Jesse blushed a little and grinned. "Were you successful?"

She paused and he waited.

"I guess I was to a certain extent," she said.

Natalie was avoiding his gaze and chewing on her bottom lip again. He could tell that she was trying to under sell her success.

"Alright. What about your family?"

He needed to know where she stood with them. Jesse watched her intently. Her far off gaze troubled him. Where did she go when she did that? Who was she thinking of?

"Earth to Natalie," he tried, hoping to bring her back from wherever she was.

"What?" she snapped.

"Your family?" he started. "I mean...never mind."

Her groan startled him.

"No, it's fine," she answered back as she blew warm air in to her hands. "Well my mother works for my grandfather. He owns..." she paused.

"Owns?"

"I don't know if it's his business anymore. Anyway, he owned a stable in the Hamptons, breeding and training horses for all the major races. The horses they trained even won quite a bit. That's actually how she met my father. He was studying to become a veterinarian and he would take care of the horses when they needed it. Eventually they went out, fell in love, got married, and had me and my sister."

So she had come from a wealthy *and* humble family. He didn't want to jump to any conclusions about her family and her relationship with them. He wasn't stupid, he could tell that Natalie was in fact a wealthy woman and lived a very comfortable life. Jesse could see it in the way she carried herself. There was a regal aura about her. He saw it in the way she walked and he definitely saw it in the way she spoke to him.

"And what about your sister?"

"Victoria and I are complete opposites," Natalie answered and stood up from the bench. Jesse noted that there was a coolness in her voice. Her body language spoke volumes too.

"When my family began to make money, everything changed. My mother trained horses from around the world and my father was taking care of them. Once the money rolled in, my sister became spoiled and selfish. Trips to the Caribbean, ski weekends in the Rockies, Mediterranean cruises, and two-week stays in Tuscan villas. My sister accepted wealth very well. She changed into someone I didn't recognize."

A few moments passed between the two. As much as Jesse hated to admit it, he was wrong about Natalie on so many levels. She wasn't the spoiled brat he thought she was. She was intelligent and career oriented. She relied on herself and not her family or their connections.

"I think I got it," he said, standing up. "You don't have to say any more." Jesse walked around her so that he could see her face.

"I need you to understand," continued Natalie. "I love my family, my parents were proud of me and loved me, and I can only hope they still love me after I have been dead all this time. It's just that...I just always felt like the odd one out. Well, until I met Nick."

Nick. Jesse had been waiting for that name to come up.

"So, Nick? He made life more interesting?"

"Yes!" she replied. "I met him at a party. Ironically, my sister introduced us. They had gone out before, she just wasn't that interested in him or looking for a commitment. Nick and I just hit it off. He was sweet, kind, and handsome. We liked a lot of the same things. I also learned that his father owned the publishing company that I worked for. In addition to writing and drawing, I also edited. My parents adored him and when he asked me to marry him, I said yes. I guess you could say that I just knew he was the one."

Jesse's jaw became tense with emotion. He didn't know what to say to her and he was seriously beginning to regret asking her these questions. She had a life. She had love. She had everything he didn't. The less he knew, the better and yet, the only way to get through the next seven days was to know everything about her.

"What do I do?" he muttered.

"What did you say?" Natalie asked.

"I said I guess we better see what we can do," he answered quickly. As he got up and started walking away, Natalie followed "I want to know more about your life," said Jesse.

"You mean my life that was, right?"

He paused and turned around to look at her.

"Yes, Natalie. Your life that was. Your life that will be again."

Chapter 7:
What Could Have Been

Darkness still loomed over Midtown and snow had started to fall from the sky. Jesse and Natalie had spent the past hour talking about her life and her family. They were both extremely tired and cold, yet Natalie felt rejuvenated. She spent seven years in Purgatory talking about her death with others like her and now she was walking among the living once more. Natalie embraced the cold weather and admired the beauty of the snow falling from the heavens. To her credit, she was doing her best to fight the cold and the sleep her body craved.

That was the big difference between living on earth and surviving Purgatory. In Purgatory, you didn't sleep. Eating and drinking were optional. You didn't feel anything but numbness. In the end, you simply existed in the realm of endless possibilities. On Earth, you felt everything. She could feel the cold winter air against her cheeks and it felt amazing. It felt real. It felt normal. While she wanted nothing more than to crawl into bed and sleep, she knew that she couldn't. Natalie was processing everything around her and vowed that no matter what the end result happened to be... she would never take this moment for granted again.

Natalie and Jesse were making their way through Times Square. It was 3AM and there were still be people lingering about. She smiled as she saw musicians playing in the street and tourists staring in awe at all the lights shining brightly.

She further reflected on her conversation with Jesse. Every time she looked at him, she wondered if she had divulged too much information. She thought maybe she was boring him with personal details of her life, but she was wrong. He was attentive, particularly when she was talking about her sister.

It dawned on her then that maybe that was the kind of girl Jesse went for. When she first met Jesse, he tried to charm her and while Natalie had found the whole thing pathetic, she knew her sister would have been flattered. She could imagine them together now. Victoria would have Jesse eating out of the palm of her hand and he in turn would enjoy the benefits that her sister would offer. Typical Victoria, she thought.

"Just typical!" she said aloud.

Jesse stopped walking and looked at her.

"What's just typical?"

Realizing he had heard her sudden outburst, she turned to him and tried to come up with an answer.

"Thinking out loud," she said.

"Do you do this often or should I find a pair of ear plugs? Hmm..."

"What?" she asked.

"I wonder if I have to bill Purgatory? I mean is that even possible? Can I expense stuff? You really only think of these things after."

Natalie rolled her eyes.

She was starting to feel more tired. It was then that she realized she had no idea where she would be staying.

"Question?" she asked.

"Answer! Or is this you thinking out loud again?"

"Very funny. Where are we staying?"

The grin on Jesse's face faded fast.

"Jesse?" Natalie questioned. "Where are we staying?"

"Look, about that..." he stuttered.

"What do you mean 'about that?'" She pointed her index finger at him. "You don't know, do you? Great! Just great! I knew something like this would happen! Redmond! Redmond!" Natalie felt Jesse's hand clamp down around her mouth.

"It is okay folks, she's just looking for our dog. Isn't that right honey? Here Redmond, come here boy."

Jesse grabbed her hand guided her around the people surrounding them. He led them to Rockefeller Center where a tall Christmas tree mesmerized Natalie. Jesse continued to drag her in the direction of St. Patrick's Cathedral. When they reached the steps of the Cathedral, Natalie stopped.

This was where they were staying? Natalie observed Jesse closely as he stood at the Cathedral's doors. Natalie heard him whisper 'Templum.' A second later, a woman opened the door and invited Jesse in.

"Natalie," Jesse said. "Come here."

Natalie slowly walked up the stairs and reached the threshold of the door. She walked inside and admired the Gothic beauty of the cathedral. The sound of the door closing brought Natalie back to reality. She turned around to find a woman standing there with golden-brown hair and green eyes. Who was she? No doubt she was someone from Purgatory.

"Very good, Jesse," she said with a hint of an Italian accent. "I have been expecting you both."

Natalie observed the interaction between Jesse and the exotic looking woman. With flawless olive skin, she looked like she just stepped out of the pages of a fashion magazine. After watching the two exchange a brief glance, Natalie started tapping her foot on the ground.

"Jesse, I believe this young lady would like to know who I am and why she is here."

Natalie watched as Jesse rubbed the back of his neck. He knew they had to come here this entire time and he failed to mention it to her.

"It seems that he has forgotten his manners," she said as she reached for Natalie's hand. "You must be Natalie Parker. I am one of many Messengers. My name is Michelangela. Welcome to your Sanctuary."

Natalie took a hold of Michelangela's hand in confusion.

"Sanctuary? Wait a minute!" Natalie turned around to face Jesse. "We're staying here?"

Jesse had lowered his head and nodded. "I know it's not ideal. I mean I was hoping for something a little more bed and breakfast like, but this will have to do. I guess you can consider St. Patrick's a religious retreat of sorts. Plus, we got a great view of Rockefeller Plaza."

"Are you kidding me? I should be happy with a room with a view? You knew we had to come here and you didn't tell me!"

Natalie took off running through the doors she had just entered. Despite the cold weather, she headed for the famed Christmas tree lit up in the distance. It wasn't supposed to be like this. She wasn't supposed to feel so alone and scared. Her weariness grew and she was starting to feel even more tired and numb. Natalie sat down beside one of lit up angels and brought her knees to her chest.

"Help."

***

Jesse watched Natalie burst through the doors outside. To say that he was shocked was an understatement. He looked to Michelangela for guidance. Instead, she just stood there giving him a look of disappointment. Jesse had done it. He had hurt Natalie and Michaelangela was clearly stunned by what had just happened.

"I knew that," he said.

"Of course I knew."

Jesse stared at the doors Natalie just exited.

"I knew what being here would do to her. She was going to be married here. It was in her file."

"Why didn't you tell her?"

"I didn't know how," he replied."Redmond told me not to tell her until we got here. That she couldn't know. Now I come across as some insensitive jerk."

Jesse ran his fingers through his hair, a nervous trait he often did when he had messed up. It was a wonder that he wasn't bald yet.

"You were scared of what she was going to do," she paused and Jesse ran his fingers through his hair once more.

"Jesse, I am well aware that you are new to this and have a lot to learn."

"We were doing fine," he explained and shoved his hands into his pockets. "We were joking. I was getting to know her and then we go back to square one all because Redmond didn't brief me on how to break it to her. He told me that I would just know. That's not fair."

"What's done is done. Think about Natalie and see that she needs you to be her friend, not the person who keeps secrets from her."

Jesse winced. Michaelangela handed him a piece of paper with one word on it. He looked at her questioningly.

"See the door over there?" she asked.

Jesse nodded as he looked at an old looking wooden door beneath an archway.

"That will lead to a set of stairs. Once you are at the top, you will see another door. Whisper 'Aperio'. Then you and Natalie will be at your Sanctuary."

Michelangela patted him on the shoulder and walked toward the doors and turned around.

"Adversus exitus optio non est."

With those words, she left him standing there looking bewildered, lost and alone. Sitting down on the wooden pew, he looked around at his surroundings. The stained glass windows were encompassed by cluster columns. He looked up and admired the pointed arches and the sculptures of many saints. It was strange that such a work of architecture could be found in a city that was constantly on the go. No matter how crazy it was on the streets, a person could find peace and solace here.

It didn't take long for Natalie to find comfort at the Christmas tree at Rockefeller Centre. She was finally home and relished in the environment she had not forgotten. The sounds of horns blaring from cars calmed her down.

Lost in her own world, Natalie was slow to see that she was no longer alone. A gentle touch to her shoulder brought her back to reality. Raising her head, she found Michaelangela looking at her with sympathy. The spell had been broken; she was dead, fighting for her life, her freedom, her second chance.

"I hate him," Natalie whispered softly to Michelangela.

"Hate is a very strong word," she whispered back, as she sat down beside Natalie.

"Why couldn't he just tell me we were going to stay there?" she said and closed her eyes.

"You are justified in your anger," Michelangela answered, hesitating for a moment. "But aside from some details about you, he doesn't know you and I don't think he knew how to tell you. He called himself an insensitive jerk, you know."

Natalie opened her eyes and stared into Michaelangela's. "Don't look surprised. He knows that he didn't handle things too well. However, Redmond didn't tell Jesse how he should tell you and I think a little latitude should be given. He's only been a Protector for less than a day."

Natalie looked at her skeptically and then looked back up

at the tree. While she had made a good point, she still hated that he had coddled her rather than be honest with her.

"I don't know. I just don't know. Here I am now, trying to get my life back and right now, I'm realizing this whole thing is more painful than I am willing to admit." Natalie stood up. "The whole time I was in Purgatory I thought about nothing except getting my life back. I never thought about what lengths I would have to go to while trying to get it back. Does that make sense?"

"It makes sense," Michelangela chuckled. "Natalie, I really think you should go back up there and talk to him. You should sleep and decide on your plan for tomorrow. You're on borrowed time and a lot of us don't want to see you waste it, especially Redmond."

Knowing that she was right was one thing, feeling normal for a little while longer was the only thing on her mind.

"Can we stay a little longer? I just don't want to go back yet," Natalie begged.

Natalie could see the Michaelangela struggling with her request. Clearly she was torn. The last thing Natalie wanted was for Michaelangela to get in trouble. Pleading with her eyes, Natalie hoped she would take mercy on her.

"Alright, but we can't stay too long."

***

One hour and cup of hot chocolate later, along with some gentle coaxing from Michaelangela, Natalie was finally ready to make her way back to the Sanctuary.

As they walked across the street back to the cathedral, Natalie wondered what Jesse had been up to. Part of her hoped that he would be gone and replaced by another Protector.

"Natalie, look at it this way. If you get your life back, you will walk through those doors in a wedding dress instead." As they approached the doors, Natalie froze. The hope in Michaelangela's words struck a chord with Natalie. She had never made it up those steps and through those doors on her wedding day. She could only hope that what Michaelangela said would eventually come true.

Natalie looked at her hopefully and even managed to smile. No longer was she going to think about the life that could have been. From now on, Natalie was going to think about the life that would be.

Chapter 8:
The Keeper's Perspective

Redmond had been keeping a close eye on Jesse and Natalie. The spark between them was palpable and it worried him because he needed them to focus on the task at hand.

"Redmond?" came a soft voice.

Looking to see who interrupted his thoughts, Redmond turned around and spotted Isa walking toward him with a worried look on her face.

"What is it, Isa?"

"Jesse and Natalie have been fighting."

"Tell me something I don't know."

Redmond frowned for a moment and looked at the mirrored vortex in his office. It was his window to the world below and his way to keep an eye on the pair.

"The fact that they were able to get along for a few hours is somewhat encouraging."

As he looked down the vortex he saw Michelangela talking to Jesse, and a smile appeared on his face. She was definitely an ally and there was no doubt in his mind that she would offer her wisdom to the quibbling duo. When Redmond heard Michaelangela say 'Adversus exitus optio non est,' he couldn't help but smile. "Failure is not an option," he said out loud. "She would have made an excellent Protector."

The vortex shifted to show Jesse in the pews looking up at the ceiling.

"Isa, I honestly have no idea what to make of him," he said and folded his hands behind his back. "He's on the clock and I need him to get his act together."

"Give him time, Redmond. He will figure it out. This is all so new to him."

"Isa, he doesn't want to do this and I'm beginning to think that this was a mistake. Then again, a promise is a promise. That will be all, Isa."

As he contemplated everything that had happened up to that point, he worried that he was asking too much of Jesse.

Turning to the grandfather clock by the mirror, Redmond scoffed in contempt. The ticking of the clock was a constant reminder that Natalie's soul was hanging in the balance.

"Tick tock, tick tock. That's all you do."

Frustrated with time, Jesse, Natalie, and the entire situation, Redmond was slowly going insane.

Before he could further ponder what kind of conversation Natalie and Jesse were about to have, a knock came at the door.

"I said that would be all and I meant it," he said.

"Redmond, didn't your mother ever teach you not to spy on people," a powerful female voice replied.

"Michaelangela." Redmond turned to face her. "It's not spying, it's observing. Thank you for getting Natalie back to the Sanctuary. I appreciate it."

Michaelangela nodded at him and he turned his attention back to his mirror and brandy.

"Redmond, I respect you as a Keeper and as a friend. Nonetheless, please tell me what you were thinking when you chose Jesse to be Natalie's Protector?"

"Angela, I am well aware that everyone around here thinks that I have made some kind of mistake with selecting Jesse as a Protector." He stopped and sighed. "Sofia and the Son would have expressed their concerns if they didn't think he was capable of it. But there's something about him and I can see why he needed to be saved."

"What do you mean 'something about him'? You admit that he was not, and is not, the ideal candidate for the job. Then why him? It's clear they dislike each other."

Redmond stood up from the chair and reached for more brandy. He looked at Michaelangela and poured her a glass while refreshing his own.

"Because I made a promise," Redmond said and handed her a glass of brandy. "And as I mentioned, Sofia and the Son approved of my choice. They thought he was more than capable of handling this."

"A promise? What kind of promise? What did you do?"

"For seven years, I have waited for Natalie to finally get selected and present herself in court. I had her Protector all lined up, but I was overruled."

Redmond turned away from Michaelangela and closed his

eyes.

"I owed someone a favour and agreed to do this for them," he admitted. "I didn't understand why he needed to be saved until I saw his death. Though tragic and painful, I saw a man who could change and I recognized why he needed to be saved."

Redmond paused and turned back to look at Michaelangela. Her body language spoke volumes. Her hands were on her hips and her head was tilted to the side. "I told Isa to bring him to me. I didn't know he was going to be this difficult. Here I was offering him a chance to be better than he was and somehow we ended up making a deal. All he has to do is help Natalie get her life back, and I would restore his life as it was."

The silence from Michaelangela irked him greatly.

"Redmond," she said. "I spent the last hour sitting with Natalie trying to convince her to go back and try to work things out with Jesse-"

"Michaelangela," he interrupted, "do you really think that the Son, Sofia, and I would put them together without really thinking this through?"

"You just said you had no choice. You made a deal with Jesse and Natalie has no idea. Jesse is only her Protector because you owed someone a favour? That's unlike you, Sofia, and the Son. How could you do this?"

"We know what we're doing." Redmond replied. "Yes, it's far more complicated, but it must be done this way."

"Who is this 'we' Redmond?" asked Michaelangela.

Redmond gave Michaelangela a hard stare. He would never underestimate her intelligence and he certainly wasn't going to bring her into this. The last thing he needed was for people to be involved.

"I have already told you. The Son, Sofia, and I-"

"No, Redmond," Michaelangela said, cutting him off. "Yes, the Son and Sofia have more power than you or I, but there's something more going on here."

Redmond was starting to get annoyed with his friend. No one else but Isa and the other parties needed to know. Friend or not, he had no intention of telling Michaelangela anything. He made a promise and he was going to keep it.

"Michaelangela, I know it's confusing but try to understand." He stepped closer to her. His eyes searched hers carefully.

"Why Jesse?" she asked. "You had a Protector selected for Natalie. What changed? What aren't you telling me?"

Redmond looked away from her once more. He needed to reassure her that he knew what he was doing.

"We've known each other for a long time," he said. "I am under orders not to tell you anything other than what you already know."

Redmond could see the hurt and betrayal in her eyes.

"For their sake and yours I hope you're right," she said. "I just want to know one thing. What if it doesn't work out and they fail, Redmond?"

"I will cross that bridge when I need to."

Redmond watched as she handed him her glass and walked out the door.

At the click of the door closing, Redmond leaned against his chair. He shook his head and glanced at the mirror in the corner. Sighing, he walked over to the mirror hoping to see what had transpired between Jesse and Natalie while he had been talking with Michaelangela. He could see the two of them talking in the Sanctuary and was hopeful that they would resolve their issues.

Explaining to Michaelangela something he didn't entirely understand himself was hard, but he made a promise and vowed to keep it.

He looked at the clock again and watched the seconds go down. Time still had a way of affecting people, even after they were dead. Only Redmond knew that when time ran out in this world, it was gone forever.

"Six days, twenty hours, fifty-six minutes and counting. Timing really is everything."

Chapter 9:
Starting Over

Jesse had been sitting in a pew at the back of the cathedral contemplating everything that had happened since he had died. He thought of his death and was thinking about Natalie and how she died. Jesse slammed his hand against the pew and heard the sound echo in the church. An eerie feeling of being watched left Jesse uncomfortable. It was then he remembered where he was.

"God's house on earth," he said. "I can't seem to escape you."

He continued to stare around his current environment and did his best to stay calm. He was worried about Natalie and hoped that Michaelangela talked some sense into her. He didn't know how much time had passed, but a noise behind him broke him from his thoughts. He turned around and saw Natalie enter the cathedral. Behind her he could see Michelangela motioning him to come forward. In a split second, Michaelangela had disappeared and he was left alone with Natalie.

"We need to talk," she whispered.

Nodding his head, he led her to the door Michaelangela showed him earlier. Together, they went up the wooden spiral of the staircase which led them down a dimly lit narrow hallway, where at the far end, stood a door. Jesse reached for the handle whispering 'Aperio.' The door opened and a furnished room appeared before them.

The floors were wooden, creaky, and old. The walls were covered with beige paint. There was the closet in the corner filled with clothes, a wooden table tucked in the corner underneath one of the windows with two chairs, and a maple hope chest carved with intricate designs. He instantly recognized The Protector's coat of arms on top of the chest situated at the foot of the bed. For a Sanctuary, it wasn't spectacular, but it wasn't bad.

"I knew," Jesse said as he stared out the window.

Natalie's eyes shot up at him and Jesse felt extremely

guilty.

"I knew that you were supposed to get married here. I read it in your file."

"How could-"

"Before you lay into me," he continued as he raised his hands up. "Redmond told me not to tell you and that it was for your protection."

Natalie raised her eyebrows at him and crossed her arms.

"I know that sounds bad, but I was doing as I was told. Don't get me wrong, I questioned him on it too. I guess he was afraid you couldn't handle it and he was right. Look at what happened."

Jesse ran his fingers through his hair. He really hated Redmond right now.

"As much as I respect Redmond," she replied, "he's not here with me. As much as I hate to admit it, you are. And you should have told me!"

Jesse was stunned by her words.

"You have to realize though that this is going to be difficult for me no matter what and-"

"Okay," he stopped her. While he was glad that their misunderstanding had been resolved, he needed her to focus on what to do next. "I'm sorry. I won't keep things from you and I will try to avoid saying something stupid."

It occurred to Jesse that Natalie had opened herself up to him and maybe now was the time to shed some light on who he was and why he constantly needed to think before he spoke.

"Maybe if you let me explain myself to you, you might be able to understand why I behave the way I do. I think it's only fair given that I know so much about you."

Jesse led her to a table in the corner with two chairs. He was tired and he could see that she was too. He rubbed his hands together nervously and carefully thought of ways to explain his background.

"I grew up with a socialite mother, a father who cared more about making money than spending time with his kids and two older brothers who bullied me and treated me like crap. I mean, they bought me a hooker for my sixteenth birthday and told me to be a man."

He looked up at Natalie to see if he could gauge her reaction, so far, she remained unmoved. "By the time I was six-teen, I had been in five boarding schools and arrested several times for my crazy partying. No one in my family cared, so I just kept doing it. I never had to apologize for anything be-cause if I did hurt their feelings they never said anything. The night before I died, I was starting to feel sorry for myself. I drank myself into oblivion because I was angry at my family for blaming me for everything. I woke up with a hangover, got in my Porsche and slammed into a dump truck. I didn't want to die, it just happened and let me tell you something, I am sorry that it did."

Jesse stopped for a moment and looked up at Natalie again. He was unsure if his explanation was having any kind of effect on her. His only hope was for her to understand. Whether she cared was a different a story. He just needed her to understand.

"For the first time in my life, people are actually listening to the words that come out my mouth. I just have to get used to the fact that people have feelings, that you, Natalie, have feelings. For what it's worth, whether you believe me or not. I am sorry."

Natalie had a look of bewilderment on her face. She seemed shocked by his declaration and he couldn't blame her for thinking he cooked his story up.

"You don't believe me, do you?" Jesse said.

"You might find this hard to believe, I mean I am having hard time believing it." Natalie paused. "I believe you."

Jesse smiled at her and he could swear that he saw a grin on her face. Maybe this whole thing wouldn't be so bad.

"I may present myself as a jerk and it's true. The one thing I want you to know is that I don't lie. Lying was never my thing and I am not lying to you now."

Jesse valued her opinion of him. He also understood that time wasn't on their side. The fact that they had wasted some time didn't help their situation here and if they didn't figure out what happened to Natalie soon, they were never going to have their second chances.

"So, should we just act like grownups and focus on the task at hand?" he asked.

Jesse looked at her and waited for her response. She pulled her chair back and stood up.

"I think we both know the situation we're in," she said as she looked at him expectantly. "Let's act like adults and do what we need to do.

"Okay," he agreed. "Now that we're starting over, turning a new leaf, making a fresh-"

"I got it Jesse," she interrupted.

"Sorry, so tell me, where would you like to start? I mean it's almost seven o'clock and the day is not quite over. We're still in the wee hours of December 10. What do you want to do now?"

"Sleep," she told him. "I just want to sleep. Between walking the streets, arguing with you, and dealing with everything else, I just want to sleep."

Jesse nodded in agreement. He was tired too. He had been fighting off sleep since they landed. Normally he was a night owl, but right now he was dealing with the fact that he was dead, becoming a Protector, and working with a perfect stranger on getting her life back. He was overwhelmed at the moment and sleep sounded like a good idea.

"Jesse?"

"What?" he said.

"We have a problem."

"Pray tell, what is the problem?"

"Take a look around the room. Tell me, what do you see?"

Natalie was either losing it or there was some merit to her request. Jesse looked around the room they had been occupying for the last while. He failed to see what problem she was referring to. Closet, table, chairs, chest, bed. Bed?

Bed! There was only one bed. In any other situation, this would not have been a problem. In this case, the thought of sharing a bed with Natalie scared the crap out of him. He turned to look at her and saw that she was waiting for some response from him.

"What is, there is only one bed, Mr. Trebek?" he said.

"This isn't funny," she replied. "What are we going to do?"

Jesse smiled to himself. He knew what he wanted to do, Natalie on the other hand was a different story.

"We can share it," he suggested. "Or, we could put a barrier between us? Take turns?" Jesse then saw her lack of enthusiasm with that prospect and knew where she was heading with this. He wasn't going to give in that quickly though.

He knew what she wanted: him, on the floor, nowhere near her.

"We could-"

"I'll tell you what we're going to do," she said, cutting him off. "You're going to sleep on the floor and I will sleep on the bed. Problem solved."

"If you knew that was the solution all along, what did you need me for?"

"I just wanted to see the look on your face when you figured it out," she answered with a gleam in her tired eyes. "Now, if you don't mind, I am going to get some sleep."

Jesse watched her walk to the bed and get underneath the covers. If he weren't so tired, he would have argued for the bed a little more. At the very least he would have tried to get her to share the bed with him. He made his way to the foot of bed near the chest and tried to decide how he was going to get comfortable. After a few seconds of changing positions, he gave up and closed his eyes. Just as he had done so, he felt something soft hit him. Opening his eyes, he saw a pillow and blanket before him. Smiling to himself, he figured that his sleeping arrangement wasn't that bad after all.

"You care - you really, truly do."

"Just go to sleep!" Natalie replied.

"Thanks for the pillow," he said after a few seconds of silence.

"You're welcome. Goodnight, Jesse," she answered back.

"Goodnight, Natalie," he replied. "Sleep well."

Chapter 10:

Appearances Can Be Deceiving

Jesse heard movement in the room and closed his eyes tighter. The majority of his night consisted of tossing and turning. He got up a few times, pacing back and forth, repeatedly thinking about his current predicament. Some of those times were spent watching Natalie sleeping, looking calm and peaceful. He shifted in his sleep once more and turned over on his back. He was up and he really didn't want to open his eyes; he just wanted to stay right where he was. Jesse found himself drifting to sleep once more, but came to awareness when he felt a pair of eyes staring at him.

"You know if you want to stare at me, at least do it from across the room. Then again, I know it's hard to tear your eyes off me."

He opened his eyes hoping to see chocolate brown eyes before him. Instead he was startled by a pair of fierce green eyes. Jesse jumped up and ran toward the door.

"Not who you were expecting?" Redmond replied.

Turning around, Jesse saw Natalie and Redmond grinning at him.

"I'm glad you two find this amusing," Jesse replied. "Tell me, who the hell stands over someone and scares the crap out of them?"

"Funny. When you thought it was Natalie you seemed to have enjoyed it."

Both Natalie and Jesse averted their eyes from one another and stared at Redmond.

"There are a few things I need to discuss with you. After yesterday's fiasco, I realized that I need to go over a few things with the both of you. First and foremost, I am going to have to alter your appearances."

"Why didn't you do it yesterday?" Jesse asked.

"Because I didn't expect the Son to speak to Natalie and I thought you two would be at the Sanctuary much sooner. Besides, I need to transform you in the Sanctuary! We cannot risk people recognizing you two, especially yourselves. Secondly, Jesse I wanted to personally deliver this to you."

Redmond tossed a book over to Jesse.

"*The Protector's Guide to a Second Life*," he read aloud. "You know, I don't think I have this edition."

Jesse noted Redmond's displeasure and smirked. Redmond was good at dishing it out, but Jesse was better at giving it right back. If the Keeper was looking for a verbal smack down, Jesse was ready.

"Thirdly, I need to speak to Natalie privately. "

Jesse took the hint from Redmond. It was clear to him that Redmond was angry at him for yesterday and he was sure that Redmond needed to assure Natalie that it was his entire fault.

"Should I leave or would his grace choose to take the conversation elsewhere?" Jesse said.

"Just read the book, Jesse."

Jesse watched the pair walk out of the room. Shaking his head, he picked up the book and stared at it.

"Terrible title. Just terrible."

***

Natalie followed Redmond along the corridor, down the stairs to the familiar pews of St. Patrick's. She noted the few worshipers waiting for the mass to start and wondered what Redmond needed to discuss with her.

"Redmond, if this is about what happened earlier-" she started.

Redmond held his hand to stop her.

"Natalie, I cannot stress the seriousness of the matter because I know you are aware of the circumstances. I am not saying this out of spite or malice. I say this simply because it is the truth."

"Redmond, Jesse and I know that we made some mistakes. That's the last I am going say anything about it." She paused momentarily realizing that patrons around them were starting to stare at her raised voice.

"Sorry."

"No, Natalie. I should apologize to you. What's done is done. However, I do have something I would like to give you."

Curiosity lit her face as she watched Redmond pull out a silver watch from his pocket. As Redmond handed her the watch, she noticed that it was not a regular watch. The numbers were counting down instead of going up. Natalie quickly withdrew her hand and dropped it in Redmond's lap as if it had burned her.

"That was not the reaction I was hoping for," he said as he handed her the watch again. "Natalie, the watch is intended for you to use. By having it, you will constantly be reminded of time and just how precious it is. Read the engraving."

"Time Knows No Boundaries," she whispered.

"The phrase is true and a clue, Natalie. This watch has some magic in it. Not the type you may think, but it can prove to be an advantage for you. Now, if we're lucky, your Protector, should he have attempted to read the book and will know what to do with it..." He saw her begin to protest this and added, "And no, I can't tell you. As much as it pains me, I just can't. Let's go see what exactly your Protector has been up to."

Natalie slipped the watch on her wrist and took Redmond's arm as they made their way back up the stairs toward the Sanctuary.

***

Jesse's patience was beginning to take a toll on him as he waited for Natalie and Redmond to return. While they were gone, he briefly glanced at the book Redmond had given him and kept an eye on the door waiting for their return. He was frustrated because he wasn't sure what kind of conversation Natalie was having with Redmond.

He picked up the book again and began to read it. He came to the realization that this book was different then the manual he read when he was up in Purgatory. He turned the first page, carefully reading the table of contents.

"Chapter One: The Protector. How original?" he read aloud.

"Chapter Two: The Protector's Medallion and The Life Locket." Jesse reached for the medallion on his neck and looked at the engraving again. "Trust God and He Will Protect You." Jesse wondered what Natalie's locket said, that is, if it said anything. He reached for the book and continued the list.

"Chapter Three: The Keeper's Watch." He paused and realized that Redmond was The Keeper, but never mentioned anything about a watch. Before he could turn to the page to find more information about the watch, Natalie and Redmond entered through the door. He closed the book and placed it back on the table.

"Read anything interesting?" Redmond asked.

Jesse momentarily looked back at the book and back at Redmond.

"Question, what does *Fidelis Deus Quod Is Mos Servo Vos* mean? I know you said it before we jumped."

Redmond's cheeky smirk annoyed Jesse. It was a simple question.

"It means the same thing your medallion says in Latin. Saying this phrase will take you right to me. Remember?"

Jesse's face reddened. The answer was meant to be obvious and he felt like an idiot for not putting two and two together.

"Okay. Well then, how much trouble am I in?" he asked.

"None," Redmond replied. "I think you know what's at stake. I don't need to remind you."

Jesse looked over at Natalie and gave her an appreciative smile. Jesse definitely knew what was at stake and he was going to do everything in his power to get what he wanted.

"Now, for the other reason I came to call on you both. Your appearances must be changed."

"Fine. So, when are you going to change us?" he said, as he walked to the mirror.

"What the..." Jesse shouted as he took in his appearance. His short black hair was light brown, slightly messy and a little longer than he cared for. His icy blue eyes were now hazel and on his left cheek appeared a pale, jagged pink scar shaped like a crescent moon. He quickly looked at Natalie and saw that Redmond had changed her too. Her soft blonde locks were auburn as Redmond said it would be, and her eyes were different colours: one blue and one green. Her face was sprinkled with faded freckles. He tore his gaze from her and glared at Redmond. The Keeper merely smiled. He made Natalie just as beautiful, if not more so.

"We look so different. Good, but different."

"I take it that by your reaction you approve?"

"Yes, Redmond. I approve. Thank you."

"Well then, my job here is done. Since I have taken up most of your morning, I shall be on my way. Please, make the most of this day and the remaining days you have left," he said.

With a stoic look on his face and a wave of his hand, he was gone.

"Ladies and gentleman, Redmond has left the building,"

"Jesse," she said.

"What?" he said as he made his way over to the chair. He picked up the book again and flipped through it. Jesse had no idea what to do next. He wasn't quite sure what approach would be best to take with her.

"So..." Jesse said.

"So..." Natalie repeated.

"When you were downstairs, you didn't happen to catch the time did you?"

"Noon," she answered.

Natalie's answer put him on edge. He watched as she carefully inspected her new features and saw a look of disdain on her face.

"You look fine," he said.

It was as if she was unhappy about the change and he couldn't blame her. He too, would have to get used to his new appearance, including the scar on his face.

Natalie gave him a small smile and while he wanted to know what was really troubling her, Jesse decided to leave well enough alone. There were more important things and that included figuring out what Natalie remembered about the week she died.

Then it occurred to him. Did she remember?

"Do you have any idea what you were doing on December 10, seven years ago today?"

Jesse observed Natalie closely and saw her close her eyes.

"Well, it is still Saturday, right?" she asked. Jesse nodded his head in agreement.

"Dinner!" she shouted.

"Good idea," he replied. "I wonder if we can get food. I usually like to eat lunch before I get to dinner, but we can figure that out. The fact that we can eat despite being dead amazes me."

"No, that's where I'll be tonight. I'm having dinner with my family."

"Okay, dinner, where?"

"21 Club."

"How fitting. Dinner at a restaurant surrounded by Jockeys."

Natalie's eyes narrowed at him and he couldn't help but smile at her.

"Now's not the time for idiotic comments," Natalie replied annoyed.

"That's not idiotic, that's ironic. There's a big difference," he countered. "Never mind. What time does this 'dinner' happen?"

"Eight o'clock. I don't see why that's relevant."

"Well, we are going to be there for dinner too."

"We are? Like a date?"

Jesse couldn't help but be amused by her reaction. He wanted to have a little fun, then thought better about pissing her off.

"Who said anything about a date," he said. "We just need to see what happens."

"I was there, I know what happens."

"Okay, you know what happens. I don't. Look, we can keep arguing over this, which we agreed we wouldn't do, or we can get started working together on this."

Leaving Natalie to her thoughts, Jesse took the time to assess the clothes in the closet. He was somewhat satisfied with the wardrobe selection.

"At least Redmond got one thing right," he muttered.

Jesse saw Natalie out of the corner of his eye and could see that she was less than impressed with him.

"Okay," she finally spoke. "We'll go."

Jesse smiled and continued to look through the wardrobe.

"So, 21 Club at eight o'clock. Any ideas as to how we should fill the time?" He yawned.

"Why don't you get some sleep? You look tired."

"Sleep? Where on the floor? I already did that, thank you

very much."

"Take the bed, Jesse. I'm going to go for a walk-" she said as she headed toward the door.

"No!" he interrupted and threw his body across the door. "No walks, no more time to waste. I don't need Redmond to come back down here."

"Calm down, Jesse. I am going to walk around the cathedral. You can get some sleep and I can try to remember more things that may help us tonight."

Jesse took a look at the bed and then back at Natalie. He was tired and came to the realization that sleeping on the floor only worked after you passed out from a night of drinking.

"Okay, I will take the bed and get some sleep. Just don't go far."

Jesse peeled his body from the door and headed to the bed

"Yes, oh great Protector!" she said. "Do you mind if I read the book Redmond gave you?"

Jesse's eyes were already closing as he muttered, "Knock yourself out."

***

Book in hand, Natalie walked down the familiar corridor that led to the back of the cathedral and sat down in a pew. Her stomach growled and it occurred to her that she and Jesse hadn't eaten since their arrival. She ignored the hunger pains and hoped that there may be something in the book regarding their food situation. Natalie turned her attention back to the book and opened it only to discover that every page was blank. She continued flipping the pages when she discovered a message Redmond had written.

For Protector's Eyes Only.
Sorry Natalie,
Redmond

Stunned by Redmond's note, Natalie sighed and shook her head. She closed the book and reached for the book about

St. Patrick's lying on the pew next to her. Natalie decided to give Jesse and hour to catch up on sleep. She was more aware of their time predicament and was certainly going to use it wisely.

"Guess I should learn more about our host," she mumbled and began to read all about St. Patrick and the Cathedral.

***

Jesse awoke to a loud bang, followed by swearing that would make even the toughest of sailors blush. He rubbed the sleep from his eyes and saw Natalie on the floor surrounded by a pile of clothes.

"I'd ask what happened, but I think that between the clothes on the floor and the bar in your hand, it's fairly obvious."

"Will you help me up?" came her exasperated reply.

He made his way over to her and picked her up while surveying the mess she created. He turned to look back at her, making sure that she didn't hurt herself.

"Are you alright?" he asked as he picked up the bar and put it back in its place.

"Yes. I was trying to reach for the box up on the ledge."

"What was in the box?" he asked.

"Absolutely nothing. Just like the book Redmond left you."

Nothing in the box and nothing in the book. What was she talking about? There was something in the book, in fact a lot of somethings were in that book. Confused by her comment, he walked over to the table where the book was and opened it.

"What are you talking about? Everything is in here."

"Well, our favourite Keeper has made it set for your eyes only."

"That..." he stopped and stroked his chin.

"That what?"

"Is interesting," he finished.

Jesse picked up the book and flipped through the pages filled with words and pictures.

"How long was I out?" Jesse asked.

"About two hours," she replied. He nodded and was about to read the chapter he was interested in from before regarding the watch, when he saw Natalie rummaging through the clothes scattered about the floor. In her hands she held two dresses and wondered which one of the two she would choose. Intrigued, Jesse made his way over to her as he watched her facial expressions change while she decided between the silky red dress and the black strapless one.

"Tough choice isn't it?" he asked.

Natalie turned around and looked at him. "It is 21 Club. I have to look decent."

Jesse could feel the walls around him get smaller and a wave of claustrophobia hit him. He looked at both dresses and then back at her. It had to be a trick because there was no way she was flirting with him right now.

"The black one...no, the red one."

Jesse never cared for the dresses women wore mainly because they ended up discarded on the floor somewhere in his room. He continued to look back and forth between the two with an agonizing look on his face.

Jesse watched her closely and became uncomfortable with the game she was playing. It was evident to him that she was toying with him.

He watched as Natalie made her way to the closet, pulling out an evergreen dress.

"What was wrong with the other two?" he asked.

Natalie turned her head and looked back at him.

"I decided to be the good girl tonight."

With that, she closed the door leaving Jesse alone with the other two dresses. He stared at both of them once more and then glanced back at the door.

"No, Natalie," he whispered. "You are definitely the devil."

***

"Are you ready yet?" Natalie heard Jesse ask through the bathroom door. He had been banging on it for the past five minutes and she could hear him pace back and forth. She knew that he was getting impatient and it made her more nervous. She was so nervous that she had only given Jesse five minutes in the shower before she chased him out. She smiled at the memory of Jesse flustered and doing his best to wrap the towel over his wet body.

Natalie stared at her reflection one more time and quietly opened the door. She could see Jesse staring at himself in the mirror, obviously giving himself the once over and taking in his new appearance. He was dressed in a black suit and white shirt with an open collar looking every bit like a GQ model. His hair was slightly messy and he had a five o'clock shadow on his face. She watched as he scratched at it. It was clear that he didn't like his beard. She waited to see what else he would do before she made herself known.

"Well, chicks dig scars right?" she heard him mutter to his reflection. Natalie could tell that he wasn't too happy that Redmond had marked his face. She, on the other, hand actually liked the scar on his face. It actually suited him and made him even more attractive, as well as menacing at the same time. Shaking off the thought, she decided that now was the time to make her presence known.

"Natalie!" he yelled. "Come on, we're going to be late!"

When Jesse turned in her direction, she saw his mouth part slightly open. His stare didn't waver and she was becoming very uncomfortable.

"Is there something wrong?" she said. "You're staring at me like I have three heads."

"Umm...you..." he stuttered. Natalie watched as he adjusted the buttons on his shirt and proceeded to wipe his hands on his pants.

"Nothing is wrong," he squeaked. "I mean, nothing is wrong," he added in a stronger tone. "You look..."

Natalie could see that he was unsure about what to say to her. "I look?" Natalie asked. Jesse tore his eyes away from her and made his way to the door. "Beautiful. You look beautiful. Now, let's go," he said.

Natalie walked to the closet and grabbed her coat. She was grateful that she would be dressed appropriately.

"You're missing the tie," she said as she searched the closet for one.

"I don't do ties and 21 Club banned the tie policy a few years ago," he responded.

"Well, maybe in your time you don't have to wear one," she said as she held one out to him, "but when I last went there ties were non-negotiable, Jesse, so, put on a tie and let's go!"

Natalie waited as Jesse marched over to her and yanked the matching evergreen tie out of her hand. He walked to the mirror and attempted to make the knot. She noticed that he was struggling and was quickly getting irritated. Rolling her eyes, she walked behind him and put her hands on his. In an instant, he let go of the tie.

Natalie focused her attention on tying the tie and tried not to think of using it as a noose. She smiled at the fact that she remembered how to do this with ease. When she finished, Jesse was wearing the perfect Windsor knot. Natalie stepped away from Jesse and put her coat on.

"Thanks. I never could do it," he admitted.

"You're welcome. Just takes practice. We better go," she replied and stepped out the door.

Chapter 11:

Meeting Mr. Perfect

The fifteen minute walk from the Cathedral to the res-taurant was awkward to say the least. Natalie wearing heels didn't help matters either. Throughout their walk, Jesse stole glances at Natalie and tried to figure out what was going on in her mind right now. He could tell that she was feeling anx-ious and he needed to reassure her that things were going to be fine. Before he could say anything, they stepped through the doors of 21 Club and Jesse suddenly felt very much in his element. He looked around the restaurant and was greeted by the sounds clinking of glasses, quiet conversations, and the aroma of fine dining. Before he could further enjoy his surroundings, he felt a tug on his jacket. He turned to find Natalie dragging him to the short, bald headed maître d with a pasty, white complexion.

"Hello, I was wondering if you have a table for two?"

"Do you have a reservation?" replied the man.

"If we had a reservation, do you really think we'd ask for a table?" Jesse said an annoyed tone.

"Jesse!" Natalie exclaimed. "Don't be rude!"

"I can't say I am surprised," the maître d' answered. "Michaelangela was right about you."

Both Jesse and Natalie's eyes shot up as they heard him mention Michaelangela's name.

"Yes, I know who you are. Redmond took care of every-thing and instructed me to give you this."

The short man pulled out an envelope from his pocket along with a note, handing it to Jesse. Jesse looked inside the envelope, surprised to find ten one hundred dollar bills. He quickly tucked the money away in his suit and grabbed the note.

"'Dinner's on me. Redmond," he read aloud. "How did he know we were coming here?"

Natalie rolled her eyes at Jesse, giving him a 'are you kidding me' look.

"Well, isn't that nice of him? So, what exactly do you do?"

"My name is Joshua and I am a Missionary. Now, follow me."

Natalie and Jesse were led up a set of stairs taking them to a part of 21 Club to which Jesse had never been. He had been to 21 Club before on several occasions, but Upstairs at 21 was a new experience all together. The room was beautifully decorated in a very authentic classic American style with murals of notable landmarks in New York City. Hints of Christmas decor also gave it a nice personal touch. Lost in the ambiance of his surroundings, Jesse bumped into Natalie. He looked around to see what caused her abrupt stop and followed her gaze. It was then that he could see the living version of Natalie in all her glory.

"Oh my God," she whispered.

"Natalie," said Joshua, "I know this is hard, but if you want your life back you have to be strong." He paused and looked at Jesse. "I have to leave, but I won't be far. If you need anything, just ask your waiter for Josh and I will come right here."

Jesse was grateful to the man for calming Natalie down because he knew that he wouldn't be able to find the right words.

"I know you're new to this," continued Josh. "Just follow her lead and let her take control. She can handle this better than you think."

Jesse heeded the Missionary's advice with a curt nod. As he sat down at the table, Jesse focused his attention on the task at hand and hoped for her sake and his that she would be able to get through this.

***

An hour later, they were no closer to learning anything relevant in regards to Natalie's death. Throughout dinner, Jesse had stolen glimpses at the table across from theirs. It was hard for him not too. The Natalie Parker from seven years ago was definitely someone he wanted to get to know. From his perspective, she seemed genuine and down to earth. She was someone you could have a conversation with and never get bored.

While Jesse had indulged in Joshua's advice, he thought the whole silent treatment was very childish. When he was younger, his grandmother had told him that patience was a virtue and while he believed that adage to be true, right now, Natalie was pushing his patience to a different level. He watched as her fiancé, Nick, stood up and headed toward the exit. To Jesse, Nick fascinated him. Who was this guy and how was he able to capture Natalie Parker's heart? His curiosity made him want to learn more about the man.

"Excuse me," said Jesse, getting up from the table. "Just heading to the men's room." Natalie nodded absently as Jesse walked away and followed Nick outside.

Jesse casually made his way down the stairs and out the front entrance of the restaurant. He gave Joshua a nod and headed out the front doors. The cold December air greeted him once more and Jesse reveled in the frigid climate. Remembering the real reason he was out there, he started his search for Nick to see where he had taken off to. He figured that Nick wouldn't have gone too far and he was right. He was standing on a street corner not too far from the restaurant with his cell phone to his ear while smoking a cigarette.

Jesse needed to know the kind of man Nick really was and what exactly it was about Nick Manning that made Natalie fall so deeply in love with him. It's not like he was jealous, he was just curious. He began to formulate a plan to engage Nick in some kind of conversation. When he saw that Nick was lighting up another cigarette, he saw his window. Jesse looked up to the sky and hoped that this would work. He casually strolled over to Nick and could hear bits and pieces of the discussion.

"Yes, Dad," Jesse overheard him say. "I know. I will talk to Natalie shortly. Just give me some time. Okay. I will talk to you later. Bye."

Jesse was intrigued by the tail end of the discussion that Nick had just had with his father. While he knew he couldn't draw any conclusions, at best he could engage Nick in some form of conversation and now seemed like the perfect time.

"Excuse me," Jesse said. "Can I bum a cigarette off you? My girlfriend isn't a fan of smoking and I could use one." Nick looked bothered by Jesse's interruption, but he nodded at him and pulled out a package of cigarettes from his jacket pocket. He handed one to Jesse and lit it for him.

"I know what you mean," Nick said. "My fiancée is the same way. She's not a fan of my smoking but sometimes the stress just gets to you and this seems to take off the edge."

Jesse nodded his head and agreement. "When's the big day?" Jesse obviously knew when the wedding was but Nick didn't know that.

"Next Saturday," he answered as he threw his cigarette to the ground and stepped on it.

"Speaking of women, I should probably get back to mine. Hope you and your girlfriend have a good night."

"You too," Jesse said as he watched Nick head back into the restaurant. Jesse finished his cigarette and contemplated the brief chat he just had with Nick. He could usually spot an asshole from a mile away. In this case, Nick was anything but that. Then again, he had overheard bits and pieces of Nick's conversation with his father which left him slightly confused and with one question. What exactly was it that Nick was going to have to talk to Natalie about?

Realizing that he had probably been gone longer than he originally intended, Jesse turned on his heel and headed back inside. He once again spotted Joshua faithfully at his maître d' station and smiled at him. When he sat back down at the table he found Natalie in the same position he had left her in.

A shift in her mismatched eyes caught his attention. Jesse looked over to see what had caused the change and saw that her family was standing up. They had concluded their evening and were ready to depart. The look of longing on Natalie's face as she watched Nick was heartbreaking. Jesse saw her starting to get up with them and he grabbed her hand gently. Natalie's eyes flashed at him and he shook his head.

"I know you want to go with them and talk to them," he said. "But you can't. Not yet."

Jesse's eyes searched hers and he was relieved when she nodded at him.

"I'd like to leave now," Natalie said.

As Natalie and Jesse were making their way out the door, they bumped into Nick who was rushing back inside. Jesse watched Natalie as Natalie watched Nick. He came hurrying back with a purple scarf in his hand and tapped on Jesse's shoulder.

"Have a good one," he said to Jessie. "Goodnight," he said to Natalie and walked out the door once more. Natalie gave him a questioning look and Jesse simply shrugged his shoulders. "Let's go," Jesse told her, and proceeded to make his way out the door with Natalie beside him.

***

The walk back to the Sanctuary had been a quiet one. Natalie had reflected on the evening and knew it was a waste. Instead of feeling overjoyed about seeing her family and Nick again, she felt saddened because the living her was so happy and energized. She thought back on the evening with regret and felt that she didn't really learn anything that would be beneficial to her later.

The one highlight of the night was when Nick had rushed back in the restaurant to grab her scarf. It had been a gift from him the Christmas before and meant a lot to her. However, one part of that brief moment had confused her greatly. Nick had acknowledged Jesse and said 'Have a good one'. What did that mean? Yes, Nick was considerate and polite, but the exchange between them was anything but courteous. It seemed more personal. It was almost as if they knew each other.

As they reached the steps of St. Patrick's, Natalie stopped and tapped Jesse on the shoulder.

"What was that?" she asked.

Jesse had turned around to face her and raised his eyebrow.

"What was what?" he asked, confused.

"You and Nick? He said 'have a good one'. He never says that to someone he doesn't know. So, why would he say it to you?"

Natalie waited for his reply and noticed that his eyes were avoiding hers.

"What did you do?" she said and crossed her arms.

"Why don't we go inside where it's warmer because I get the feeling that you aren't just crossing your arms to prove a point."

Yes, she was cold and, yes she was trying to prove a point. They were also out in public, and the last thing either of them needed was to cause a scene. Natalie nodded in agreement and headed up the stairs. She heard Jesse whisper 'Aperio' as they reached door to the Sanctuary. Once she heard the click of the door, she waited for his reply.

"Well, dinner was good," Jesse started. "I know you didn't have much-"

"Jesse," she hissed. "What did you do?"

He was hesitating and they both knew it. She wanted answers and she wanted them now. Jesse took off his jacket and loosened his tie. It was clear to her that he was stalling and it worried her because she was scared at what he may have said or done.

"Okay," he said. "I talked to him."

"You talked to him? When?"

Natalie didn't recall Jesse leaving the table and she didn't see Nick leave his table either.

"You were so zoned out getting caught up in the past, you didn't see Nick leave the table," he answered and pulled the tie off. "When he did, I followed suit."

Natalie sighed and pulled off her coat and laid it flat on the bed. How did she miss them both leaving the room?

"And?"

"I was curious," he said. "I went outside and he was on the phone with his dad having a smoke. So, I bummed one off him and he mentioned how his fiancée, who would be you by the way, didn't like him smoking, and I said my girlfriend didn't either."

"Girlfriend?" she asked.

"Yes, girlfriend," he repeated. "What was I going to say? That I'm really with your dead fiancée and we're trying to figure out how she died? I needed to think fast and that was an easy, believable answer."

Natalie stared hard at him. She wasn't impressed by what he had done, then again had she been more focused, it never would have happened in the first place. Now she was curious.

"Anything else?" she asked.

Jesse rubbed his five o'clock shadow and shook his head.

He was lying and she knew it.

"Jesse!"

"What do you want me to do Natalie?" he asked as he touched her shoulder. "Nothing happened. I wanted to get an idea about what kind of a guy he was. He seems like a catch. I wish I could snap my fingers and take us back so you could see for yourself how harmless it was but I can't."

Before she could process his words, the walls around the room began to shake and they grabbed on to each other. Natalie felt her body levitate along with Jesse's and closed her eyes. When the shaking had stopped, she opened her eyes. She was standing in entrance of the restaurant.

"What just happened?" Natalie asked as she let go Jesse.

"I don't know," Jesse replied just as confused.

"Well," came a voice. "Looks like you figured out the art of time travel."

Jesse and Natalie turned around and saw Joshua standing there with a smile on his face.

"Time travel?"

"Yes, Natalie. Time travel."

"Well, that's convenient," Jesse said. "Why didn't Redmond tell me we could do that?"

Natalie rolled her eyes.

A book hit Jesse on his head. "Ouch," Jesse grunted.

Natalie bent over to pick it up, she opened the book and laughed. "Yup, this was meant for you." She handed it to Jesse, who read it out loud.

'Jesse, I told you to read the book! Had you done that, you wouldn't have been surprised. Read Everything! Sincerely, Redmond.' Chapter Three: The Keeper's Watch? What watch is he talking about? Redmond gave me no watch!"

"Jesse," she asked. Natalie held out her wrist to him and he reached for it, inspecting it as he did so.

"When did you get this?" Jesse asked as he examined the watch.

"Redmond gave it to me earlier today when we were in the cathedral," she replied. "Joshua? What does this mean?"

"Hang on, I'm looking for it," he replied.

After reading a few pages of the book, Natalie waited for Jesse to find what he was looking for. "Here it is," he said then continued to read the passage.

"For Time Travel to occur, both parties must be present and touching. The Protector must be wearing their medallion and their Ward must wear the Life Locket and The Keeper's Watch. The Protector and the Ward must be touching as the Ward thinks of the place they wish to go and they will be transported to the designated time within the timeframe. It is important to note that your previous presence in the timeline is erased. All interactions with people you meet are gone, once you reappear again in the same moment. They will have no memory of you at all."

Jesse stopped reading, looked up at Natalie, then Joshua.

"So, whatever we did before didn't really happen because we're back again. Meaning that my conversation with Nick won't happen this time. Right?"

"Correct," said Joshua "Once you go back again, whatever you did before and whoever you talk to won't remember because it never happened. Now if you will both excuse me, I have a restaurant to run."

"Keep reading," she said to Jesse as Joshua left them.

"'The Keeper's Watch will act as a countdown clock to remind the Ward how much time remains It will act as a time clock, so that the Ward is aware of the current time and it will act as a date clock to remind the Protector and their Ward as to where they are within the timeline.'"

"Jesse, do you realize what this means?" she said. "We can skip a few days and go the day I died and see what happened. That's what Redmond meant. The watch could save us time!"

"Where did you want to be when we were back at the Sanctuary?" Jesse asked.

"You said that if you could take me back to see Nick when he went outside that you would and since I didn't believe you, I wanted to see what happened myself."

"So, you just wished you were in another place and then you were?"

"Yes," she said. "But it only works when we touch."

From Natalie's perspective, Jesse didn't seem to like that she held this power. This ultimately put him at her mercy. True, she couldn't do it without him, but she controlled where they would go. Natalie then remembered why they came back here in the first place. Jesse's conversation with Nick. She deserved to know.

"Now, there are two ways we can do this," she told him. "One we wait for Nick to go back outside and see what he was actually doing or two, you tell me the truth."

The look on Jesse's face spoke volumes. She knew that he was stuck between a rock and a hard place and whichever option he chose, Natalie would know the truth.

"What's it going to be?"

Jesse stuffed his hands in his pockets and shook his head. "He was on the phone with his dad," he muttered. "When he finished, I approached him."

Natalie folded her arms and tapped her foot.

"I haven't known you for long, but I know you must have gotten close and heard the conversation," she said. "What did you hear?"

Jesse sighed. "'Yes. Dad I know. I will talk to Natalie shortly. Just give me some time. Okay. I will talk to you later. Bye.' That's all he said, I swear."

Natalie unfolded her arms and let them drop to her sides. 'I will talk to Natalie shortly.' What did that mean? She believed Jesse when he said there was nothing more. Because even if she thought he was lying, she could still wait for Nick to go outside and listen for herself. In addition to answering the question as to why she died that day, she had another question. What did Nick need to talk to her about?

"Natalie," Jesse said and waved his hand in front of her. "The watch. What does the watch say now?"

"The countdown clock says 5 days, 23 hours and 57 minutes. The time clock says 7:57 PM Eastern Standard Time and the Date Clock reads December 10, 2005."

"7:57?" said Jesse as he turned his attention toward the door. "Well, that means that you will be walking in the door any minute now." Sure enough Natalie, Nick, and her family walked in. Natalie didn't have time to comprehend what was going on and before she could, she felt Jesse move her out of the way.

She was within feet of them and there was nothing she could do or say. When they had been there before, she watched them from afar and now that they were this close to her, she was overcome with emotion. Her mother was smiling. Her sister was checking herself out in her compact and

Nick was helping her living form with her coat. Her father did the same with her mother and spoke to Joshua. Natalie watched as they headed toward their table when she heard her father's voice.

"Jack Knight, is that you?"

Natalie's mouth parted in surprise and she quickly looked at Jesse and saw that his eyes were widened. They together stood in shock as they watched their fathers shake hands with each other.

Chapter 12:
Time Travel

Confusion. It was the only word that Jesse could come up with as he watched his father talking to Natalie's. How did they know each other? Natalie's dad was a veterinarian; his father was a real estate tycoon. The two of them running in the same circles didn't make any sense.

Jesse looked over at Natalie and saw that she wasn't as surprised. Did she know something he didn't? Jesse grabbed Natalie's hand and walked out of 21 Club for the second time that night.

Throughout the entire walk back to St. Patrick's, Jesse ignored Natalie's request to slow down. He picked up his pace as he walked along the busy streets and refused to let his emotions get the better of him. Storming into the Sanctuary, Jesse led Natalie into the room, slammed the door, and proceeded to pace the floor. Redmond had warned him that he could bump into his living form, but Jesse never considered the odds of bumping into his father. He began to wonder if fate really was a bitch or if there was a logical explanation to all of this.

Jesse cracked his knuckles as he thought about his dad. Jack Knight was a lot of things. Rich, successful, and well known. However, Jesse knew there was one aspect of Jack Knight's life that consumed him more than anything. His father had made it his personal mission to make Jesse's life a living hell.

"How the hell do our fathers know each other?"

Natalie flinched as Jesse stalked around the room. Immediately, he felt guilty for his tone. He wasn't angry at her: he was angry about his father.

"I'm not sure. I do know that I have met your parents before."

Jesse's eyes bulged out his sockets. Was she kidding? What were the odds of that happening? Turning his attention back to Natalie, he thought it best to question her on the nature of their parent's association.

"Met before?" he asked.

"Yes. I'm certain your parents have been to the Hamptons for various horses races and polo matches. I had no idea you were related to him."

"How many Jesse Knights do you think exist?" he asked.

"That's not the point. In case you haven't noticed, I have been dead for a few years, forgive me if I don't remember who your father is. We only met not too long ago, Jesse."

Jesse couldn't fault her for that. Making his way to the bed, he sat and began to rub his neck.

"Why did you run out of there like that?" she asked.

He had no intention of explaining his relationship with his father to her and he certainly didn't owe her one. Raising his head, he locked his eyes onto hers.

"So, time travel?"

"That's it? You're going to change the subject-"

"Yes," he stated. "This isn't about me, it's about you."

Jesse only hoped that she would let it go for now. He pleaded with her silently to just drop the issue.

"Time travel it is," she said, defeated. "But clearly you have problems."

"Clearly," he agreed. "Well, where do you want to go? Where in the time space continuum do you wish to see? Where would you-"

"Jesse, shut up!"

"Well?"

"Perhaps you should read over the rules of time travel while I decide where I want to go," Natalie suggested.

"How hard can it be?"

Natalie raised her eyebrows at him and tossed over the book.

"Considering you didn't know how it happened in the first place, I suggest you figure out exactly how it works."

Opening the book, Jesse turned to the time travel chapter and started to read. Out of the corner of his eye, he watched as Natalie curled herself up on the bed still wearing the dress. Images filled his brain and he sighed. She was going to kill him.

***

Thirty minutes later, Jesse had read and reread everything about time travel. He practically had the chapter
memorized and knew how to successfully travel within the
given time frame. He had to admit, it was far more complicated then he initially thought. Jesse rubbed his eyes and
looked over at Natalie. She was still curled up in the fetal
position asleep on the bed; the dress she was wearing was
riding up her legs, leaving very little to Jesse's imagination.

"Help me," he pleaded.

Spotting the blanket in the closet, Jesse went to grab it
and cover her up. As he placed the blanket, Natalie moved,
rolling over onto Jesse's hand, trapping him between the
blanket and her body.

"Crap!"

Jesse saw Natalie's eyes fluttering open and he waited for
hell to break loose.

"What are you doing?" she questioned.

Jesse stumbled backwards, landing hard on the floor.
Rubbing his side, Jesse stood while trying to hide the smile
on his face.

"I was trying to cover you up," he admitted. "You looked
cold. When I put the blanket on you, you moved and, well, my
hand-"

"I think I get it," she said as she covered herself up.
Walking toward the closet, she pulled out a pair of faded
jeans, a pink t-shirt that read 'I'm With Stupid', and a white
hooded sweatshirt. She proceeded to make her way to the
bathroom, shutting the door with the click of the lock.

"So, what did we learn about time travel?" she asked
through the door.

"We?"

"Fine, what did you learn about time travel?"

Jesse smiled. He could still feel warmth in his cheeks and
hoped that she didn't know what kind of effect she was currently having on him.

"Well, we can go anywhere within the timeframe. You
pick the memory you want to see, provided that you remember it and that's where we'll go. We traveled to 21 Club because that's where you wanted to go and because that's
where you were going to be."

"What does that include?" she asked as she stepped out of

the bathroom.

Jesse gave her a quick once over and sighed. Her hair was up in a ponytail and her outfit made her look irresistibly cute.

"Well?"

"It means we can go from the moment we arrived in the timeline to the moment you died."

Natalie nodded at the information and Jesse continued. "Courtesy of the watch, we can go forward and backward as many times as you wish. Not only that, we can watch from every possible angle. It's like instant replay!"

"Take me to the hospital."

Jesse's smiled disappeared instantly. Out of all the places to choose, why there?

"We can go-"

"Jesse. Take me to the hospital."

The tone in her voice resonated with him. This was her life, he was only there to help her and do what she asked.

"Okay, okay. Let me change."

Grabbing some jeans, a t-shirt and a sweater, he stripped down to his boxer shorts right in front of her.

"Umm, Jesse?"

Realizing that he was changing before her, Jesse thought now was the time for a little payback.

"What? Nothing you haven't seen before."

He smirked when he watched her turn away from him and stared out the window. He wanted to feel guilty for making her uncomfortable, but he was amused at how easy it was to get under her skin.

"Ready?" he asked.

Natalie whirled around at glared at him. He was now fully clothed and decided to match her clothing style. His jeans were darker than hers. His t-shirt was black and tight, the way he liked it. The shamrock green hoodie was his way of paying homage to St. Patrick, their current landlord.

"Yes, but I think shoes might be required."

He nodded and they both put on sneakers.

She pursed her lips and Jesse smirked. Not wanting to risk another argument, he took Natalie's hand in his and let her memories consume them. The jolt from the time travel left him somewhat disoriented. It was the sound of the heart monitor beeping and the smell of a sterile environment infiltrating his senses that made him realize where he was.

"Oh my God!" Natalie whispered.

Jesse turned to Natalie and saw that she was staring at herself. The sight sickened him. Natalie's head was wrapped in bandages, several cuts and bruises covered her face.

"So, this is how my life ended. I remember briefly waking up in the hospital. It was weird. I was pulled somewhere, then came back here and then it was just grey."

Jesse kept his mouth shut for one of two reasons. The first being that he had nothing comforting to say. The second, he was pretty sure he was going to be sick. The look on Natalie's face overwhelmed him. He just stood beside her and let her take everything in.

"I can't believe it," Natalie cried.

The sound of the machine crashing brought Jesse back to reality. Hearing footsteps running toward the room, Jesse pulled Natalie behind the curtain. They couldn't get caught. The last thing he wanted to do was explain to a bunch of doctors and nurses why they were in the room. Peeking their heads out, Jesse and Natalie watched as the medical staff tried desperately to revive Natalie. It was then that they both saw Natalie's eyes open.

"You did come back."

"No, I didn't."

"Clear!" they heard the doctor yell as she shocked Natalie.

"She's bleeding internally!" someone shouted.

"We're losing her!"

"She's flat lining!"

The sound of Natalie's heart stopping got Jesse's attention. Instantly, he could feel Natalie shake in his arms. He needed her to get them out of there and fast.

"Please, Natalie. You got to get us out of here."

Jesse could hear someone about to open to curtain. Crap, he thought to himself. Before he had time to think of a possible excuse to give, Jesse felt himself being pulled once more.

"Ow!" Jesse yelled in pain as he landed on the floor. "Damn it! I really have to work on the landing."

Jesse stood up and realized that Natalie had taken them back to the Sanctuary. Breathing a sigh of relief, Jesse found

Natalie lying on the floor silently sobbing. He was too scared to approach her. Dealing with crying women was not his forte. For one, he didn't know what to say to them and two, he had a habit of making things worse.

"Are you..." Jesse started. He couldn't ask her that. Of course she wasn't okay. She just watched her death. She heard her heart stop. He had never felt so powerless in his life. He couldn't comfort her. He couldn't do anything for her.

"Jesse," she whispered.

"Yeah," he responded.

"I need to see something else."

He wasn't sure if he heard her correctly. She wanted to go somewhere else? Hadn't that scene been enough for her? Hell, it wasn't his death and he had seen enough.

"Natalie, I don't-"

"I just need to see it."

"Natalie, it will be the same result."

"Not there, somewhere else."

Jesse raised his eyebrow.

She hesitated for a moment and he waited.

"I think it's better if I just take you."

"Natalie, I don't think that's a good idea. I mean you just went through hell. Do you really think you can-"

Before Jesse could finish the sentence, Natalie touched his arm and he felt himself being pulled apart for the second time in five minutes.

"Son of a bitch!" Jesse yelled as he fell hard on the ground. "There has got to be some kind of manual for that."

Jesse stood up awkwardly and brushed the snow off his body. Disoriented and unsure of where they were, he looked for Natalie. Her recovery from their fall didn't seem to faze her as much as it did him. She was on her feet and took off quickly. He watched as Natalie walked around the corner and Jesse chased after her. She stopped abruptly and it gave him the chance to catch up to her. Where exactly were they and why was she so intent on being here?

"Natalie?" Jesse said as he tried to get her attention. "Natalie!"

He followed her gaze to the direction of a dry cleaner and saw a woman walking out. From where he was standing, he could see that she was on her phone. What was so fascinating about her? He looked to Natalie once more, again, she was focused on the woman and nothing else.

"Nat..." He stopped. He could hear the sound of a car screeching on its breaks. Turning toward the sound Jesse could see that the car was skidding out of control.

"No!" he shouted.

Jesse held his breath. He knew exactly what was happening.

Chapter 13:

Going Forward and Going Back

Natalie closed her eyes as she heard the sound of her body hitting the car and watched as her lifeless body made contact with the cold pavement.

She felt a warm hand grab her arm and her eyes met Jesse's shocked, sympathetic ones. Natalie focused her attention back to the scene. She had a sudden urge to vomit as she saw the sight of her own blood pouring out of her body. Shards of glass from the car's headlights surrounded her.

The sudden urge to move closer overwhelmed her as she begged her feet to advance.

"Natalie!" Jesse shouted. Ignoring him, she moved forward again with more confidence.

"Natalie!" he shouted louder. Natalie could feel Jesse grabbing her roughly, spinning her around to face him.

"What are you doing?"

Shaking him away from her, she walked toward her motionless body. His footsteps weren't far behind as he easily picked her up into his arms, carrying her out of site into the alleyway across the street. Natalie began flailing her arms about, kicking him and screaming at him in the process. When his hand clamped over her mouth, she had enough. Opening wide she clamped down hard on his hand.

"Ow!" he roared. Dropping her from his body, she could hear him groaning in pain.

"You bit me! You actually bit me!"

Seeing her chance, she broke free, running off in the direction of her body.

"What do you think you're doing?" Jesse asked as he ran in front of her.

Natalie glared at him. Was there anything she could do to get rid of this guy? "What am I doing?"

"Yes, what are you doing?" he asked rubbing his hand.

Natalie stared at Jesse. He had no ability stop her. What she was doing was her business, not his.

"Answer my question! What did you think you were doing? Did you think you could stop it?"

"I can try!"

"You can't! Natalie, look at me. Look at yourself! What good are you to yourself if you walk over there? You can't change anything!"

"So, I am supposed to just stand here and watch? Take a good look Jesse! No one's around. No wonder I died, there was no one to save me!"

"I get it, okay? I get it!"

"No you don't!"

"What do you think you're going to change?"

"I can stop myself from dying!" she replied

"I hate to break the news to you," he said. "You're still going to end up dead! We can't mess with the past."

His honesty broke her. She knew there was nothing she could do. Tears she'd been holding in finally let go.

"It's not that easy," he admitted. "If it were, then they would have just told us to do this in the first place."

On the one hand, he was just doing his job. On the other hand, this was her chance to know what happened that day. Catching Jesse off guard, she grabbed Jesse's hands, placing them in her own.

Natalie felt her body being pulled as the world rewound itself around them. She had taken them back to minutes before her accident for a second time. Natalie landed roughly against Jesse as he took the brunt of the fall against the cold sidewalk.

She watched as Jesse became disoriented by the stunt she just pulled. She wasn't feeling well herself, but the summers at Coney Island spent riding the roller coasters repeatedly helped her overcome the wave of nausea.

Sensing that Jesse's attention was not on her, Natalie slipped out of his sight, hoping to finally make it to her body. Before she could even take a step, Jesse grabbed her.

"You know, I am getting really sick of doing this. If it didn't work the first two times, what made you think that it would work this time?"

Natalie pushed Jesse away. "I'm getting sick of it, too!"

"Enlighten me here, Princess. What do you think you are going to accomplish?"

Natalie wiped away the tears in her eyes.

"I have spent seven years trying to figure that out! Seven years wondering. Waiting. I just want to stop it from happening. I-"

"But you can't," he said. "No matter how many times you go back, the result is going to remain the same."

"I want to see it again."

Jesse stared at her. The look in his eyes told her that he was trying to process her current mindset. Hell, she was trying to figure it out. She needed him to understand that she was trying to find some kind of closure.

His tall frame leaned casually against the wall of the alley, staring at her as if trying to read her mind.

"Okay," he said and nodded. "We'll do this your way."

Stunned, Natalie held her breath as Jesse came closer to her. Placing his hands in hers, she watched as he waited for her to make the next move.

"Again," she whispered.

Once more they were pulled back. They were frozen in place as time spun back around them.

For Natalie, it was about the moment that changed everything. She kept trying to see her face. Before the car hit her, while the car hit her, and after it hit her. She saw terror, fear, dread and pain. As she watched her body hit the cold, hard, icy pavement, she saw the blood covering her face, the shattered glass surrounding her unmoving body. It was then, right there, that she saw death. No hope, no happiness, no life, just grey, dragging her away to Purgatory.

"Again," she said.

Every time she felt herself being pulled back, she prayed. She prayed for someone, anyone to save her. For someone to just push her out of the way. She kept waiting for a voice to yell at her to get out of the way. No matter how many times she waited for it, it never came. She thought that if she watched enough times, that maybe once, she would be alive and stay that way. That she could make it to the limo, to the cathedral, to Nick, to her family, to finally saying the words 'I Do'.

"Again."

The sight of her lifeless body, along with the cold reality of death infiltrated her mind.

"Again," she whispered.

Emotionally she was drained. Collapsing to the ground, she felt Jesse cradle her in his arms as a parent would a child. Closing her eyes, she felt content.

"I'm sorry," she heard him murmur into her hair.

"*Templum*," Jesse said.

A glowing warmth surrounded them and they were gone.

***

Darkness filled the room as Jesse watched Natalie sleep. She'd exhausted herself during the ordeal and Jesse didn't want to admit that the whole situation affected him, too. Slowly, he made his way over to her and looked at the watch. They had spent a day reliving her death and none of it made sense to him. How could she just die like that? Why on her wedding day of all days? There were so many questions, but not enough answers. He was also feeling extremely guilty for saying 'Templum' to bring them back to the Sanctuary. Jesse hoped that the cost wasn't going to affect her too badly.

"I guess we'll have to wait and see. We have a lot to figure out."

Jesse saw her stir and held his breath. He hoped she would stay sleeping for a little longer. He wasn't sure he was ready to deal with her just yet. If he were honest with himself, he would admit that the whole experience of watching Natalie die repeatedly affected him more than he thought.

Carefully, he left the Sanctuary. Walking down the corridor, Jesse found a door that he hadn't noticed before. "Well, I'm already dead. What's the worst that could happen?" he muttered as he opened it. Sure enough, it led to a set of stairs.

The sounds of the city echoed as he climbed the wooden steps. Reaching for the handle of the door, he was greeted by the cold, crisp air of winter. It was dark out, yet it suited his mood. As he took in his surroundings, he peered over the ledge of the cathedral. Thousands of onlookers littered the streets as they admired the famous Christmas tree without a care in the world.

"If they only knew."

In the distance, he could hear tires screeching to a halt.

The sound still affected him and he felt like he was going to be sick again. The sounds of the crash made him relive the moment his car collided with the dump truck. One stupid decision changed everything.

Tires screeched once more and Jesse turned his attention in the direction of the sound.

"Lucky," he said as he saw the car stop before it hit the bus.

At twenty-nine, he was on top of the world. He owned a club he named after himself, The Knight Club. Sure, it lacked originality, but it did not stop Manhattan's social crowd from stopping by. He hired a bunch of people to run the business and benefitted greatly from it. It was another part of his life that his family didn't approve of. The frustration of the past few hours weighed on him heavily and he felt now was time to let it out.

"You couldn't accept me for who I am!" he yelled out.

Ultimately, the reason Jesse lost control that day was because of his father and that part he remembered well.

***

"You're doing well," his father said.

"You seem surprised," Jesse countered.

Jesse watched as his father's eyes grew into slits.

"Well, with your last name, it is no surprise that you're a success."

"Yes, Dad. That's the reason."

Jesse glared at his father and in turn Jack did the same. Father and son were prepared to engage in a battle of wits and Jesse was determined not to let his father get to him.

"I need your signature on something. There is a housing project we want to develop in Upstate New York."

"Just like that? You invite me over, which is a rare feat for you, and you want my John Hancock?"

"Jesse!"

"Ask me nicely," he said.

Jesse saw anger flare in his father's eyes.

"Listen here, you're going to sign it-"

"Or what? I control the company, I can fire your ass right

now. The only reason I won't is because it is not what gran would have wanted. So, I repeat, ask me nicely."

"You control the company in name! When was the last time you were at a meeting?" his father demanded. "You always send a proxy on your behalf.

"My mother had no right to leave you control in the will. She was going crazy in the end."

"Don't you dare talk about her like that! She's the only person who gave a damn about me. So show her some respect!"

Jesse's anger only intensified as he watched his father stalk over to him. As a child, he found his father's size an intimidating feature, but since he grew up, he could match his father, if not best him.

"Did it ever occur to you that she felt sorry for you?"

"Sorry for me?" He roared back. "Really? You ignore her, you ignore me, you throw her money around like no tomorrow and I'm the one she felt sorry for? You know what, I'm glad she felt sorry for me, especially since I have a father like you!"

Jesse saw that his father was about to punch him. Raising his hand, he stopped his father from making contact with his face.

"Care to try again?" he taunted.

"The only thing I am sorry for is having you as my son. You were an accident the moment you were conceived. I already had the sons I needed to one day run the company, you, I did not need. You're pathetic!"

"Looks like you're going to need me dead before you can get that thing signed."

Turning around, Jesse saw his entire family standing there guiltily.

"Jesse," his mother began as she entered the room.

"Don't. You haven't exactly been mother of the year."

Walking out the door, Jesse turned around to look at his family.

"Thanks for the invite," he said and headed toward the front door. "As always, your hospitality could use some work. I guess it's a good thing we're not in the hotel industry. We'd lose a fortune!"

With that, he slammed the door. Heading for his Porsche,

Jesse drove off and didn't look back.

The sounds of carolers down below broke Jesse from his memories. He felt wet drops on his cheeks. Wiping them away, Jesse looked up to the heavens in contempt. He closed his eyes and remembered what happened after he stormed out.

The accident itself had been his own doing. Once he left his parents' house in Connecticut, he drove to his club and locked himself in his 'office'.

Pulling out a bottle of scotch, he started drinking, wishing that the scotch could burn away his memories as it burned his throat.

By the sixth glass, Jesse was feeling the effects of Mr. Johnny Walker. The scotch was doing little to ease his pain.

"Boss?"

"Yeah?" he said.

"Got some ladies down here wanting to meet you."

Since drinking alone wasn't doing anything for him, Jesse decided that drinking with beautiful women would liven things up.

"I'll be down in a sec."

Taking another swig of scotch, Jesse went down the stairs to meet a flurry of women.

The rest of the night consisted of shots, making out, shots, groping, shots and more scotch.

Hours later, morning light crept its way into the room Jesse was occupying. Looking around at his surroundings, Jesse checked to see that he was clothed. Relieved that he was in fact wearing his pants, Jesse got up and felt the familiar ache of a hangover.

The room was full of women and while the sight was appealing, he needed to leave. Finding his Porsche was another story. Reaching for his phone, Jesse checked the GPS and found his car two blocks away. The roar of the engine bothered his already throbbing head and all he wanted to do was to crawl inside his bed and forget.

Pulling away, Jesse reached for the flask in his glove compartment. Stepping on the gas, Jesse darted out on to the street like a mad man. Increasing his speed, Jesse played back the words his father had spoken to him the night before.

"The only thing I am sorry for is having you as my son.

You were an accident the moment you were conceived. I tried to convince your mother to get an abortion. I had the sons I needed to one day run the company, you, I did not need."

"Damn you!" he yelled.

Accelerating more, Jesse gripped the wheel tightly. Blinded by his rage and hatred for his father, his family and his life, he drove through the intersection, heading straight into the dump truck crossing his path.

***

Jesse tore himself from the memory, looking up once more at the heavens.

"Help."

Deciding that he had had enough of New York's winter air, he headed back to the room. Seeing that she was still in her slumber, Jesse walked over to the table and picked up the guidebook.

He read the introduction about being a Protector and what they did. The definition of the term threw him by surprise.

Protector: A man or woman with noble pride and loyalty to whomever they serve. Someone who understands pain, and loss: has the ability to honour and defend those in their protection. They will do everything in their power to keep their ward safe from harm's way.

He read about the different types of angels that he could turn to for guidance. He also found the chapter of Latin phrases interesting and discovered that some of the phrases could be helpful down the line.

As he made his way through the rest of the book, one chapter caught his eye; Ceterus Angelus. Jesse quickly flipped to the Latin phrases chapter and found the definition.

"The Other Angels," he said quietly. "Sounds better in Latin."

Remembering that Natalie was still sleeping, he glanced over to make sure that she was still out.

He read about the Defenders, the Messengers, the Missionaries, and the Saviours, agreeing that they all reflected Edward, Michaelangela, Joshua and Isa's personalities. He hadn't met the Guardians, the Advisors, the Soul Searchers or the Healers and he seriously doubted that he ever would, but out of all the positions that existed in the Afterworld, one type of angel confused him.

"The Advocate?" Jesse whispered.

Jesse wasn't completely inept. He had heard of the Devil's Advocate and he assumed that that term was associated with the Devil.

"'The Advocate is an Angel with powerful control. They possess the ability to give ultimatums to those who need help. The Advocate, not to be confused with its counterpart, The Devil's Advocate, acts with the sole purpose of doing good and only good to those they make offers to. While each ultimatum has risks, The Advocate never misleads or lies and wants to aid those searching for answers. He or She is to be trusted and their intentions are never questioned.'"

Jesse turned the page and listed before him were the different kinds of ultimatums the Advocate could offer to Natalie.

"All Ultimatums and Deals come at a cost," he read aloud. "What cost?" he pondered.

"'The 24 Hour Deal is the only deal of its kind with powerful consequences of both good and bad. Quite simply, the deal allows a ward the chance an extra 24 hours within the time frame.'"

Jesse paused and carefully thought about what that could mean for them. They could potentially have another day at their disposal just in case. He continued to read the passage and read the rest aloud.

"'While it may seem ideal, the temptation of time should only be used under extenuating circumstances and should not be taken lightly. This deal is one of high risks and high rewards. Should the ward succeed, their second life will start anew. Should the ward fail and not renew their second chance at life, the ward will spend eternity in Purgatory tormented. Never again will they see their loved ones. The soul, will never rest in peace.'"

"I think we should consider it an option."

Jesse whirled around and found Natalie sitting on the edge of the bed, shocked to find her sitting so calmly. Was she crazy? Did she not hear what he said?

"Me and my big mouth," he muttered. "Are you insane?" Jesse asked. "Did you not listen to what can happen to you?"

"Look, we don't know exactly what that means," she replied.

"Hmm, what does it mean?" he paused and tapped his index finger to his chin. "Well, let's see...tormented in Purgatory for eternity. Sounds clear to me."

"I know that I showed a moment of weakness earlier. I panicked, I got scared, and I lost control-"

"You didn't lose control Natalie," he interrupted. "You lost your mind. Do you realize we wasted another day?"

"Yes," she whispered.

"Now, you want to take a chance with this deal and you don't even know all the circumstances behind it?" he said.

"Okay, I screwed up. I got caught up in something and did not handle it well. But I never saw that car coming and for the first time since that day, I saw it Jesse. I saw it come right at me and hit me and take my life away from me. If we can buy time, we can and will," she said.

"But at what cost?" Jesse answered. Upon reflecting the loss of his own life moments before, he knew that being reckless and foolish cost him everything. He didn't want Natalie to do something that they would regret later.

"Fine," she said. "But can we at least talk to him or her? The deal is so vague and it doesn't mean we make a deal with him. We're just weighing out the option should it come to that."

"It's not necessary," he stated. "We're doing fine right now. This is my life we're talking about!" he said and brought his hands to his face.

"Your life?"

Realizing what he just said, he turned away from her and cursed himself for saying it out loud. He could feel her eyes burning a hole through his head and knew she was going to let him have it.

"What about your life? Before it was none of my business..."

He turned back to look at her and saw her staring back at him with hatred evident in his eyes.

"It still isn't your business," he said.

"Then stop making it my business," she told him. "Either

you tell me what you meant or you get the Advocate here."

Seeing as he had no choice, he picked up the book and read the part about summoning the Advocate. He knew what he had to do. It would be the only way to shut her up and the only way he could make her see that this was not the only solution. He raised his eyes once more and watched her watching him.

"Causidicus, Causidicus, Causidicus," he whispered.

After a few minutes, nothing happened and no one appeared before them. Jesse read the phrase in his head again and checked the phonetic wording. He looked toward Natalie who seemed unimpressed by him and he didn't blame her.

"Did you say it right?" she said.

Before he could give her a reply, he was interrupted by a knock at the door. Jesse and Natalie looked at each other expectantly, neither knowing what to do. Three more knocks echoed into the room and Jesse made his way to the door. Anxiety was slowly building within him and he had no idea what awaited him, or them, on the other side.

Chapter 14:
The Advocate

As Jesse opened the door, he saw a man standing there, wearing a black suit without a tie.

"Oh look," said Jesse as he made his way toward the bed, "it's the Advocate we ordered."

"May I come in?" said the Advocate in silky, smooth voice.

Natalie nodded yes and the mysterious Advocate entered the room.

"Allow me to introduce myself," he said. "My name is Antonio Delgado."

Jesse rolled his eyes as Antonio kissed Natalie's hand. The guy literally looked like he belonged on the cover of an erotica novel. He had slicked-back black hair, with golden brown skin and deep brown eyes. The tight, white t-shirt beneath his suit left little to the imagination and Jesse definitely believed that his pants were just a little too snug.

"So, could someone tell me why I have been summoned?"

"We did not summon you," Jesse said. "She summoned you," he added, pointing at Natalie. "She wants to talk to you."

"All right," said the Advocate. "Then you won't mind if she and I have a conversation together in private."

Jesse's jaw tightened. Yes, he did mind, but this was Natalie's call and not his.

Accepting defeat, Jesse made his way to the door.

"Natalie, don't do anything stupid," he said to her. "Don't do anything stupid...please."

***

Natalie sighed as Jesse left the room.

"I take it he hasn't exactly embraced the role as one should."

"No, he hasn't," she answered as she turned around to Antonio.

Patricia Bandurka

As her eyes met Antonio's, she was instantly lost in his warm, brown ones. To say that he was attractive was an understatement. His olive complexion suited him perfectly. His hair was slicked back and his suit fit him to the letter. She caught him staring at her and then remembered why he was here to begin with. What could he do for her? More importantly, what could she stand to gain and what could she lose? As she appraised him, she in turn noticed that he was doing the same thing.

"Let's begin with why you asked me here."

"I thought that you might be able to offer insight regarding my current situation."

"That's not the reason," he replied. "You either wanted me here so that you could get rid of him or you think that I can give you something he cannot. Which one is it? "

Natalie felt like a five year old all of a sudden.

"Okay, maybe I did ask you to come here under false pretenses. In my defense, I needed some things cleared up."

"Care to explain?"

"I overheard Jesse," she said.

"Overheard Jesse? What exactly did you overhear?"

"I heard what you can do," she said. "That you make deals, in particular the 24 hour deal. We argued and I kind of manipulated him into getting you to come here."

Antonio raised his eyebrows. "Well, it appears that Jesse has underestimated you."

"After the way I behaved yesterday and the time I wasted, I just need to talk to someone who isn't Jesse or Redmond."

"Natalie," said Antonio, "the 24 hour deal is not as simple as that. I don't just offer it to anybody. I understand your frustration, but Natalie, you are nowhere near the point of requiring me or my services."

"Can't you-"

"No," said Antonio. "Natalie, the 24 hour deal is everything Jesse said it was. It's a high risk deal. One that does have great outcomes and rewards." He paused and looked away from her. "But, the consequences should someone fail are also devastating."

"So, it is possible-"

"No. Natalie, that offer is only made under certain cir-

95

cumstances and right now it does not apply to you."

Feeling like she had been slapped. She stepped away from Antonio.

"Should you feel this way in a few days, then you can call me again and we can discuss other possibilities. I know you don't trust Jesse and I also don't blame you for that. However, he knows when to make a deal."

Deal? What deal? Before she could ask any questions, Antonio strode to the door.

"Natalie, the longer I stay, the more time you waste. Just remember one thing. I am an Advocate and I will expect my '*Quid Pro Quo*'. If you are desperate and wish to talk again-"

He pulled a coin from his pocket and tossed it in her direction.

"That's a Causidicus coin. When you want to see me, flip the coin and say 'I Want to Make a Deal'. If the coin disappears in your hand when you open it, it means that I will make you one. If it is in your hand when you open it, it means that I have nothing to offer and you have nothing to give in return."

Antonio smiled. "Take care, Natalie. I really hope you don't have to use that."

With that, he walked out the door, leaving her more confused than before.

***

Wasting time seemed to be a common theme the past few days. Jesse anxiously paced the creaky floors and tried his best to not think about whatever they were talking about. It's not that he didn't trust her, he didn't trust the Don Juan. He contemplated entering the room, but thought better of it. As he sat on the wooden floor, he wondered what the Advocate could offer her and how it could potentially ruin his chance to get his life back.

Jesse was about to open the door when he saw Antonio stepping out. Antonio smiled smugly at him and Jesse wanted nothing but to punch it off his face.

"You better keep your eye on her."

"Tell me something I don't know," he agreed. "So, on a

scale from one to ten, how screwed am I?"

"You are not screwed. She just needs to think."

"Think? Think about what? We wasted more time-"

"It's not that easy Jesse. I am the one person who thinks that time is never a waste. She's looking for answers and options. All you have done is added more pressure."

"So, it's my fault," he said.

"No," replied Antonio. "No, it is not your fault. In fact, I am willing to wager that she has no idea about the arrangement you made with Redmond?"

Jesse looked away from Antonio and headed to the door.

"That's what I thought," Antonio said. "You have no immunity. Since you are not trying to become a Protector, your life is in her hands. I know why you didn't want me alone with her. If she knew what was at stake for you, you might have a better chance working together. Don't underestimate her. She may be able to help you more than you think."

With a snap of his fingers, Antonio was gone, leaving Jesse with more questions than answers.

Jesse hated to admit it, but Antonio had a point. Shaking his head in confusion, he entered the room to find Natalie sitting on the bed in a daze. He closed the door and waited for her to say something.

After a few moments, Jesse gave in and broke the silence.

"So, what did you talk about?" he asked as he walked toward her.

Natalie was ignoring him and Jesse was becoming frustrated. He crouched down beside her and looked right into her multi-coloured eyes.

"I said, what did you talk about?"

He didn't know where the threatening tone came from. He surprised himself in the process as her eyes widened. She stood up quickly and headed toward the bathroom.

"Deals that can be made. Deals that have already been made."

He blocked the entrance to the bathroom and glared at her.

"What did he say to you?" he said. "We made a deal to talk to each other."

"Funny," she rebutted. "You seem to have made a few of your own."

"What did he tell you?" he demanded. "Tell me."

His face was mere inches from hers and Jesse saw fear in her eyes. He backed away from her and took a deep breath.

"What are you going to do, Jesse?" she asked. He could hear a hint of panic in her voice. His breathing became heavy as his jaw clenched tight.

"You want me to tell you what happened between myself and Antonio?" she said. "Why should I? You're not telling me the truth!"

"Nat-"

"Don't," she said. "You're pathetic!"

Something snapped in Jesse. He no longer saw Natalie standing before him. *The only thing I am sorry for is having you as my son. You were an accident the moment you were conceived. I already had the sons I needed to one day run the company, you, I did not need. You're pathetic!*

In that moment, all Jesse saw was his father's menacing face staring and laughing at him. He closed his eyes tightly trying to rid the words that were still fresh in his mind.

"I'm not pathetic," he said and pushed Natalie against the door. "You are!"

The thud of a body hitting the wall broke Jesse from his trance. When he opened his eyes, he saw Natalie against the door staring back at him in shock. They were tears streaming down her face and she was rubbing her back.

"Natalie-" Jesse said and reached out to her.

"Don't," she whispered. "Don't ever touch me again."

Natalie ran toward the door and in one quick motion she pulled the necklace off, throwing it on the floor. She repeated the same move with the watch from her swollen wrist, tossing it on the bed.

"Natalie," Jesse said as he walked toward her, but stopped when he saw her flinch.

"I didn't mean-"

"Don't touch me!" she said again in a whisper. "Don't even think about following me. Just stay the hell away from me," she said with more confidence.

With that, she walked out the door and took off.

Jesse stood rooted to the floor for a few seconds and walked slowly to the door and opened it. He peered outside hoping that she might be there, wishing that last few minutes didn't happen.

He looked down the corridor and saw nothing but the door leading to the cathedral.

Jesse hung his head and walked back into the Sanctuary. He bent over to pick up the necklace, clutching it to his chest. He then walked over to the bed, carefully picking up the watch too. What he saw on the watch made him sick to his stomach. The glass on the watch had shattered.

"What did I do?" he said aloud. "What did I just do?"

Jesse laid back on the bed, holding onto the necklace and the watch for dear life, letting the tears fall from his eyes.

Chapter 15:
A Chance Encounter

Natalie took off running as fast as she could, her eyes burning from her own tears. She ignored the cold air assaulting her face and the looks from strangers. Natalie was on autopilot, guiding herself on Madison Avenue, heading anywhere that wasn't near Jesse or anyone else for that matter.

Without realizing it, she had managed to find herself in Central Park, heading toward Gapstow Bridge. Slowing her pace, she made her way up the bridge. Falling to the ground in defeat, she cried out in pain. She was lost in her own world of emotions and wondered how she ended up feeling this way.

Before she could contemplate further, she heard the sounds of footsteps approaching.

"Miss," came a deep voice. "I don't mean to interrupt. It's just, well, I saw you running through the park…" The male voice hesitated. "Are you alright?"

The voice sounded familiar, too familiar. Natalie could feel him come closer and cowered away from him as he kneeled down, handing her a handkerchief.

"Are you alright?" he asked again.

She gently lifted her head, her eyes meeting the man's before her, confirming his identity. Jesse.

"Don't you think you've done enough?" she said, standing up.

Natalie saw the look of bewilderment on his face and turned away from him.

"I'm sorry," he said. "I can see that you're in distress. It's cold and it's almost 6am. God only knows what kind of idiots are out here right now looking to take advantage of a woman who's alone."

Was he serious? He cared about what happened to her? She was in more danger being alone with him.

"I'll take my chances," she said.

"Let me at least take you some place warm."

"No!"

"I'm not going to hurt you. I just…" he said fumbling over

his words. "Consider this something that I need to do to get on Santa's good list."

"Cause that doesn't make you sound like a weirdo? Even after what you've done?"

Natalie did a double take at Jesse. He looked different. His hair was black, his eyes were a shade of midnight blue and the scar on his face was gone. What was he trying to pull?

"You think that because you got Redmond to change back your hair, your eyes and got rid of the scar that everything would be okay? That nothing happened?"

Natalie saw confusion written in his features.

"Don't even try to deny it," she added.

"I'm...confused? Have we met before? Who's Redmond?"

So, he wanted to play dumb, she thought.

"I don't have time for this Jesse. Play stupid all you want, I'm going."

"Wait a second," he questioned. "You know who I am?"

"We spent almost three days together-"

"What?" he asked in a surprised manner. "Alright, I'll admit that I have been with a few women, but I can assure you that I would have remembered spending three days with a beautiful red head. Trust me when I say, I don't know who you are."

It finally dawned on Natalie why Jesse was acting like he didn't know her. Given her current emotional state, she could kick herself for not realizing sooner. The different hair, the eyes, and the lack of scar. Yes, it was Jesse, but it wasn't the same Jesse. Could it be? Was this the Jesse from this time?

"You really don't know who I am?" she asked.

"I really don't, but I wish I did," he said. "Is there someone I can call for you? I really don't think you should be out here alone."

Natalie continued to examine Jesse and couldn't fathom how in a city populated with millions, he was the one she would run into. It couldn't be a coincidence? As she continued to watch him, she noticed that in turn, he was doing the same thing to her.

It was a staring contest and at the moment neither one wanted to be the first one to break.

Natalie could see that Jesse had had enough and ran his

hand through his hair, breaking the silence.

"Can I take you somewhere?"

"No!" she said. "I mean-"

"Okay," he said, backing away a little. "Here, take this," he said as he pulled his coat off and handed it to her. "You're going to freeze."

Without another word, he turned around and began to walk away.

Natalie seeing this, called out him.

"Wait, you're giving me your coat?" she shouted.

Jesse turned back to her.

"I think you need it more than me. Unless, you wouldn't mind giving it back, but much later."

Natalie's eyes widened at his comment. Was that a suggestive tone in his voice?

"Wow, that sounded bad. I'm sorry. Just take the coat."

Natalie watched him walk away once more and could not believe what was happening.

Bewildered by his act of kindness, Natalie called out to him.

"Wait!"

Jesse turned on his heel and walked back to her.

"Thank you," said Natalie.

Natalie waited for him to make the next move and could tell that he was doing the same thing. Seconds passed, though it felt longer, when Jesse broke the silence between them.

"I know this may seem random but I was going to spend the day pretending to be a tourist. I do it every year at this time. I go to all the touristy things and have some fun. So, why don't I make you a deal?"

"Don't use that word!" she said louder than she intended.

To say that he was startled by her outburst would have been an understatement.

"Use a different word."

Natalie knew that this Jesse must being thinking that she was crazy and she couldn't blame him. She was beginning to think that she was in the process of going crazy too.

"Okay," he said carefully. "How about offer? Proposition? Proposal? Plan? I would have more words for you, but I left my thesaurus in my other coat."

Natalie smiled and found herself feeling quite surprised and charmed by this Jesse.

"Alright, what is your offer?" she asked.

"Well, if you'd like, you can spend the day with me."

She saw hesitation in his eyes. With a nod, she willed him to proceed.

"We take turns. We each choose three places we want to go today. I'll go and then you and so on and so forth. One rule though, we get to ask any three questions that we want. So, if I pick the first place we go to, you get to ask me the first question. I figure I can keep you away from wherever it is you don't want to be and I don't have to spend the day by myself."

Jesse paused and waited for her approval. "At 11:59pm, we'll be back here and when the clock strikes twelve, Cinderella can make her way back home."

Natalie was definitely intrigued by his offer. The irony was not lost on her. Escaping Jesse by being with Jesse. The idea of spending the day with him became more and more interesting. It occurred to her that there was sadness in his words. It was clear to Natalie that he was alone and for the moment, so was she. She could get to know this Jesse and maybe get a better idea of the kind of guy he was and what changed him.

"I don't have any money on me," she said.

"I figured you didn't, considering you didn't have a coat, but that's not a good enough excuse. Since this is my idea, I'll pay."

"Why do I feel like a hooker?"

Natalie watched him smile at that. At the moment, she felt exposed to him and very vulnerable to him.

"You know, you seem to be able to twist my words the wrong way," he said in a reassuring voice. "I promise, I am not going to treat you like a prostitute, and I definitely don't want you to feel like one. Like I said before, I want to get on Santa's good list and this will be my Christmas gift to you."

"You don't even know who I am," she replied as she shook her head and pointed to herself.

"True, but you know me."

He was right somewhat, she thought. She knew a part of who he was, but she didn't know the real him and he had no clue about her. Before she knew it, he had his hand extended toward hers.

"I'm Jesse Knight."

She looked at his hand and became nervous. Natalie placed her hand in his tentatively and introduced herself for the second time in her life.

"Natalie...."

She could see him waiting for more to follow, but decided against telling him anymore than that.

"Natalie...?" he repeated.

"Just Natalie."

"Shall we?" he asked as he offered her his arm.

Natalie hesitated for a moment, but when she saw the look he was giving her, she knew that this Jesse wouldn't hurt her. She linked her arm through his and let him lead the way.

***

Three hours later, Natalie found herself on the ferry headed for Liberty Island. Once they had left the park, Jesse had taken her out for breakfast and bought a coat for her to wear since he needed his.

She didn't know how he had managed to get Saks to open at seven o'clock in the morning and thought it best to not ask questions. From Saks, they took a cab to Battery Park, stopping at a bakery for more coffee and some bagels.

Presently, Natalie was drinking her third cup of the day while taking in the view before her. Lady Liberty was slowly becoming bigger as Jesse stood silently beside her. For whatever reason, she could feel his eyes on her constantly. It seemed that he wanted to say something and just wouldn't.

As the boat approached the dock, Natalie started to formulate what questions she would ask Jesse. There were so many things she wanted to know, but with only three questions to ask, she knew she needed to choose wisely.

They got off the ferry and made their way over to the statue itself.

"Well, there she is," said Jesse. "Ever been here before?"

"Yes. It's been awhile though," she said.

Once again, she could feel Jesse's penetrating gaze on

her.

"You?"

"I come here once a year," he said.

The sentimental way he spoke just now captivated her. She could hear the regret in his tone and knew there was more to the man before her.

"Why?"

"Does this count as your question?" he asked back.

Did it? She didn't think it did, but he seemed to think so.

"I'm just kidding," he laughed out.

"Well," he paused. "Lady Liberty reminds me of someone I used to know."

"You know someone just as old as her?" she said as she pointed up to the statue.

Natalie saw him laugh at her attempt to make a joke and smiled.

"No. You know, I can't say anything without you being able to read me. It's like you know me or something."

"Or something," she whispered to herself. "Speaking of knowing, I think I have my first question."

"Go ahead," he replied as he turned to focus his attention on her.

Natalie began posing questions in her head, trying to figure out exactly what she wanted to ask him.

"It can't be that hard," he said, breaking her out of her concentration.

If he only knew, she thought to herself again. If only this Jesse knew what she was going through.

"Okay. What's your relationship like with your family?"

Yes, it was a question that had been bothering her since he admitted that he was a screw up and intensified more when she saw his reaction to his family that night at 21 Club.

"That's an interesting question," he said and leaned back into the bench. "Then again, I'm not that surprised given that you seem to know a little bit about me." She watched as he took a sip of his drink and wondered if her question was too personal. She knew the current Jesse hated talking about his life, but figured this one would be a little more open.

"I guess if you do this sort of thing every year, I just wondered why you don't do this with your family."

"I suppose you won't accept, 'it's complicated'," he said,

using air quotes.

"You did make the rules," she pointed out.

"Good point," he sighed. He led her to a bench and sat down. "My family and I aren't close. My parents do their thing, my brothers, both older, live their lives with their families, and me, I'm the proverbial black sheep."

Natalie had heard this from Jesse before. She had questioned his truthfulness then, but she could see that he wasn't lying now because he had no reason to. She saw him flinch as he put his arm behind the bench, no doubt having seen her tense up at the movement.

"Sorry."

"It's okay," she said.

"It's hard to live up to their expectations. I mean they're not horrible people. To be honest, I don't blame them for making me the outcast. Things in life just get complicated and it's just the way it is. So, does that answer your question?"

Natalie didn't know what to say. She didn't want to console him, she didn't want to feel sorry for him, but the voice in her head told her that there was more to Jesse Knight.

"For now," she replied.

They sat there for a while, finishing off their coffees while watching tourists take pictures.

"Well, we should go. We got more things to see!" Jesse said and proceeded to jump off the bench. He reached for her and she took his hand tentatively.

"Since it's your turn, where are we going?" he asked.

Natalie looked at the skyline once more and knew where she wanted to go.

"You'll see," she said as she made her way to the dock.

"You know," he said with a grin on his face. "I know New York pretty well and judging by your gaze, I can already tell where our next stop is."

"You couldn't possibly know."

Jesse winked at her.

"You realize that does take the fun out it for me."

"That wasn't my intention, but I'll put this into perspective, Natalie. How can we not go to the Empire State Building? Come on, Princess."

Before she had the chance to respond to his comment, he reached for her hand once more and pulled her in the direction of the ferry.

Chapter 16:

Jesse versus Jesse

The sound of car horns blaring around him woke Jesse up from his sleep. Stirring in the bed, Jesse began to wipe the sleep from his eyes and found the locket and watch clutched firmly in his hands. The events from the night before came flooding back to him and he hated himself for what happened. He lost control and instead of seeing Natalie, all he saw was his father. He believed himself to be a monster and could only imagine what she thought of him.

Jesse looked around the room to see if there was any sign of her.

"Natalie?" he called out.

Jesse stood slowly, making his way over to the bathroom. He knocked softly, waiting patiently for a response.

"Natalie?" he said as he knocked once more. "I'm sorry. What happened...What I did wasn't about you. All I saw was my father and I had no right to take it out on you... I...Look, I would rather apologize to you in person. Could you open the door?"

Anxiety crept over him. He knew she was angry and hurt. He felt extremely remorseful for scaring her. Jesse knew that his anger was the cause of most of his problems and while he would lose it mentally and emotionally, he never lost it physically, until last night. The second she had said that he was pathetic only reminded him of the last words his father had said to him. Jesse knocked on the door once more and called out to her again, "Natalie?"

Jesse counted to ten in his head and waited.

"I'm coming in," he said.

Opening the door slowly, the only sign of Natalie in the room was the green halter dress hanging on the back of the door.

"Damn it," he whispered.

He walked back out into the main room and he could feel the panic set in. His heartbeat was elevating and his palms were getting clammy. The realization of how badly he had hurt her was something he wasn't proud of.

"Okay," he said aloud. "Maybe she's in the cathedral or she just took a walk?"

Refusing to give up just yet, he fled down the stairs, entering the corridor that led to the cathedral. Carefully, he walked up the aisles looking for her.

After ten minutes of searching, he still had not found her.

"Where are you Natalie?"

Jesse ran back toward the Sanctuary hoping that she may have returned. He entered the room and found it the way he had left it, empty and cold. He sank onto the floor holding on to the locket, his only link to her, and looked at the watch as it continued to countdown. So many thoughts were rushing through his head. One, where was Natalie? Two, how would he explain this to Redmond? And three, how was he ever going to make it up to her?

Jesse didn't know where Natalie was, but he was sure of one thing. He was definitely in hell.

***

Past Jesse, or PJ as Natalie had so dubbed him, excused himself once they boarded the ferry and Natalie was left alone. Deep in thought, she failed to notice his return and continued to think about what made him change to the angry man she had the run away from.

As they got off the pier, she watched him hail a cab to take them to the Empire State Building.

An hour later, they were riding up in the elevator towards the top. As they walked out, Natalie realized that they were the only two people on the observation deck. She looked at Jesse who just smiled as if everything was normal.

"Since your choice of location was rather obvious, I made a call and had them clear it for a while. We've got about fifteen minutes. Natalie, New York is yours to be seen."

Natalie walked out, looking at the city below her. It amazed her how a person's perspective could change in just a moment. She loved the Empire State Building and not just because of the romantic clichés.

As she continued to look around, Natalie felt a tap on her

shoulder and saw Jesse with two cups in his hand.

"Hot chocolate?" he offered. "I figured you might want a change from coffee."

She nodded and gladly accepted the cup and the two began to walk around the deck.

"It's beautiful up here," she said to Jesse. "You can see everything!"

"So, who are you running from?" Jesse asked.

Natalie spat out the hot chocolate and glared at him.

"It's my question," he reminded her and took a sip from his cup.

Natalie winced and then remembered their arrangement. It was only fair, she had asked him a question and now it was his turn to ask her.

"Come on, who are you running from?"

"I'm running from life," she said.

"You're lying and I don't know why. Seems like you are running from someone who hurt you."

Natalie felt helpless, more so now than she did the first time she met the other Jesse. The Jesse she met in Purgatory was arrogant and a pain in her butt. This Jesse was as well, to some extent, but he seemed genuinely interested in her and her problems. Why else would he want to help her? To this Jesse, she was a stranger that he was taking pity on and right now, she didn't know what to do.

"Yes," she said.

"So, who's the guy?"

In spite of herself, Natalie smiled. How could she explain Jesse to past Jesse? Was it even possible?

"What makes you think it's a guy?"

Jesse was about to respond, but Natalie held her hand to him, indicating that he was right.

"Okay," she said as she stared at him. "You win. He's unlike anyone I have ever met. He thinks he knows everything about me when he doesn't, he makes things about him when it isn't, and he doesn't like my fiancé for some reason-"

"Your fiancé?" he interrupted. "You not only have one guy in your life, you have two?" Well, there go my chances. Can I ask then why do you care what this guy thinks?"

That was an interesting question. Did she really care about what Jesse thought?

"Getting to question number two?" she said.

Jesse smiled awkwardly at her and looked away. Natalie smiled and decided to answer him anyway.

"To be honest, I think he's just trying make sure that I don't mess up," she explained.

"Like a brother?"

"No! Not like a brother!"

"Well, not knowing the particulars or the people, it sounds to me like he is just trying to be your friend and protect you."

PJ's choice of words intrigued Natalie.

"Protect me?"

"You know, make sure you're okay and that you don't make a mistake with your life. Or maybe he has feelings for you."

Natalie choked on her hot chocolate. Feelings? As in 'In Love'? Jesse?

"Sorry. I overstepped. If it were me and I had someone like you in my life, I'd be in love with you in a minute."

His admission left her speechless. Unable to answer him, she stared at the view surrounding her.

"Do you like the view? Our time is almost up and we have places to go and things to do."

Had it really been fifteen minutes? Had PJ admitted he could fall in love with her? A sudden wave of nausea hit her.

Meeting PJ's eyes, she nodded somberly, following him to the elevator. The doors opened and they stepped inside.

"Enjoy the view, Mr. Knight?" asked the elevator operator.

"Yes, we did Bernie!" he answered as he shook the man's hand. Then looking at Natalie, "Yes we did."

***

Jesse paced the room back and forth, hoping that Natalie would enter.

"Come on, Natalie. Please don't make me go to Redmond," he said to the empty room. Jesse grabbed the book, trying to locate the chapter about how to get back to Purgatory.

"Where is it?" he said as he roughly flipped through the pages. He flipped through to the Keeper's chapter and found the phrase. Jesse glanced at the door one last time hoping that she would enter, sparing him the anger Redmond would unleash on him.

"If I weren't already dead, I'd wish I were," he said. "Here goes. *Fidelis Deus Quod Is Mos Servo Vos.*"

Jesse felt himself being pulled away, falling rapidly through Natalie's memories, only this time, she wasn't falling with him.

Closing his eyes, he waited for the hard landing to come. When it didn't, he opened his eyes again and found himself on a carpeted floor staring into a burning fire.

"That wasn't so bad."

Jesse tried to warm himself up, but the cold air seemed to linger. He turned to explore his surroundings only to be greeted by five familiar faces.

"Redmond," he said as he nodded at him.

He looked around and saw Isabella, Michaelangela, Joshua and Antonio.

"Well, at least the gang's all here," he said. "I'd ask what you are doing here, but I have a feeling that you already know."

"No, we don't," said Redmond. "Why don't you enlighten us and tell us why you are here?"

***

"FAO Schwartz!" Natalie shouted as they entered the famed toy shop. Natalie turned toward Jesse, returning the smile that was beaming off his face.

Out of all the places in town, Jesse had taken her to the one place that could make anyone feel like a kid.

***

"What am I doing here?" Jesse repeated.

"Indeed, Jesse," asked Redmond. "What are you doing here?"

111

Jesse could feel the walls close in on him as five pairs of eyes assaulted him. At that moment, he wanted to say that his being there was just a mistake and that everything was okay, he just knew that they would not buy it. Hell, he didn't know if he would buy it.

"Okay," he hesitated and began to pace. "I don't know where Natalie is."

Silence filled the room as the others tried to interpret what Jesse had just said. He watched as an array of emotions appeared on their faces. He watched Redmond's face in particular as the Keeper processed the information.

"What do you mean 'you don't know where she is?'" asked Isabella.

"I mean that I don't know where she is. We got into a fight-"

"Surprise, surprise," said Michaelangela.

"What did you do?" asked Antonio.

"Yes, what did you do?" Joshua repeated.

"Enough!" Redmond bellowed.

Jesse and the others flinched at his tone and backed away from the angered Keeper.

"What happened, Jesse?" Isa asked gently.

"I watched Natalie die over and over again yesterday," he said. "I watched from every possible angle. Being the Protector, I was obliged as she put herself through pain and scrutinized her death repeatedly." He looked up at Redmond, watching as he listened to his story.

"We got back to the Sanctuary and she passed out from crying. I didn't know what to do. I was scared. So, I let her sleep it off. I started reading the Protector's book and read the part about the Advocate." He glanced at Antonio and continued. "Without realizing it, I read it out loud and she heard me. She tricked me into summoning him and I did. Next thing I knew, I was sent outside in the hall while they talked."

"What happened next?" Redmond asked.

"I went back in and asked her what they talked about and Natalie said that 'I made quite the deal' and I asked her what she knew-"

"Did you tell her?" Redmond turned to Antonio.

Jesse saw a guilty look on the Advocate's face.

"I may have alluded that Jesse had a deal-"

Redmond held up his hand to silence Antonio.

"I will speak with you later," he said to Antonio. "What happened next Jesse?"

Jesse took a breath. Closing his eyes, he relived the experience a second time, wincing as he heard the sound of her body hitting the wall. Shaking off the memory, he opened his eyes and continued.

"I pushed her," he confessed as he turned his back to them. "I pushed her...I didn't mean-"

"You pushed her?" Redmond asked with hint of rage in his voice. "You are supposed to 'protect' her. I trusted you with her. How could you do that?"

"It wasn't her that I pushed-"

"You just said you pushed her. If not her, then who?"

Jesse turned away from their disapproving eyes. He had seen those glares before and he felt like he was experiencing déjà vu.

"It wasn't her," he whispered. "It was him. I pushed him."

"What?" said Isabella. "What do you mean?"

"Do you know the last words my father said to me before I died?"

Jesse was greeted with silence and continued. "We got into a fight and he said that I was a mistake."

He leaned against the wall for support. "He said that I was pathetic."

"Jesse," Redmond said. "I-"

"Let me finish. When she said those words, I swear all I saw was him. Not her. Never her. All I could see was my father's stone cold eyes staring back at me and a vindictive smile on his face."

He turned around to face them, and felt a tear streaming down his face.

"So, I pushed him because that is who I saw. I didn't see her, just him. I know that it's not a good excuse, but I swear to you all, I didn't mean to hurt her."

"I think the four of you should leave us," Redmond said as he looked at Isa, Michaelangela, Joshua, and Antonio. "Isa, inform the Soul Searchers that Natalie is missing. Joshua, let your fellow Missionaries know what's going on. They may be stationed at locations across the city and may find her. Antonio, I will see you shortly and Michaelangela, go read Natalie's file. It might give some insight on where she might go."

They all nodded in agreement and silently filed out of the room.

"Redmond, I-"

"Your shield will link you to her locket. Why didn't you use it?"

Jesse turned, meeting his eyes with Redmond's. He looked down at the floor and sighed.

"I was going to do that, but I have a problem." He reached into his pocket and pulled out the locket. "I believe she has to be wearing this in order for it to work."

Jesse looked up once more, watching Redmond contemplate the current situation. He didn't know why, but he wanted to know what was going on in Redmond's head.

"The watch," said Redmond. "I gave her the Keeper's watch."

Jesse immediately winced as he heard that.

"You won't find her that way either."

Jesse pulled out the watch and handed it to Redmond.

"I guess Natalie and my father were right."

"About what?" Redmond replied as he clasped his hands together.

"I am pathetic."

Jesse saw Redmond walk toward him and placed his hands on his shoulders. "You're a lot of things. I can assure you, but that's not one of them. We will find her and you will make things right. I know you didn't mean to hurt her, but actions have consequences, Jesse, and we're going to have to face them."

"What happens now?" Jesse asked.

"Now we wait and hope that Natalie returns."

Chapter 17:
Soul Mates

According to the clock above her, thirty minutes had gone by since Natalie had last seen PJ. She was beginning to wonder if he had ditched her and found someone else to spend the day with. Currently, Natalie found herself surrounded by a mountain of stuffed animals. She looked around the store in awe and spotted the collection of dolls across the room. Getting up, she made her way over, gently lifting the Raggedy Ann doll, reminding her of the one she had when she was a child. Tears came to her eyes and she found herself wishing that she was a child once more.

"Why me?" she whispered.

She held the doll in her arms wishing that it could protect her like it had when she was younger and that's when PJ found her.

"Hey, you have to check out the piano," he said. "It's-" PJ noticed her crying. "What's wrong?"

"Don't you ever wish you could be a kid again and stay that way forever?" she said barely above a whisper.

PJ pulled out a Kleenex and handed it to her.

"Sometimes," he replied. "But that's why I come here. Probably more than I should. I just feel safe here."

Natalie saw that he was about to touch her. Before she could react, PJ pulled back. It became obvious to her that he was picking up on her reactions to his touch and she felt guilty for doing so.

"What is it about here that makes you feel safe?" she asked.

"Is this your question?" he answered.

Natalie simply nodded her head.

"I guess when you're a kid you don't have to worry about anything. You are loved no matter what, or at least you think you are. You can just have fun and do whatever. There are no consequences or worries. Granted, I still do whatever and people may not like that about me, at least here it doesn't matter."

"So, you don't care who you hurt?" she asked.

"I do care," he replied. "I just don't let it bother me."

Natalie saw that he was avoiding her gaze and could see that he was in pain over things he had done.

"You asked me why I don't do this with my family," he said, finally looking at her. Natalie nodded. "I have said and done things I am not proud of, but sometimes people say things because they were hurt first. Being alone is just something I have gotten used to."

In that moment, Natalie came to the realization that Jesse was like everyone else. He wanted to be loved for who he was without trying to be someone he wasn't.

"Well, who do we have here?" Natalie smiled as he held the doll carefully in his arms.

"That would be Raggedy Ann," she said.

"Ahh, well you know what Raggedy Ann needs?" he asked.

Natalie raised her eyebrow in confusion and watched Jesse stroll over to the dolls.

"Raggedy Andy," he replied.

Natalie laughed and stood up, placing the Raggedy Ann doll back on the shelf.

"What are you doing?" he said.

"Putting the doll back."

"Oh, no you don't!"

PJ walked up to the doll and picked it up. He then walked to the cash register.

"Jesse! What are you doing?" she yelled as she ran after him.

"Mr. Knight, more presents for your nieces and nephews?" the cashier asked.

"Nope. This is for the young lady you see rolling her eyes at me," he replied.

PJ waved at Natalie, signaling for her to come over.

"There you are Mr. Knight," she said.

"Thank you."

They walked outside, stopping in front of the giant teddy bear. Natalie peaked into the bag and smiled.

"Alright, where to next?" he asked.

***

Jesse watched Redmond closely as he paced the floor. He couldn't help but wonder what the Keeper thought of him. At the moment, Jesse wasn't thrilled by what he had done to Natalie. The look of shock on her face and the tears flowing from her eyes haunted him. He was angry at his father and he took it out on her in the worst way possible.

Jesse walked toward the fireplace for warmth. Since he awoke that morning, he had felt cold and numb. He wasn't sure what was happening to him, all he knew was that he was considerably uncomfortable. He turned when he heard the sound of the door opening and saw Isabella standing there. She had a solemn look on her face and he knew that she had no news regarding Natalie.

Before he could ask what else could be done, he felt the room getting colder and still could not fathom what was going on. Without warning, he felt a sharp pain in his side and fell to the floor. Taking in a few breaths, he clutched at his side, waiting for the pain to subside.

"What's happening to me?" he said in pain.

***

Natalie winced as she watched PJ fall for the tenth time. She glided past him, lapping around him once more.

"You know," he yelled as he attempted to pick himself off the ice. "I know that I said we can do whatever the person wanted, but this is ridiculous!"

She laughed and skated towards him.

"What, you never ice skated before?"

PJ was on his feet again, gripping the rail for dear life. He gave Natalie an exasperated look and took another fall.

She cringed as he took down two more people with him. Skating over to PJ once more, she apologized to the couple he collided with. She placed her arm around him and steadied him as best as she could.

"I didn't skate as a kid," he said. "I skied, I never skated!"

Natalie shook her head at him, while keeping a firm hold.

"I see," she replied. "Well, come on. You have to at least do one lap around the place."

She laughed when she saw the fear in his eyes. She

grabbed his hand in hers and guided him around the ice.

By the tenth lap, PJ got the hang of it, but wouldn't let go of her. For Natalie, the anxious feeling in her stomach had returned. She knew it was his turn to ask the question. She just hoped she could answer it.

"I'm going to sit down," he said, breaking her out of her thoughts.

"Are you okay?"

"I'm fine. Maybe I'll ice the bruises that are beginning to form. Hmm..."

"What?"

"I wonder where I can get some ice," he said.

Natalie could tell that PJ was waiting for some kind of reaction out of her. She simply shook her head and skated away.

"Okay, that was a bad attempt at a joke!" he shouted out to her.

***

Isa rushed to Jesse's side and began rubbing his back.

"Jesse?" Redmond asked.

"It's cold in here," he replied.

Closing his eyes, he leaned into Isa's touch. The warmth of her hand made him feel somewhat better.

"Redmond," Isa said. "He is cold. Jesse, how long have you been feeling like this?"

"Since I woke up," he answered as he sat up.

Taking a breath, Jesse closed his eyes and wished that it would just go away. He just wanted to be back in his room, in his bed, and not deal with any of this. His head was pounding and he could hear a ringing in his ears. There were voices in his head and the sound was growing louder. He put his hands to his ears and rocked his body back forth, willing for the pain to end.

"Make it stop!" he pleaded.

"Jesse," he heard Redmond call out to him. Jesse could hear the voices getting louder, as his head began to pound with pain. What was going on?

"Voices," Jesse whispered. "I can hear voices."

The silent exchange between Isa and Redmond scared him. They knew what was going on.

"We need to keep him calm," Isa told Redmond.

"I had no luck finding her," said Michaelangela entering the room. "I read her file to see where she might be, but came up empty. I thought for sure she would be with her living form, but didn't see her anywhere...what's the matter with him?"

"Stay with him," Isa said. "Just keep him calm and relaxed.

In an instant, he felt Michaelangela rubbing his back in soothing circles.

Jesse desperately tried to listen to the conversation between Redmond and Isa, but to no avail. All he could hear were the soft voices in his head. He closed his eyes once more and passed out.

The door of Redmond's office opened and Antonio came into the room.

"Redmond I...what is wrong with him?"

Isa and Redmond exchanged glances. Redmond motioned for Antonio come toward them. He nodded, allowing Isa the chance to explain.

"They're soul mates," Isa said.

"You're kidding right?" Antonio whispered. "They hate each other!"

"Yes, soul mates," Redmond divulged. "There's a connection between them. A strong connection."

"Wait," Antonio said. "How long have you known about this?"

Redmond rubbed his beard and looked at Isa.

"Not long actually," he admitted. "Natalie told me that Sofia and the Son needed to see me," Redmond stated. "They both explained the connection to me, but advised me not to say anything to anyone."

Redmond stopped and waited for Antonio to process everything he had just said.

"Isa knew before I did and she was specifically instructed to save Jesse," he told him. "There's a reason Jesse is Natalie's Protector and now you know why."

"That can't be everything?" Antonio said. "There has to be more to it than that."

Redmond wished he could have explained more to him, but alas, he could not. Redmond was still trying to figure things out and he too was confused about the entire situation.

"I can only tell you what I know," he told Antonio and patted him on the shoulder. "I wish I could tell you more, but even I am not privy to everything in this case and you have no idea how frustrating that can be."

"How does this explain why he is cold?"

"My best guess is that she must be somewhere cold," Redmond concluded.

Antonio gave them both a frown.

"The stronger the bond, the stronger the connection," Isa answered.

Redmond turned his attention back to Jesse. There was little he could do to help him. He was worried about the emotional and physical toll Jesse's body was taking, he could only hope that Natalie would come back soon.

Chapter 18:
Needs and Wants

For the past hour Natalie skated freely as the cold air kissed her face. She felt alive, yet reality reared its ugly head. She wasn't alive. She wasn't free. She was living on borrowed time. Time she promised to use wisely.

Natalie found PJ watching her with a smile on his face. Heaven help her, she couldn't help but smile back. Eventually she would have to go back to the Sanctuary and she would have to face Jesse, the real Jesse, because the one she was with right now was too good to be true.

Natalie skated over to him and gladly accepted the cup of hot chocolate in his hands.

"You look good out there," PJ told her. "You even did that spinny thing," twirling his index finger to emphasize his point.

She smiled at him and took another sip.

"Well, Madame Skate Queen, are you done?"

Natalie nodded her head and proceeded to take off her skates. With her shoes back on, she led PJ to Ben & Jerry's.

"You're kidding me right?" he said. "You want ice cream?"

"I always have ice cream after I'm out in the cold," she answered. "Besides, they might have ice for you."

"Trust me. Where I am bruised, ice cream will not cut it."

The pair entered the iconic ice cream store. Natalie instantly felt like a kid again. The bright colours, the smell of hot fudge, and children making messes everywhere made her smile. They headed to the counter and Natalie looked carefully at the menu. She knew exactly what she wanted. The server looked at the pair expectantly and Natalie looked at PJ.

"Don't look at me," he said. "This was your idea."

Natalie smiled. "We'll share the Brownie Special," she told the server and turned to PJ. "It's the best of both worlds. Hot brownie and cold ice cream."

"Ahh, I see," he nodded in agreement. "So everyone wins."

"Exactly!" she exclaimed.

After PJ paid, they headed to a table and sat down. It didn't take long for Natalie to dig in to her favourite treat.

"I believe I have another question to ask," Jesse said as he shoved a piece of brownie into his mouth.

Natalie tensed, but she knew that it was only fair.

"Alright."

"Are you happy?"

Natalie looked up at Jesse, and then glanced out the window.

"What makes you think I'm not?" she answered.

"Nope. No answering questions with questions."

Natalie groaned, giving the waitress a dirty stare as she delivered the ice cream.

"I am happy," she said.

"Liar," he said. "I think those two guys are making you miserable," he added.

"What's the term you used before? 'It's complicated'?"

"Somehow, I still think you're lying. So, let's go back to the last question. Why are you running from those guys?"

"I already answered that."

PJ was beginning to infuriate her. Their day had been fine up until this point. She was now beginning to think he wasn't that different from his counterpart.

"Okay, then which one is making you unhappy?"

"Why does it matter? And I don't care that I answered a question with a question."

"Fine, but you agreed to answer any question that I asked."

Damn their deal. No matter what else she wanted to call it, it would always be a deal. Natalie looked around, watching others in the shop staring at them. She knew she couldn't run. Where could she go? She ran from one Jesse, she couldn't run from both.

"I am unhappy," she admitted louder than she intended. "I am not really living the life I want." Technically, that wasn't a lie. "I just want my life back,"

"Okay, so your friend is giving you a hard time. Forget what he thinks and just live your life," he said in an authoritative voice.

"It's not that simple."

"It can be. What power does this guy have over you?"

"I need him," she said.

Did she just say that? Did she really need Jesse? She knew that she had to have his help, but after saying it out loud, she knew she needed it. Now for the hard part. How could she make past Jesse understand Jesse without making herself sound crazy?

"You need him?" he asked.

"I need him to help me get my life back together. In a way, he already has and he doesn't even know it. He may be a conceited, arrogant jerk, but he is the only one who can make everything okay again," she said smiling at him. "Don't take it personally," she said. "I doubt my fiancé will understand when I tell him. I hope you can accept that."

The grimace on his face and nod of his head indicated that he could accept it. Whether he wanted to was entirely different.

Together, Natalie and Jesse polished off the rest of the ice cream and headed back out into the December cold.

"Jesse, do you know what time it is?"

"Almost five o'clock. Cinderella doesn't wish to go back early, does she?"

Natalie's eyes widened as soon as she heard the time. She had been gone for quite a while and thought about what Jesse, present Jesse, was doing right now. She would be lying if she said she hadn't been enjoying her time with PJ, but she couldn't run forever. She still needed to figure a few things out and she was confused now more than ever.

Natalie looked at PJ and knew what had to be done.

"Jesse-" she started.

"I know," he interrupted. "I didn't mean to come on so strong. I just-"

"That's not it," she said and placed her hand on his arm. "You have given me a few things to think about but-"

"But you can't do that if you're with me," he said and shoved his hands into his pockets.

"No, I can't."

Natalie handed him the bag with the dolls in it and took off the coat he had bought for her.

"Don't," he said. "Keep it. I hope you find what you're looking for," she heard him say.

She watched as he walked away from her and suddenly

felt a wave of loneliness surround her.

***

Redmond sat down at his desk, watching as Isa and Michaelangela tended to Jesse. He spent the better part of the hour contemplating their next move. It was clear to him that Jesse was the key to getting Natalie back.

His thoughts were broken by Antonio, who had brought him something to drink.

"Thank you."

Antonio nodded and walked to Jesse and the others.

Redmond took a low sip of the brandy and sighed. He was following the rules, but even this was uncharted territory for him. It wasn't often that a Protector and their Ward were soul mates.While he trusted Sofia and the Son, he felt uneasy about not being completely honest with everyone. Especially Natalie and Jesse.

Redmond finished his brandy and stood up slowly. He watched as Jesse was writhing in pain and he hated that there was little he could do to make things better. Deciding that enough was enough, he walked over to Isa, Michaelangela, and Antonio. He had made an executive decision.

"We need to go to the Sanctuary," he said.

Redmond heard Jesse speak and kneeled by his side.

"What is it?" Redmond asked Jesse.

"I'm sorry," he whispered and passed out once more.

Redmond frowned and looked at Isa.

"Templum," he said and they were gone.

Chapter 19:
Me Looking At You, You Looking At Me

Natalie had spent the past few hours walking around Manhattan. Every now and then she would ask someone for the time and worried about the potential harm she was causing by running away.

Past Jesse had given her a lot to think about and that included her relationship with his future counterpart. The more she thought about it, the more she thought about the odds of running into his past self. She knew that it couldn't have been a coincidence. Granted, she had often wondered whether he was telling the truth about his past, but there was no reason for his past self to lie to her.

She was standing among thousands of people in the middle of Times Square. People who were rushing around her just minding their own business without a care in the world, and here she was trying to find answers and the courage to go back to the Sanctuary and face Jesse.

"What am going to do?" she said as she pulled out the Raggedy Ann Doll from the bag. She frowned at the doll when she realized she wasn't going to get a reply.

***

Jesse woke up and was feeling very disoriented. As he stood up, he saw Redmond and Isa in the room with him and was grateful for not being alone.

"How long was I asleep?" he asked Isa.

"A few hours," she replied. "Your body has taken quite a toll. How do you feel?"

"Better," he stated.

Jesse winced and rubbed his eyes. Redmond walked over to him, handing him a glass of water.

"What's wrong?"

"Lights," Jesse replied. "I see lots of lights."

The door to the Sanctuary burst open. Jesse, Isa and Redmond's eyes darted to the entrance.

"The Soul Searchers have closed in on her, but they keep finding the Natalie from this timeline," Michaelangela said. Noticing the disappointment on their faces, she concluded that they wished she were someone else instead.

"Sorry, they are doing their best."

The door opened once more. Joshua entered the room. "I have informed a few of my people," he told the group. "We did some research on potential locations Natalie may turn up, but haven't found her yet. Have you heard anything?"

Jesse walked over to the window, ignoring the question and conversation that followed. The pounding in his head had returned and he didn't know how he wanted to deal with it. More flashing appeared before him, only this time they were far more vivid. The cold took over his body once more and for the first time he heard her and it scared him.

He wasn't prepared to tell the rest of them what was going on. He could care less. Leaning against the glass of the window, Jesse closed his eyes and focused his attention on the voice. It was hers and he knew it.

"She's okay," Jesse began. "She's safe."

Jesse expected one of them to say something, when nothing was said he sat on the bed.

"What did you hear?" Isa asked breaking the silence.

Jesse had only one option. Lie. He knew that this could have repercussions, but if Natalie did not want to be found just yet, he was going to let her have her freedom.

"I couldn't make all the words out," he told them.

"Are you sure?" Redmond asked.

"Yes, I'm sure" Jesse answered.

***

Natalie finally found her nerve and decided to head back to St. Patrick's. Along the way she felt like she was being pulled off course. It was as if her body was telling her that she wasn't ready to go back yet. She found herself in front of the entrance to Central Park and headed back to Gapstow

Bridge. It was only fitting that she would want to end her day the way she started. Since leaving past Jesse, she wondered about what the rest of their day would have consisted of. She liked the element of taking turns where they were going and asking questions about each other, but it felt like cheating and she didn't want Jesse, past or present, to expose himself to her like that.

She placed the bags on the bridge and pulled out the dolls. Natalie smiled at them.

"I knew you needed both of them," came a voice. "You can't have Raggedy Ann without Raggedy Andy."

Natalie whirled around and found past Jesse standing on the other side of the bridge.

"Jesse?" she said as her eyes lit up in bewilderment.

"I realized that we never got to ask our final questions," he said and walked up to her. "I have been trying to find you since I left you and for some reason, I had a feeling you might be here."

"How were you so sure?" she asked.

"Intuition? Dumb luck? Going to every possible tourist destination I could think of," he stopped and then looked at her. "Then I thought, if it were me and I were running away and looking for answers, I'd go back to the place that I went to first. You obviously came here for a reason, so I hoped that you might come back."

Natalie didn't know what to say to him. They were back where they started and for her, she felt like she had come full circle.

"It's almost midnight," he said. "Ask me a question."

PJ's tone was daring and his eyes were filled with determination.

A question? What could she ask? The whole point of leaving him was because she didn't want to take advantage of him. She needed a safe question. One that was simple and one that he would answer.

"Okay," she said. "Are you happy?"

Natalie waited for his response, but when he said nothing she asked again.

"Did you hear-"

"I heard you," he spoke. "Truthfully, no. I am not happy. Today. For a few hours I was." PJ stopped and leaned against

the bridge. "And I have you to thank for that. I wasn't thinking about me or my problems."

"I'm sorry, I shouldn't have asked," she said.

"No," he said shaking his head. "Don't be sorry. Not about
this."

Natalie saw tears pooling in his eyes, she knew that he
was not going to let them surface in front of her. Instead she
looked out around her, letting Jesse compose himself.

"Last question?" she choked out.

Past Jesse leaned in slowly. Natalie knew exactly what
he was going to do and she found herself leaning into him too.
She closed her eyes and when their lips met she let herself
go. As he deepened the kiss, she let her arms wrap around
his neck. She had had her fair share of kisses, but there was
something different about this kiss. Natalie's need for oxygen
caused her to pull away from him and he groaned. When her
eyes met his once more she saw longing and understanding.

"What's your last question?" Natalie asked him as she
touched her lips.

Past Jesse smiled at her. "I was going to ask if I could
kiss you," he replied.

Natalie's eyes widened.

"What would have happened if I had said no?"

PJ shrugged his shoulders and grinned sheepishly.
"That's why I didn't ask."

"Jesse-"

"I know," he said. "You have to go."

Natalie slowly stepped away from him. Giving him a sad
smile, she clutched the bags in her hands and took off running into the night.

***

Jesse had been pacing around the room for the past
twenty minutes. He had lost the connection with Natalie for a
while and worried that something terrible had happened to
her. About an hour or so ago, the connection between them
had been restored and he wondered why he had lost it in the
first place.

"Jesse, sit down before you wear a hole in the floor,"

Michaelangela said as she stood up. "You are making me nervous."

Jesse nodded and walked over to the bed. He sat down and picked up the locket and examined it closely. When he looked at the watch he was stunned to see that it was whole once more. He sighed as he watched the minutes count down.

"We'll find her," Isa told him.

"I hope..." Jesse started. He looked at the door and saw her beneath the threshold of the door. He blinked to see if she was real. His hazel eyes focused on one green and one blue eye staring back at him at the threshold of the door.

Standing up, Jesse stared at her with relief evident in his eyes. He walked over to her, while maintaining a safe distance.

"I'm only going to ask once and only once," he said with intent. "Where were you?"

Seeing her nervously look around the room worried Jesse. He started to panic and dreaded what her answer would mean to them and to everyone else in the room.

"I was with you."

Chapter 20:
Back to Reality

"What did you just say?" Jesse asked.

"I said that I was with you," Natalie repeated and placed the bag she was holding in her hand on the floor. "Not the whole time though."

Natalie was unsure how Jesse and the others would take the news. She was still in shock about everything that had transpired in the last 24 hours and that included the kiss she just shared with past Jesse. She could still feel his lips on hers and hoped that no one could tell that she was blushing.

When her eyes caught Jesse's, she could tell that he was trying to process what she had just told him.

"You mean-" he started.

"I mean that I was with you," Natalie confirmed. "I'm sorry for worrying everyone. Running away wasn't the best solution, but at the time," she looked at Jesse and then back at the others. "It seemed like a good idea."

Natalie wasn't sure what Jesse was feeling, much less thinking, but the expression on his face showed that he was experiencing some kind of inner turmoil. To her, he seemed a bit unnerved about her admission of spending time with his living form.

"Isa, I think it's time you all went back. Also, please inform Antonio that Natalie has returned."

"Of course."

"Wait," Jesse said. Everyone in the room paused and looked at him. "Natalie…"

Natalie's heart was racing. She had no idea what Jesse was about to do and she could practically see the sweat coming out his pores. "I'm sorry," his voice cracked. "I never should have hurt you like that. I'm supposed to protect you. I promise to do everything in my power to change that."

He turned away from her and looked at Redmond, Isa, Michaelangela, and Joshua. "I'm sorry for putting you all in this position. You trusted me and I abused that trust and because of it we lost time. I hope you can try to forgive me."

Natalie watched the four of them closely and saw them give Jesse a stern glare. She was relieved when they nodded at him. The last thing she wanted was for this to get out of hand and for them to make things more awkward between her and Jesse. They all nodded and seemed somewhat satisfied with his apology. Within seconds, Isa, Michaelangela, and Joshua were gone.

"Natalie," Redmond began. "I realize that you were in an awkward situation-"

"Redmond, I-"

"Let me finish," he said. "You've lost another day and I know you know what's at stake here. Do you realize what could have happened? Natalie-"

"Redmond," she interrupted. "I think you should go."

Natalie could see that Redmond was clearly caught off guard by her statement. When she looked at Jesse, she saw that he too seemed surprised by her request. While she knew what Redmond was trying to do, she needed to talk to Jesse alone and the last thing she wanted, much less needed, was for Redmond to come between them.

"You can't fix this one or try to make it better," she said. "This is between me and Jesse."

Redmond walked toward her slowly, placed his hand on her shoulder. "Okay."

With a final look at Jesse, Natalie heard Redmond utter a phrase and in a flash, he was gone. She was now alone again with Jesse and while she knew that they would have a lot to deal with, she came to the conclusion that she needed him now more than ever.

***

Jesse took a deep breath and closed his eyes, releasing the anguish he had been holding since Natalie returned. Reaching into his pockets, Jesse pulled out the locket and the watch.

"I believe these belong to you," Jesse said turning to Natalie. "You better put them back on."

Jesse walked over to Natalie, gently placing the locket and watch in her hands. He made it a point to not touch her.

Avoiding her gaze, he made his way over to the bed and sat on it. Running his fingers through his hair, Jesse proceeded to massage his temples, trying to rid the ache.

Minutes later, he felt the weight of the bed shift. He could tell that she was trying to get his attention, yet he wasn't sure if he was ready to give it.

"I've never done that before," he said and looked at his hands. "I've never..." Jesse's hands started to shake and the urge to vomit was overwhelming.

"Jesse," Natalie said and tentatively touched him.

He pulled away from her touch and stood up from the bed.

"Don't," he said. "I hurt you because in that moment, all I saw...all I heard was my father and I-"

"Jesse."

"I've never done that. Ever. I'm so sorry, Natalie. Throughout my life, I've been angry and I have said a lot of things, but I have never..." He paused and looked at her. "I'm supposed to protect you," he said and shook his head. "And I can't even do that right. You ran away because for one moment I was angry, not at you but at my father. I feel like an idiot for what I did and I don't blame you if you hate me too."

Uncomfortable with their proximity, Jesse stood up and walked over to the bathroom. He leaned his hands against the door frame for support and fought the urge to vomit. He was still disgusted about what he had done to her and vowed that he would only touch her when he had to.

"Jesse," she repeated. "Wait a minute."

He propped himself up from the door frame.

"Yes, I am angry at you," she continued, walking towards him and I am worried about what you're capable of. I'm not going to forget what happened here and I know you won't. It's something that will always be between us. But Jesse, I am not scared of you."

Jesse turned away and went inside the bathroom. He closed the door and slumped onto the floor. She wasn't scared of him? How could she not be? He was scared of himself.

"I spent the better part of the day with your living counterpart," he heard her say through the door. "I know that could not have been a coincidence. The city's filled with millions of people and out of all those millions, you were the one that found me."

Jesse closed his eyes as he listened closely to her words. The second that she told him that she had spent the better part of the day with his living self, he started to wonder what that had meant. What exactly were the odds of him from seven years ago running into her? Carefully, he pulled himself off the floor and reached the door handle. He opened it and saw that Natalie was waiting on the other side.

He walked past her and sat back down on the bed.

"I find it interesting that out of the millions of people that live in the city, I ran into you on that bridge in Central Park," she said. "I could've ran into anyone but I ran into you. Something tells me that there was a reason that you were the one on that bridge with me."

"Bridge?" Jesse said. "Gapstow?"

Natalie nodded her head at him. "The one and only. I learned a lot about you today." Jesse began to shake. He was worried about what she may have learned. Jesse now realized how vulnerable he really was to her and understood how she may have felt when he bombarded her with questions about her life. He didn't know what his past self may have said to her and that scared him more than anything.

"I think you will have noticed that I'm not the same person I was seven years ago," Jesse told her. "I'm different from that wide-eyed twenty-one-year-old. I don't even really remember what I was like back then."

"It's okay because I see part of him in you," she said. "It's funny that by running away from you, I actually ran toward you."

Jesse couldn't quite explain the range of emotions he was feeling. Maybe her seeing how he used to be wasn't a bad thing after all.

"You think I haven't thought about the fact that there's millions of people in the city and it was me that you ran into," he told her. It explained so many things. Why he could feel her, see her, and smell her. "I think a part of me knew that I was with you too. It occurred to me that maybe it was a guilty conscience and that I was being tortured because of what I had done to you."

"Jesse."

He waved her off and continued. "You said you only spent

part of the day with me," he pointed out and stood up again. "I guess you got sick of me and realized that you should get away before I did something to you again. And yet you didn't come back here. So, where did you go?"

Jesse was curious about where Natalie had ended up. If she hadn't been with him, he wanted to know what she ended up doing instead.

"I decided to end it early because I knew that I needed to get back to you here," she said. Jesse noted the hesitation in her voice and the way she fiddled with her fingers. It was clear that there was something she wasn't telling him.

"I'm sensing there's more to it than that."

"I ended it early because I didn't want to take advantage of you or your past," she admitted. "I didn't think that would be fair. At least not that way."

Jesse did a double take at Natalie. She didn't want to exploit information from him and learn about his past because she thought it would be unfair. What exactly did the living version of himself say to her?

"So I walked around the city and I went to my favorite places," said Natalie. "I mean it was your idea to just go play tourist have fun." She laughed. "You know the funny thing, I actually did have fun."

Jesse found himself smiling at her. The living him had made Natalie happy and he was grateful that the old him hadn't morphed into a complete jerk yet. He was even more grateful that she was somewhat charmed by his character. It made him wonder how he could have become such a monster.

"I went to Grand Central, got lost in the library, and finally made my way to Times Square and just watched tourists in awe of everything going on. Then I started to make my way back but couldn't. Not yet."

There was a look in her eyes. One that he had never seen before. She seemed wistful about everything.

"I found myself going back to the bridge and I just stood there. In that moment, I had never felt so free, so alive, and so alone at the same time. Then all of a sudden you were there. It was like you knew I would be there."

"What happened?" he asked. There was a tone of dread in his words. He watched her closely. He was extremely curious as to how his night with Natalie ended.

"We asked our final questions and I left," she answered.

Jesse raised his eyebrow at her. For some reason he didn't quite believe her. Her short response only piqued is interest further and while he wanted to know, he wasn't going to demand an answer from her. The last time that happened, he hurt her, she ran away, and they ended up wasting the day.

"That's it?" he asked.

"That all," she replied. "Although there was one thing you said that got me thinking."

"Oh? What did I say?"

"Well, I talked about you to past you," she said.

"This already sounds like the start of an interesting conversation," he said.

"Past Jesse thinks that in regards to our relationship, you're just trying to protect me and now I know that you being my Protector isn't a mistake. You're my Protector for a reason and I know that you are the only person who can help me get back what I lost." She stopped and he watched as she approached him cautiously. "Only you can help me get my life back."

Jesse stood up and faced Natalie. He crossed his arms about his chest and sighed.

"Natalie, I don't even know where to begin," he said. "Maybe you should find the living me. He seems to have a better idea about what needs to be done."

Jesse didn't want to admit that he was jealous of himself. For one, there was nothing to be jealous of. They were one in the same. However, Natalie seemed taken with his living counterpart and he hated that.

"Jesse, you are him. He is you. What would you do if you were me?"

Now there was an interesting question. Jesse paced the length of the small room and thought about what he would do. Then it hit him. He snapped his fingers and spun around to look at Natalie.

"I would ask myself what led me to the place where I died."

"What?" she asked. "I don't get it?"

"Think about it," he told her. "Why were you at the dry cleaners on your wedding day? Wouldn't you already have your dress? Wouldn't you have someone else pick up the dress for you? Natalie, why exactly were you there?"

"I was picking up my wedding dress," she answered. "My sister had spilled red wine on it at my rehearsal dinner. I was showing the dress to her and she tripped on the rug in my room and spilled the wine."

"So, had that not happened you never would have been at the dry cleaners that morning," he stated. "You never would have been hit by the car. I think we have been going about this the wrong way."

"What do you suggest we do then?"

"We need to write down everything that happened to you that week," he said "Maybe we can prevent it."

"Jesse, you said it yourself. We can't prevent my death."

'Damn it' he thought and sat back on the bed. They couldn't prevent it. Their goal was to find out why she died in the first place.

"Okay, then we need to know what you did that week."

"Jesse, that week was hectic. Do you know how busy things can get the week before you get married?"

"No, I don't," he said. He had no idea. He'd never been married. He wasn't even close. He'd actually have to be in a relationship to even consider getting to that point. "This is the part where you tell me."

Rolling her eyes, she joined him on the bed once more.

"Lots of things happened," she replied. "I don't remember,"

"Liar! Were you a Bridezilla? Trust me, been there done that. My sister-in-laws made the Bride of Chuckie look like a saint."

Natalie laughed at his joke and he smiled at the memory.

"It was a bad week. Everyone has them!"

"True. But not everyone ends up dead!"

She winced at his response and he wanted to smack himself for being insensitive.

"I don't know. Nick and I got into a fight, my future father-in-law wanted me to stop writing and become 'Susie home maker', and my sister spilled red wine on my wedding dress. And that all happened in one day!"

"How?" Jesse asked barely above a whisper. "Tell me."

Her hesitation worried him. He was pushing her and he knew that his approach could blow up in his face, but he needed to do it.

"It was the little things," she groaned. "Nick had two things to do. Show up at the wedding and plan the honeymoon. We argued over that for a week!"

Seeing that Natalie was working herself into a fit, he went into the bathroom and brought her a glass of water. She smiled gratefully at him and drank it. Calming herself down, Natalie resumed her story.

"Nick's father wanted to close the children's section of his publishing company. In reality I think he knew that it would be the only way for Charles to get what he wanted. Me, a stay at home, socialite wife."

Jesse smirked when he heard that. She was definitely not the type.

"My sister could not fathom as to why I was making things so difficult. It only got worse. She wanted to see my wedding dress, but I wanted everyone to wait. I also didn't want her opinion. So, when I did show her...well you know what happened next," she stressed.

"I, uh...I don't know what to say."

"You know, I wasn't sure if I wanted to get married anymore," she said.

Jesse's eyes shot up at that. He didn't know if his ears were deceiving him and he didn't dare ask her to repeat herself.

"Don't get me wrong. I wanted to get married to him, just not like that."

Jesse felt jealousy flow through him and fought the urge to make a comment about Mr. Perfect. His mind wandered as Natalie told her tale. It struck him that Natalie wasn't the type to make a big deal about anything and he was beginning to see that she wanted her wedding be one thing. Hers.

"I guess there is only one question I want to ask you," Jesse said. "Are you ready to face that day all over again? Wait! Let me rephrase. Can you face that day all over again?"

Natalie nodded her head. "I don't have a choice," she responded. "We need to know. So, yes. I am ready."

Jesse's eyes locked onto hers. For the first time since this adventure of theirs began, they were finally on the same page. They may have been reading a different book, but they were on the same page.

"Okay," he said. "Let's do this."

Natalie's smile reached her eyes and found himself smiling too until she stretched her hand out to him. He stared at her hand and caught a glimpse of bruises around her wrist. He was suddenly overwhelmed by the image of him pushing her against the wall. He quickly looked away and stood up.

"We better go!" he said as he headed toward the bathroom.

"Jesse."

Leaning his hands against the door frame for support, he feared feeling of guilt would never go away.

"Jesse," she repeated. "It's okay."

Jesse relaxed his shoulders and walked into the bathroom. Shutting the door behind him, he slid to the floor and covered his face with his hands.

"No. It's not. I'm sorry, Natalie. So sorry," he whispered. Natalie Parker was far more forgiving then she should have been and Jesse Knight certainly felt unworthy of her forgiveness, or a second chance.

Chapter 21:
Facing the Past

"Natalie, come on!" Jesse shouted as he banged on the bathroom door.

"This isn't going to work!" Natalie shouted back.

"Yes, it is!"

"No, it isn't!"

"Yes, it is!"

"No, it isn't"

"Yes, it is and don't say no it isn't!"

Natalie opened the door and stormed out. Jesse's mouth dropped open and he couldn't stop staring at her. It was almost as if she hypnotized him.

"We can't just walk into the party. People will know that we don't belong. Jesse? Hello! Earth to Jesse!"

Snapping out of his trance, Jesse focused his attention on her and not the black dress.

"What?"

"Where were you?"

Heaven. He was in heaven. The black dress was made for her. Flowing just above her knee like a curtain while straps showed off her slender shoulders. Her auburn hair framed her face in a simple up do, bringing out her mismatched coloured eyes.

"We can't just walk in there," she said and adjusted the dress.

He watched her carefully as she made her way to the jewelry box and pulled out a pair of diamond studs.

"Look, can you honestly say you remember everyone who was there that night?" Jesse asked, but he already knew her answer. Her silence proved his point and he continued. "We're dressed for the party and we look like we belong. As long as we don't draw attention to ourselves, we'll be fine." Although he had a feeling that she was definitely going to draw some attention from a few men at the party. "Now, where exactly are we going?"

Jesse watched as she fastened the earrings in place. It

always amazed him to what lengths women went to get ready. While he appreciated it he didn't think Natalie required that much time to get herself put together. He watched in fascination as Natalie tried to remember where she had been that night.

"The stables!"

"What?"

Natalie walked over to him and took his hand. Jesse shuddered at her touch. The fact that she was willing to be around him, let alone hold his hand, unnerved him.

"I was at the stables! And you still need a tie! Honestly, Jesse!"

Jesse looked in the mirror and saw his lack of tie. He didn't do ties! He was happy with the charcoal suit and open collared white shirt.

"Come here."

Stepping towards Natalie, she wrapped the royal blue tie around his neck. Days ago, he was certain that she would have used the tie as a noose. Right now, he still thought that she would.

"Why blue?" he questioned.

"What?"

"This shade of blue, why did you pick it?"

"It matches your eyes," she said barely above a whisper.

"Hazel."

"What?" she looked up at him and he saw her cheeks redden.

"My eyes were blue. They're hazel now."

Jesse smiled as Natalie's cheeks turned an even darker shade of red.

"Let's go!" she said and grabbed his hands.

Feeling the familiar pull around his body, he held onto Natalie's hand tightly. Watching her memories pass by, he waited for the hard landing to come. When it didn't happen, he looked at his surroundings. Natalie's hand was still clutched in his and they were on a bed of hay. Jesse turned his head to face Natalie and could see a tearful smile across her face.

"Well, that was a better-"

"Shh," Natalie hissed.

"What?" Jesse asked.

Natalie pulled Jesse behind the stacks of hay. Placing her finger to his lips, she whispered and pointed.

"I'm right over there."

Peeking his head around the hay, he could see the living Natalie petting and talking to a horse.

"What are you worried about?" he said as he pulled himself back and looked at her.

"I believe you said that we shouldn't draw attention to ourselves!" she whispered back. "Besides, if she sees us, if I see us, we may be kicked out of here sooner."

"Oh, I thought you were afraid we'd scare the horses."

"Shh," Natalie hissed once more as a pile of hay fell over. "Great! Now you've done it!"

"Is someone there?" they heard the other Natalie ask.

Natalie and Jesse stared intently into each other's eyes, praying that they would not be caught.

"Oscar! What are you doing here?"

They heard a dog bark and both Jesse and Natalie sensed that the dog was coming in their direction

"Oscar?" Jesse mouthed at Natalie.

"My dog," Natalie answered.

"Obviously," he whispered. "Why would you name your dog Oscar?"

"Are we really going to do this now?"

Silence came as they waited for the coast to clear.

"Come on boy, let's go!"

Once they heard the footsteps disappear, they stepped out into the open.

Natalie smacked Jesse on the arm.

"Ow," Jesse said and rubbed his shoulder. "What was that for?"

"We almost got caught!"

"We were fine."

Sighing in contempt, Natalie linked her arm through his and they made their way toward the house.

Jesse stared in awe as Natalie led them to the front door. He was amazed by how right it felt to be with her like this.

As they walked up the steps, Jesse hoped that everything would go according to plan even though technically, they didn't have one.

"Invitation?" the doorman asked.

Natalie gave Jesse the death glare and both were startled when they realized that the man was Joshua.

"I'm just kidding," Joshua said. "It's a good thing I'm here. Trust me, you wouldn't have been admitted without one."

Natalie gave Jesse an 'I told you so look' and he focused his attention back to Joshua.

"What are you doing here?" Jesse questioned as he looked at the Missionary all spiffed up in the penguin outfit.

"My job," he said. "Like I said, you wouldn't have been admitted. Now, get in there." He winked at them.

The foyer was impressive. White marble floors and high ceilings with expensive crown moulding. There were expensive paintings that accented the room, along with impressive pieces of colonial furniture. Yes, Jesse was in the Hamptons. The champagne was overflowing, the caviar was out in full force, and a variety of perfumes were wafting about the room. He looked around and could see members of high society strutting around and making small talk with each other. He shook his head in amusement and then he wondered if his parents were going to be here. Jesse felt the tie around his neck tighten. He didn't know what he would do if his father was here and he certainly didn't want to find out.

"Okay, now that we're in, let's get to work," Jesse said as he fought the urge to loosen the tie. "Where did you go once you left the stables?"

Jesse waited again. Her eyes shut once more and he could tell that she was struggling to remember.

"Nick!" she blurted out. "I went to talk to Nick."

Jesse nodded.

"Where?"

"The balcony."

Grabbing her hand gently, he nudged her to lead the way. They glided across the room to the doors of the balcony. Trying to act inconspicuously, they headed outside where they heard raised voices.

"Nick! I asked you to do one thing, just one thing!" Natalie shouted.

"Natalie, calm down, okay?"

"Calm down? I don't know where we are going! I don't know what to pack! You had one job and that was to pick our honeymoon destination!"

"You are worrying for nothing. With the jet, my name and our passports, we can go anywhere and buy things."

Jesse couldn't believe the words coming out of his mouth.

"Nick! A honeymoon is supposed to be romantic."

"And being spontaneous isn't?" Nick answered as he pulled her into his arms and kissed her.

Jesse's jaw muscles clenched and his fists tightened. He took a deep breath as the jerk continued to speak.

"Nat, come on. Trust me. This will be a honeymoon we'll never forget. Plus, being spontaneous is romantic."

"You know I hate it when things aren't planned! You know that I-"

"I know. Can we finish this later? Trust me, it will be okay. People are waiting for us. Come on."

Jesse watched as Natalie walked into the baboon's arms. He looked over at his Natalie once more and sighed when he saw a smile of contempt on her face. As he turned his attention back to the happy couple, he could see that the other Natalie was not entirely convinced by her fiancé's words.

"That wasn't as bad as I remembered."

"He called you 'Nat'," Jesse said.

Natalie blushed and Jesse walked further out onto the balcony where Nick and Natalie had stood moments before.

"Okay, so that wasn't the part of the night that made you miserable, but you have to admit that you weren't exactly too happy with him. He talked down to you."

Natalie jerked her head and frowned.

"No, he didn't."

"Yes, he did."

"No, he didn't."

"Yes...I don't want to get into this again," he said. "Where to next? That is to say, what other bad things happened? Unless they are all like this and you really were a bridezilla."

Not amused by his tone, Natalie grabbed Jesse's hand and led him to another memory. Flashes of memories wrapped around them once more and they found themselves gripping onto each other.

They landed roughly onto a couch with Natalie on top of Jesse.

"Hmm, I seem to be experiencing a case of déjà vu, but I

was on top," Jesse quipped as he remembered their very first landing.

Natalie pushed herself off him. She led him into one of closets nearby.

"You know, I've had first dates start out like this," he said trying to break the mood. He could tell that he had upset her before with his comment. Then again, that was his jealousy talking.

Natalie glared at him.

"I know, I know. Shh!" he said as he raised his finger to his lips.

They heard the door open and close. They held their breath and waited.

"Natalie, are you okay?" asked a voice.

"What do you think, Dad?"

"Natalie, your father and I are worried about you," replied a feminine voice.

"Mom, today is not turning out exactly as I imagined. I am getting married in two days! Things are going from bad to worse."

"Honey," her father started.

"You know he wants me to quit writing. They both do. My future husband and father-in-law want me to quit writing and play Mrs. Socialite!"

"Natalie-"

"They are closing the children's section down!"

Jesse could hear the torment and pain in her voice.

"I love him, but why is he asking me to be somebody I'm not?"

Jesse listened intently to her words. Something didn't add up to him. Natalie said that she did have a confrontation with Nick and Nick's father. One question entered his mind, why did Natalie take him here? Why were they going out of order?

"Natalie?" he said. "If you already had your argument with Nick's dad, why are we here?"

Natalie raised her head and let the tears pool in her eyes.

"I just wanted be near them," she whispered.

And that's when Jesse understood. Natalie had spent seven years in Purgatory trying to remember. Trying to hold onto whatever she could. She was just a little girl who needed comfort and being close to her parents would give her the motivation she needed in order to get through this.

Jesse reached to open the door, but Natalie stopped him.

"I don't want to see them, not like this."

"They don't know who you are."

"Please."

Jesse sighed and nodded in agreement.

"We need to move," Jesse told her.

Nodding, she clasped their hands together and disappeared out of the closet.

With a graceful thud, Jesse and Natalie landed on the dance floor. Couples waltzed their way around them, as the music floated in the air. As they stood on the floor, they received a flurry of curious stares.

"I think we should dance," Jesse said.

"What? Why?"

"Remember that whole 'let's not draw attention to ourselves.'"

"Yeah," came a hesitant reply.

Natalie gave Jesse a questioning look and realized what he was saying.

"Oh!"

"Yes, oh!"

"Can you even waltz?" Natalie said.

Jesse grinned. Placing her right hand in his left, he took her into his arms and they glided across the room to Hubert Giraud's 'Under Paris Skies.'

Saturday's dancing with his grandmother turned out not to be a waste after all. The astonished look in Natalie's eyes consumed him. He knew she was shocked that he could lead her around the dance floor. The one thing on his mind was the fact that people still waltzed these days. He twirled her around the room as gracefully as he could while continuing to search for the living her.

"There you are," he told her.

"What?" she asked in a daze.

"Let's head that way," he said as he twirled her once more.

Jesse managed to get them as close as he could without raising suspicion.

"Natalie," said Mr. Manning, "I need to discuss something

with you. In private."

"Now?" she replied.

"Yes, shall we?"

Jesse and Natalie watched as the pair left the dance floor. Natalie was ready to run after them, but Jesse held her back.

"Wait," he instructed. "We don't want to look like snoops. Remember, we can't cause a scene."

Jesse guided them carefully out of the room. Once they were out, Jesse wiped the sweat off his brow.

"Where did you go?" Jesse asked.

"The library."

"Hmm, a publisher in a library. Insert joke here."

Natalie walked off in the direction of the library and Jesse chased after her. He saw her stop outside a closed door.

"Well, that can't be good," Jesse sighed.

"If you had gotten us off the floor faster-"

"Even if I had, how would we get in? We would have to be there beforehand.We can't just go back-"

"Yes, we can!" she told him.

"To when though?" Jesse asked.

"We have to leave before I do. I mean-"

"I know what you mean. So, we must get across the floor quicker."

Natalie and Jesse grabbed each other's hands and waited for the pull. Once again, they were on the dance floor. 'Under Paris Skies' was beginning once more, as Jesse and Natalie took the familiar waltzing position.

They danced around the couples again and proceeded to make their way toward their desired exit. Natalie saw herself dancing with Nick's father and brushed pass them. They continued to waltz out of the room, stopping once they were out of sight.

"Okay," she said. "Hurry up! They're coming!"

They rushed into the room and shut the door behind them. Jesse admired the library and appreciated the simplicity of it. The walls were painted burgundy and were lined with mahogany bookshelves and collections of books by various authors. Before Jesse could inspect the rare collection of books, he spotted Natalie out of the corner of his eye looking for something.

"Natalie, what are you doing?"

All of sudden he heard a loud noise, revealing a wet bar from the bookcase. Jesse looked on in amazement as he watched the rest of the bar unfold.

"Son of a-"

"Jesse!" Natalie whispered. The sound of footsteps broke Jesse from his shock and he felt Natalie roughly push him behind the bar.

They managed do get down in time before the door burst open. Jesse continued to look at the liquor, amazed by the supply of booze.

Nudging him, Natalie pointed to her ears signifying for him to listen.

"Is this about the new book?" the other Natalie asked.

"Actually, it has something to do with it," replied Mr. Manning. "It will be your last."

Jesse couldn't fathom the emotions Natalie must have been feeling. It was clear to him how much her writing meant to her and this arrogant prick was taking it away from her.

"Mr. Manning-" Natalie started.

"Natalie, please call me Charles. We're going to be family soon."

"Okay. Charles, I don't understand."

"We are dropping the children's section," he told her. "With only three authors on our billet, I just don't think it's worth it."

"But I thought that I was-"

"There you are!" Nick said as entered the room. "What's going on? Dad? Are you doing what I think you're doing?"

"You mean you knew?" Natalie demanded.

"Natalie, this was my decision," Charles said. "I have been debating this for a while and now seemed to be a good time. Besides, you'll be married to my son, you won't have time to write."

Jesse could feel Natalie shaking with rage beside him. She was angry and he could see why. The short, pudgy man controlling her career was as oily as his hair and he wanted nothing more than to rip the moustache off his face. Nick must be counting his blessings because he certainly didn't look like his father.

"So I'm expected to be some socialite wife?"

"Dad, would you excuse us?" asked Nick.

"No! It was his idea, I want to hear his answer!"

"Natalie, I don't have to explain myself to you," Charles said. "My son can provide for you and-"

"Sweetheart," Nick said, interrupting his father. "You always talk about how much you miss training horses, I thought that you would prefer to do that, but if you still want to write, I am not going to stop you."

"No. He is. I-"

"Nick! Natalie! Everyone is looking for you!" came a female voice.

"Victoria, not now!" Natalie yelled.

"Victoria, did you find..." Natalie's father started, but stopped. "What's going on?"

"Oh nothing!" Natalie said. "My future husband and father-in-law have decided that I should be subjected to living life as a 1950s housewife!"

"Drama queen much?" said Victoria.

"We need to get out of here," Jesse whispered to her.

Jesse searched Natalie's eyes and worried when she didn't acknowledge him.

"Come on, Natalie," he said as he wiped the tears falling from her eyes. "I've heard enough and so have you. Let's get out of here."

Chapter 22:
Tears, Troubles and Takeovers

For the second time that evening, Jesse landed on a stack of hay. Rubbing his behind, Jesse followed Natalie down to a pond. Before he could speak, he saw a flash of blonde hair running toward the stables.

"Is that you?" Jesse asked as his eyes continued to follow the figure.

"What do you think?"

Jesse could hear a hint of sarcasm in her voice. There was no doubt in his mind that she was frustrated with everything. Both versions of Natalie were clearly agitated by the events of the evening. In addition to her frustrations, he was surprised by her vulnerability. The only other time he saw her like this was when they watched her death repeatedly. Since meeting Natalie, he never once saw her as being weak and it was evident to him that she was the type of person to bottle everything up.

"I know it hurts."

Natalie raised her eyebrow at him. "I mean, I know what it's like to have your family gang up on you." That's when Jesse saw a look of sadness on her face. He recognized the pity right then and there. Whatever the living him had told her had struck a chord. Before he could contemplate things further, Jesse felt a familiar pull.

"Where are we?" Jesse asked.

"My room. I came here after the argument to clean up."

Jesse was about to reply, but Natalie dragged him into the bathroom.

"Well, at least it's not a closet," he said.

Natalie pressed her finger to his lips. Giving him the 'now's not the time look' he waited.

"Nat?"

"Victoria?" Jesse mouthed to Natalie.

Natalie nodded her head as they peeked out the door.

"What is it, Tor?"

"I'm sorry about before."

"Don't worry about it."

Jesse could feel Natalie's fingers dig into his back. Fighting the pain, Jesse focused on the conversation.

"So, where's the dress?" Victoria asked.

"I have told you before, you will see it on my wedding day."

"Fine, but what if it's hideous or something? You need to have a second opinion."

"Why?" asked Natalie. "I have no doubts about the dress!"

Jesse didn't know what disturbed him more-knowing what was about to happen, or that he was about to watch what was about to happen. The fact that Natalie was holding onto him more firmly only made him more uncomfortable as things progressed.

"Natalie, as your maid of honour, don't you think I should see it? I promise not to say anything."

Jesse could see the hesitation on past Natalie's face. A part of him wanted to tell her what was going to happen, but the other part of him knew that he needed to see this play out. He watched as she walked into her closet and pulled out the dress. Victoria was sitting on the bed swirling the glass of wine.

"Here it is," Natalie said to her sister.

Jesse's mouth dropped as he watched the dress appear before him. Closing his eyes, he tried to picture her in it and the very idea of her in that dress captivated him.

"Natalie?" he said as he turned to her.

Shaking her head she pointed out the door indicating that he watch. Obediently, he turned back, watching the scene unfold.

"I take it you approve?" Natalie asked her sister.

"Yes. Sweetheart bodice, a beautiful brocade design! Oh and I love the wine-coloured trim. So Christmassy!"

Jesse could see Natalie smiling at her sister's approval. He just wished he could see Victoria's face right now.

"Oh and there's a shawl!" Natalie said as she walked back into the closet.

Once more Jesse observed, waiting for havoc to break out. He watched Victoria approach the dress with caution. He could see her delicately touching the dress and then watched her pull her hand back as if she were burned. Victoria headed back to the bed and sat down.

"See the shawl goes-

Jesse watched as Victoria turned sharply toward Natalie. The wine jumped out of the glass straight onto the dress.

"No!" Natalie shouted as the wine hit the dress.

"Oh my God!" Victoria yelled as she picked up the glass. "Natalie, you scared me! I was looking at the dress and I-" she said with tears evident in her voice.

"How could you-"

"It was an accident!"

"What? Why the hell are you carrying wine?" she said through the tears that were now forming.

Jesse let the fight play out, when something occurred to him. How convenient this whole situation was.

He may be a guy, but even he knew that a wine glass in the vicinity of a wedding dress was a faux pas. Women like Victoria didn't exactly strike him as the type to be that 'clumsy'.

Screams pierced the room and Jesse flinched from the sound.

"Natalie." At that moment he doubted anyone could hear him.

"What?" she said.

"I need to see it again."

Knowing that it came out wrong, Jesse hoped that Natalie wouldn't start a fight while there was another one going on.

"What?" she asked.

"I need to see something. Just take me back to one minute ago, please."

Without any kind of acknowledgment from her, Natalie just took his hand, rewinding the scene before his eyes.

Shifting to the other side of the closet, Jesse used the mirror as a way to see everything at a better angle.

"See the shawl goes-"

Jesse watched Victoria turn quickly. "Damn," he muttered. Victoria was good. It really did look like an accident. Jesse knew better. If his suspicion was right, Victoria had done it on purpose. She wasn't so much as startled as she was guiding the wine to the dress.

The yelling started once more and Jesse grabbed

Natalie's hand once more. Letting the scene play out this time, he observed the two engage in an intense fight. The door opened to reveal Nick and Natalie and Victoria's parents.

"What's going on?" Nick asked.

Natalie was about to charge at Victoria, but her father managed to hold onto her before she had the chance to get at her.

"She spilled wine on my dress! Red wine!" Natalie said as made another attempt to get to her.

"It was an accident!" Victoria cried.

"Girls!" Mrs. Parker said in an attempt to gain some civility.

"Annie," said Nick. "Why don't you and Tom take Victoria out of here and I will calm her down.".

The couple nodded and obliged Nick's request, who turned his attention to his crying bride-to-be.

"Hey! Hey, look at me."

"She ruined it!" Natalie sobbed. "And now you've seen it!"

Jesse watched Nick pull her into his arms once more and clenched his fists.

"It can be fixed," said Nick. "Look, I'll call my dry cleaner. He is the very best in New York. My sister got grape juice on her cotillion dress and he got it out. It took a couple days, but she looked beautiful and no one knew."

Before he knew what was happening, they were back at the stables, this time landing gracefully on the hay. Jesse brushed himself off and watched as Natalie made her way to the lake once more.

As if on cue, Jesse watched Natalie's figure run down to the stables and he realized right then that they had come full circle.

"I don't know what's worse," his Natalie said. "Having lived through it once or having to go through it all over again,"

Seeing her looking so defeated made him feel helpless.

"It wasn't your fault," Jesse said.

"Yeah? Well I'm in there telling myself otherwise!" she shouted as she pointed to the stables.

"Why don't we go in there and hear what you have to say."

"Jesse, could I just be alone for a while?"

Jesse was about to protest, but thought differently. Being on his own would give him the chance to learn more about Nick and his family. Not to mention his involvement with Victoria.

"Alright. One hour. We'll meet on the balcony. Okay?"

Natalie simply nodded. Jesse wanted to say more, but figured that it would best if he didn't push her.

***

Watching Jesse walk away, Natalie sat on the stack of hay and cried. She was doing that a lot lately and felt weak for doing so. The fact that she was dealing with this for a second time bothered her more than before. The night was supposed to be wonderful and a prequel for her wedding day. Standing up, she walked over to the entrance of the barn and stared at the house. The faint music of another waltz filled her ears and she remembered her dance with Jesse. She sighed at the memory. Not because she didn't like it, but because she liked it too much.

"Nick," she voiced out to the open skies. Why didn't she get goose bumps around him? Why didn't her stomach do flips? Why didn't her heart skip a beat?

"Great! I sound like a sappy romantic."

When she met Nick, she didn't give him a second thought. Sure, he was handsome and intelligent, but their first meeting was under interesting circumstances. Looking up one more time to the night skies, she let the memories of the past infiltrate her mind. Nick was the perfect guy for her and she loved him. Her first meeting with Nick felt like something out of a romance novel. He was with her sister at the time. Although it was not serious, she vividly recalled her sister saying that Nick liked her and since Victoria wasn't one to commit, she tossed Nick out like garbage two weeks later.

The sound of a dog barking, no doubt Oscar, broke Natalie from her memory.

Looking at the watch on her hand, she sighed as the numbers counted down and then cringed. Realizing that she had to meet Jesse soon, she made her way back to the house. Staring up at the heavens once more, she couldn't help but wonder.

"What if?"

***

Jesse hated leaving Natalie alone, but seeing how badly things happened the last time he forced her to do something, he decided that leaving her be was best. Making his second trip up the path to the house, Jesse decided that now was the time for some fun. He approached the door once more, patting Joshua on the shoulder as he walked into the foyer. Grabbing the glass of scotch that he longed for, Jesse carefully made his way around the room.

In the corner, Jesse could see Nick talking to some guys in an animated conversation.

"He has no idea where she is right now," Jesse muttered as he proceeded to take a sip of his drink.

Walking towards the circle of men, Jesse casually leaned against the wall and listened to the conversation.

"Come on, Nick! You excited for the big day?" one guy asked.

"You're a lucky guy," added a shorter man.

"Yup! Can't wait," replied Nick.

Jesse noticed his change in demeanor and wondered what was getting the jerk so flustered.

"That's it?" said another guy. 'Can't wait'?"

"Look fellas," said Nick, "I have a lot on my plate. Business meetings, signing authors, socializing with the people in the book world. My only worry is to show up at the wedding and say 'I do.'" The other guys laughed.

"Sounds about right, Nicky!"

Jesse knew that this was guy talk. He himself would be the first guy to admit that he would rather talk business and stupidity, but not from the guy getting married.

All his guy friends gushed about their brides to be almost to the point where Jesse needed to puke or drink. The fact that Nick was talking shop angered Jesse.

"So lover boy, where are you taking the future Mrs. Manning on your honeymoon?"

"Didn't know you boys worried about stuff like that. My answer. None of your business! Let's talk Knicks. When I get back, who's in for some court side seats?"

The guys all laughed once more.

Jesse took a swig of scotch. Deciding that he had had enough of the way he was talking about Natalie, he wanted to make Nick pay. And making him look like a jackass seemed like the thing to do.

Jesse turned to leave. As he did, he bumped into someone.

"I'm sorry," said a voice.

'That's okay..."

He stopped when he realized who he had bumped into. It was Natalie, not his Natalie, but the Natalie from this time.

"Excuse me," she said and walked toward Nick and his friends. Now, he was intrigued. The only interaction he had seen between them had been on the balcony earlier. Jesse casually shifted closer to see what would happen.

"Hey Nat!"

"Hi guys."

Jesse noted that she seemed uncomfortable with his friends.

"Everything cool with you and Vic?" said Nick as he stroked her arm.

"Yes."

Jesse could feel his body tighten as Nick touched Natalie. Judging by his touch, Nick was placating her and could he tell that Nick didn't really want her there.

"You need something else, sweetheart?"

"No, just wanted to see you," she admitted.

"Aww, she just wants to be around her Nickykins!" said the short guy.

"So, Nat, when's the next book coming out? Steph and Aiden are waiting for it."

"Soon-"

"Natalie's going to take a break for a bit," Nick interrupted.

Natalie looked up at Nick, giving him a smile through gritted teeth.

"That's too bad," said the short guy. "The kids love your

stories."

Seeing Natalie looking so detached broke his heart. If she wasn't going to stand up for herself, he would. Making his way over to the corner of the room, he looked at the time and saw that Natalie wouldn't meet him for another ten minutes.

Pulling out the Protector's guide, he flipped through the chapters.

"Where is it?" he said in an exasperated tone.

Chapter Eleven: Protector's Powers
Jesse thumbed through the options until he spotted the one he wanted.

Taking Over Another Body

Taking over another body requires a simple phrase. Abeo, pronounced A-Bay-Oh, the phrase means change. Look at the person you would like to morph into and say the word three times. Your body will join the other person's and you will have full control.

To return back to yourself, say Reverto, Rev-air-toe once.

WARNING: Use with caution. Use wisely.

Jesse put the book away and walked to Nick.

"Abeo, Abeo, Abeo," he whispered.

Jesse saw his body beginning to fade and glide over to Nick's. In one quick motion, Jesse felt a jolt and could see that he was in fact in Nick's body.

"Time for some fun," he said quietly.

Jesse made Nick walk over to an older gentleman.

"Nick my boy, congrats! Natalie is a fine young lady," said the man who resembled the monopoly man.

"Hey pops, anyone tell you look like Uncle Pennybags?"

"Nick!" Natalie scolded.

"What? Not my fault he's bald and has the weird mustache."

Jesse was having fun. Taking over Nick's body was becoming quite the amusing experience. He proceeded to make Nick make a spectacle of himself.

"Nick, son, why don't you have a drink?" Mr. Manning

said as he handed his son a scotch.

"What the hell's the matter with you?" his father hissed.

"Nothing. Just being me."

Jesse made Nick walk out of the room, making him trip onto the floor splitting his pants in the process. Bursts of laughter exploded in parts of the room. Deciding that he had done his job, Jesse decided to get out of the body. The fact that he was in it for that long disgusted him.

"Reverto," he said.

Jesse walked out of the body and ran onto the balcony, laughing all the way. As he got there, he could see Natalie, his Natalie, standing there looking anything but amused.

"How could you?" she said, and stormed off.

Jesse looked up at the heavens and sighed. He took off after her and was surprised at how well she could run in those heels.

"Damn it!" He caught up to her just in time to see her swipe keys from the valet parking attendant and get into a Range Rover. She was definitely a woman on a mission.

He swiped keys from the valet and clicked the horn to see where the car was. When he found it, he hopped into the car and revved the engine. When he felt the car come to life he slammed on the gas and followed her.

"Damn it!" he shouted. How was he going to explain this to Redmond? He'd already messed up once. He couldn't afford this right now. Neither of them could afford it.

Chapter 23:
A Fight to Remember

"You're a jerk!" Natalie yelled as she stormed through the doors of the Sanctuary.

Jesse had finally caught up to Natalie. The drive was nerve wracking—to the point where he thought he was going crash a few times. He had to give her credit. She knew how to drive. He was sure that he broke more than one law on the way back to the city. They had ditched their cars on a side street and he tracked her all the way back to St. Patrick's.

"I know!" he said and ducked at the pillow coming at him.

"You made my fiancé look like a fool," she cried. "You ruined the night!"

Jesse smiled as he thought about making Mr. Perfect look like an idiot. Natalie may not have been impressed with what he had done, but the guests certainly got a laugh.

"I did not ruin the night," he told her. "The night was already ruined."

She rolled her eyes and Jesse knew he wasn't making things better.

"Come on. I was just joking."

"Why is everything a joke to you?" she said. "I thought things were going to be different since…"

Jesse's grin immediately left his face. He looked away from her.

"Jesse-" Natalie began.

"No, I deserved that," Jesse said and undid his tie. He was beginning to feel a severe case of déjà vu. He counted to ten in his head and then turned to look at her.

"It's not a joke," he said while nervously running his fingers through his hair. "I thought it would be funny. Clearly, I was wrong. But you want to know something? I'm not sorry." He watched as Natalie's eyes crossed in confusion. "How can you want to be with a guy who treats you like that?"

"What?" she answered. "Nick?"

"No," Jesse said. "The Easter Bunny. Of course, Nick. Do you realize that he treated you like a client rather than a fiancée? He would rather talk about bestselling books and which authors he was looking to sign rather than talk about you becoming his wife. Everyone was asking him about the wedding, which by the way is in two days, and the only thing on his mind was what he was going to do when he got back from his honeymoon with you."

"You don't know him like I do," she said. "There is a lot of pressure on him. He has a lot to think about."

Jesse walked up to her slowly. She stepped back and he stopped advancing. Scaring her was not his intent. Making her see what he saw these past few hours was. He held his hands up and looked at her. He needed her to see that he wasn't going touch her.

"If it were me marrying you," he said and placed his hands on his chest, "I don't think I would be able to tear myself away from you. I don't think I would be able to talk about anything but you and how lucky I am. Nick Manning sees you as his meal ticket-"

"Stop it!" she yelled, wiping the tears that were suddenly streaming down her face. "You don't know what you're talking about!" He's perfect for me. He's kind. He's handsome. He's polite. He makes me laugh."

"He's boring and what you really mean to say is that he's nothing like me."

"You're, well, I mean you're..."

Jesse took another step closer to her and stared intently at her lips.

"I'm what, Natalie?" he whispered.

Jesse could feel Natalie shaking and she was doing everything in her power to look anywhere else but at him.

"You want to know the difference?" she hissed. "With Nick, I wouldn't be another notch on your belt."

Jesse pulled back from her. So, that's what she really thought of him. That he was a womanizer who looked for one night stands. He could feel his fists clench tightly and his windpipes collapsing. He slowly approached her again and he could see fear in her eyes. He wasn't sure who he was more scared of that moment. Her or him.

"Let's get one thing straight," he spoke with a hint of pain and anger in his voice. "Once the time runs out and we watch you die again. I want you to think of this moment. Because when you die - not if you die, but when - there will be no more second chances and you'll be back in Purgatory or someplace much worse."

Before he turned to walk away, Jesse turned to look at her one more time.

"I think Eddie was right, you do belong there."

Jesse regretted the words the second he said them and found her charging at him. He didn't have the chance to duck when he saw her fist coming at him. The sound of her knuckles making contact with his face was like fireworks going off. He compared the punch to the moment his car collided with the dump truck. Fast, painful, and unforgiving.

"You are exactly who I thought you were!" she spat and rubbed her fist. "I guess the Jesse I spent the day with was nothing but an illusion. Now get out!"

He stumbled out the door and heard it slam shut behind him. He heard her sobbing behind the closed door and fell to the floor. He didn't know what hurt more, his eye, his pride, or his heart. Jesse was right about one thing. The woman could throw a punch.

Chapter 24:
Figuring It Out

Natalie heard Jesse's footsteps fade away. In that moment, she had never felt so alone in her life. The venom in his words had hurt her deeply.

"Where's the Jesse I met in Central Park?" she sobbed. "Where is he?"

Walking over to the bed, Natalie wrapped the covers around her, curling herself into the fetal position, and sighed. Her hand and her head were throbbing. The moment her head hit the pillow, she could smell Jesse's cologne suffocate her.

"Why is this so hard?" she groaned.

The effects of the day were finally catching up to her. Closing her eyes, Natalie let the warmth of the bed and the scent of Jesse take over all of her senses.

Within seconds, she was asleep and let the dream world consume her.

***

"I've been waiting for you."

Natalie opened her eyes and whirled around, trying to find the owner of the voice to no avail. She wasn't in the Sanctuary anymore. Instead, she found herself standing all alone on one side of Gapstow Bridge wearing nothing but a simple white sundress. She was confused by her surroundings. The current weather definitely threw her. It felt more like summer rather than the dead of winter.

"You're just dreaming," the voice came again. She turned toward the direction of it and standing on the other side other bridge was a black haired, blue-eyed, unscarred, Jesse.

"I'm grateful that you made this a summer setting," he said. "I'm not opposed to winter," he added and she saw him slowly advance to the middle of the bridge. "It's just colder."

Natalie fought the urge to smile at him and could feel

herself losing the battle. She walked toward him and took in the ambiance of their location.

"It's okay, you know," he said.

"What's okay?" she asked.

"This. You. Me. Here."

Even in her dreams, he confused her. Natalie pulled herself up on the ledge of the bridge and sat down. She carefully surveyed the surroundings and was secretly happy that she had picked this place and that it was a warm summer night rather than a freezing cold one. Darkness was starting to claim the day and in the distance, she could see the glow of the silver moon rising. The pond was oddly still and she couldn't see another human being anywhere near them.

"It's beautiful here," she admitted.

"It's your dream, Princess," Jesse replied as he sat down beside her.

Natalie could smell his cologne and groaned. She couldn't escape him. He was everywhere. He was in her life, her world, her head, her dreams, and pulling on her heart. Shaking her head in defeat, she faced Jesse.

"Then why are you ruining it? Why can't you just be the you I spent the day with?"

She watched him as he grinned at her.

"Who says I'm not?" He responded and smiled wider at her. "Natalie, this is how you see me," he told her and pointed to himself. "Look around you," he paused and she humoured him. "Look at where you are. Out of all the people you could be talking to right now, why me?"

Why him indeed? For so long, she dreamt of Nick. Her parents and family. The stables and her books. Why was she here? With him? Now? Here of all places? Because they fought? Because they were both hurting? Because he was the only one who could make things right again?

"I don't know!" she exclaimed. "I want to hate you. I really want to hate you. Yet for some reason, I just can't." She stared at the pond, hoping for clarity.

"How can you be a selfish jerk and then a sweet and caring guy? I don't get it. I don't understand and for the life of me, figuratively speaking of course, don't know why I care."

"Natalie, it's your dream. Just ask."

"It's not that simple and you and I both know it."

Natalie heard him scoff at that. He jumped down and pulled her gently down.

"You want to know why you care?" he asked. "I'll tell you. It's because you're scared."

Natalie lifted her eyes to meet his and stared at him.

"I am not scared of you!"

"I didn't say you were scared of me," he told her.

"What?" she asked.

"I didn't say you were scared of me," he repeated.

"Pray tell, oh wise one. What am I scared of?"

Natalie wasn't sure if she wanted to hear his answer. Because while she knew this whole thing wasn't real, a part of her was curious to know what it would mean to her and for them in the end.

***

Jesse had been walking aimlessly on the cold streets for a few hours thinking about his recent fight with Natalie. There was no doubt that a nice bruise was forming on his face and he was somewhat grateful to be out in the freezing cold.

As he continued to walk, he found himself back on the steps of St. Patrick's. He turned and stared at the Christmas tree at Rockefeller Center, wishing that his life could be as it was before.

"God, I am an idiot!" he yelled out loud.

Before he knew it, he was teleporting back to the Gate of Purgatory. He ran through the corridors he went through the first time. Jesse was frantically looking around for the man that brought him here in the first place. The only thing he wanted to do was confront Redmond and hurt him the way he was hurting now

"Come on out Redmond!" Jesse yelled as he banged on Redmond's door.

"Don't hide from me! Show yourself!"

Jesse continued to pound on the door and slowly fell to his knees crying out.

"I don't want this! Do you hear me?" he bellowed. "I don't want to help her. Answer me, damn it. Someone just answer me."

"Redmond's not here," replied a soft voice.

Jesse looked up and through his tears saw Sofia staring down at him.

"Come with me."

Jesse slowly stood and followed her to her chambers. As they walked into the room Jesse remained silent and watched as Sofia poured a glass of water. She handed him the glass and motioned for him to sit down on the brown leather chair by the fireplace. The room reminded him of Redmond's office, but with a subtle feminine touch.

"Did you want some ice for that black eye?"

Jesse gently brought his hand to his bruising face and winced. Shaking his head no, he took a sip from his water and stared at the burning embers.

"I've been trying to help Natalie as best as I can and I'm failing!" he said. "My problem is that I have no idea what I'm doing here or why I was chosen to do this. You must have some idea as to the kind of person I am. What could possibly have made you think that I was the one for the job? This whole thing has been one giant mistake. What made me worth saving?"

"I don't make mistakes," she answered.

"You don't make mistakes?" Jesse shook his head. She was entitled to believe what she wanted. Then again, so was he.

"That's funny because before I died, my father pretty much said I was one."

There was an edge in his voice and he wanted to see how she would respond to it.

"Your father was wrong and we both know it," she said. "You're right for this job and I believe you will succeed in helping Natalie and the reason I believe that is because I believe in you."

Jesse stared hard at her. She believed in him? She believed that he would succeed? Had she not been kept apprised of what exactly had been going on?

"Stroking my ego isn't helping."

"That's not what I am doing," she answered.

"Have you paid any attention to what has been happening down there? We have a love/hate relationship. Mainly hate. I mean, between the two of us, there's some serious mood whiplash going on. We are not getting anywhere."

"That's interesting to hear considering the words you said to her before you left. It seemed as though you were anticipating her death."

Jesse froze.

"You heard that, huh," he said and scratched the back of his neck.

"Well, I have been kept apprised of what has been going on between you two."

"I regretted saying that the moment I said it," he told her. He massaged his temples and sighed.

"I know."

"I just keep playing her death in my head over and over and it can't be an accident. I mean that's just easy...isn't it?"

Jesse stopped and realized what he just said.

"Son of a bitch," he said and stared hard at Sofia. "Please tell me it's not that easy! It can't be."

***

Natalie stared at dream Jesse waiting for him to explain himself. The grin he sported annoyed her and she wished she could wipe the look off his face.

"You're scared that I'm right. That there may in fact be some merit to what I said regarding Nick."

"That's ridiculous," she said and turned away from him. "I think that you're jealous."

"What if I am?"

Natalie turned back to face him and was surprised by the sincerity in his blue eyes.

"Don't joke," she exclaimed. "Not about this."

"Okay," he paused. "When you first saw me, what did you think? Before you thought I was an arrogant jackass."

Natalie looked up at the moon and brought herself back to the moment she first laid eyes on Jesse Knight.

"I thought you were annoying," she muttered.

"That's stating the obvious. What did you really think? The first thing that came to your mind."

Natalie looked away from him. Shaking her head, she took a deep breath.

"I thought you were handsome," she mumbled.

"I'm sorry, I didn't quite catch that."

Natalie's fists clenched. He heard her and they both knew it.

"I thought you were handsome," she repeated.

His smirk irritated her and all she wanted to do was wipe it off his face. She was beginning to feel the urge to punch him again and would be justified in doing so. She did it once, she could definitely do it again.

"Good," he said. "Because when I first saw you, I thought you were beautiful."

Natalie shook her head at him and crossed her arms.

"I know you said that you don't lie, but dream you really sucks at it."

Natalie started to walk away from him, but Jesse ran in front to stop her.

"Natalie," he said and gently placed his hands on her shoulders. "I don't lie and I know you know that." Jesse led her to the ledge of the bridge. "Look at your reflection in the water and tell me what you see."

Natalie rolled her eyes and complied. She peered into the murky water and could see that her hair was blonde again. Her wide brown eyes stared back at her. She looked like her and yet, she didn't feel like herself. Looking further into the water, she started to feel her feet lift off the ground. Before she could fall in, she felt a pair of strong arms grab her.

"Gotcha," Jesse whispered against her ear. He held onto her tightly, and she focused her attention back on the water.

"What do you see now?"

Natalie saw Jesse with brown hair and hazel eyes. She saw his scar and a smile on his face. Then she looked at herself. Auburn hair once more. Freckles on her face. One blue eye and one green eye. In her entire life, she had never seen herself as anything other than a plain, blond haired, brown eyed girl who no one ever noticed.

"I've been hiding."

"Hiding what?" Jesse asked as he turned Natalie to him.

"The real me."

For the life of her, Natalie couldn't believe she admitted to not being her true self. She looked at her reflection in the water once more. For the first time, she saw herself and liked what she saw. She saw a strong woman and not a mousy one. Provocative and not plain.

"I was Betty and my sister was Veronica. Nick somehow ended up being Archie."

Natalie heard Jesse give a low chuckle and smiled. Then she remembered how he could also make her feel angry and sad. It was then that she remembered what Jesse had told her about belonging in Purgatory.

"You still push my buttons!" she said as she dug her fingers into his chest. "You still say things and hurt me. This wouldn't be happening right now except because of that stunt you pulled. You know what that makes you? "

"Jughead?" he replied.

Natalie groaned.

"Why can't-"

"Why can't I be serious? Okay, I will tell you. It's simple. You don't want me to be. In reality, you are you and I, for one, like you. I bet you never went around New York by yourself and actually saw the city. You only saw what you needed to and you, Natalie, are a lot like this city. You have beauty, you have character, you are a powerhouse waiting to be seen and heard."

Natalie stared at Jesse and carefully took in everything he was saying. Part of her wanted to believe him, yet the other part of her doubted the honesty in his speech. Before Natalie realized what was happening, Jesse was at her side once more.

"For some reason, Natalie, I can only be the real me when I'm with you."

"But-"

"Shh," he said as he placed his fingers on her lips.

Natalie stared into his eyes. She could see them changing from pools of blue to hazel intermittently. His hair was also changing back and forth from black to brown. The two Jesses were one in the same and she knew it.

"Sometimes our truest reflection is the one we keep hidden because we're waiting for the right person to find us."

With that Jesse placed a kiss on her lips and everything felt right. Any anger and pain she was feeling was gone. In that moment, it felt so right and natural for her to kiss him like this. She had shared kisses with several men over the course of her life, but something about this kiss was different than any other kiss she had ever experienced. Because this kiss was one she never wanted to end. Before she could further process what was happening, his lips left hers and he walked away without saying a word.

***

"She won't believe me," he said as his voice cracked. "She just won't."

He heard Sofia's footsteps approach him and saw her sit down in the other chair again.

"Then show her. You still have time to prove to her and prove to me that we were right about you," she paused. "That I was right about you."

Jesse saw sincerity in Sofia's eyes.

"Your Honour-"

"Please, call me Sofia."

"Okay, Sofia. It took me roughly 106 hours to figure this out. You want me to help her realize what went wrong in the remaining 62 hours? Half of our time is gone and the way things are happening between us now, that's impossible."

"Only if you believe it is."

Jesse shrugged his shoulders and shook his head. The complex nature of his relationship with Natalie just became even more complex within a matter of hours.

"You're in love with her aren't you?"

"What?" Jesse asked bewildered.

"Are you in love with her?" she asked.

Jesse stood up abruptly and paced. He could feel his heart rate elevating and panic set in. His breathing became labored and he felt like he was about to pass out. He closed his eyes and stopped his pacing. He couldn't lie because they both already knew the answer to that question.

"Yes," he said barely above a whisper. He felt a hand on his shoulder.

"Then help her. You don't need any more motivation then that."

Jesse nodded and let Sofia guide him out of the office. She led him all the way back to the Gate. He was surprised to find Redmond standing there.

"I'll let Redmond take it from here," Sofia said and gently touched his cheek. "I believe you two need to talk. Good luck Jesse."

Jesse looked on as she proceeded to leave him with Redmond "Jesse," she said as she turned back toward him. "Try going back to the beginning. You might just find what you're looking for there and I meant what I said. I don't make mistakes."

Jesse looked thoughtfully at her and wondered what she meant by that. Back to the beginning? Why did she have to speak in riddles?

"I do hope you don't plan on attacking me." Redmond stated and broke Jesse's gaze from Sofia's retreating form. "I would hate to have to hurt you."

"What?"

Jesse had no idea what Redmond was talking about.

"Yes, I believe you were calling me out."

Jesse realized what Redmond was referring to and looked at him sheepishly.

"It's fine. Surprisingly, you are not the first in this category. Now, you better get back to Natalie."

"Are you insane?" he said. "Given everything I have just learned, I can't face her. Not yet."

"Jesse-"

"Furthermore, how could you not tell Natalie this? How do you do that? Have casual conversations with her when you know how she died?"

"I know you are upset with me and I don't blame you," Redmond admitted. "But that's why I have Protectors. It's their job to figure out the truth. The truth about what really happened to Natalie hurt me too and I hate that I wasn't allowed to tell her."

"And when she learns it, then what?"

"Then she gets her life back," Redmond said. "We made a deal and I will honour that because I am a man of my word. Only you can help her."

"While I appreciate the vote of confidence, you will have to forgive me, but things just got a little more complicated."

The portal suddenly opened before him and he looked through the vortex and watched as images of Natalie's life swirled below. How the hell was he going to prove it to her?

"It's time to go, Jesse."

Jesse nodded at him. A feeling of dread overwhelmed him because he knew that the next few hours were going to take a toll on both he and Natalie. Before he could jump, there was one thing he needed to know.

"Redmond? Will you promise me something?"

"Depends on what the promise is," he said.

"Just promise that no matter what happens, she will be okay."

"Jesse, I made that promise to her and to myself a long time ago and now I am going to make that promise to you. Now jump!"

He shook his head at Redmond and jumped over the edge back to reality.

Flashes of Natalie's life appeared before him. He knew what he had to do make everything right for her. Before he knew it he was back at the Sanctuary and saw Natalie asleep on the bed with tear stains on her face. He slowly made his way to her and hated the idea of waking her up, but he knew he had to.

***

Natalie felt herself being pulled from the dream. She found herself leaving with some answers, but definitely had more questions.

She opened her eyes and was greeted to Jesse's hazel ones. Wiping her eyes, she looked up at him and smiled. It was then she realized that she was no longer dreaming and remembered their fight. She uncovered herself and stood up from the bed.

"I thought I told you to get out?" she said with pain and anger in her voice.

"You did, but I came back and I deserved that."

"You deserve a lot more than that," she said and headed to the bathroom. She shut the door and sat down on the toilet.

"My eye still hurts if that makes you feel better."

Natalie covered her face with her hands. It didn't make

her feel better. Not in the least.

"Look, I went up to see Redmond and saw Sofia instead and then Redmond came and well, let's just say I figured a few things out," he said.

"What things?" she questioned and pulled her hands from her face.

"I think…no, I know what happened to you. I just have to prove it to you."

Natalie got up and opened the bathroom door. She took in his haggard appearance and could see that he looked tired and that he was in a lot of pain.

"Go on."

"I need you to trust me," he said and she watched as he rubbed his neck. "I know that's asking a lot, but you told me that I am the only person who can help you get your life back. You told me so in this very room. I need you to believe in me, so that I can show you the truth."

Natalie listened intently as he spoke. There was something in his speech and demeanor that sent chills down her spine. Why did he need to prove it? Why couldn't he just tell her? He was asking her to trust him because he knew what transpired on the day she died.

"Fine," she said and stepped closer to him. "Show me."

Chapter 25:
Time Waits For No One

"Okay. Sofia suggested that we go back to the beginning."
"And?"
"Well, that would be where?" asked Jesse.
Natalie thought back to where they first began. Nothing had really happened their first day together.
"21 Club. That's where we started. Jesse, we didn't exactly go to a lot of places. I mean, between traveling back and forth through various places and watching my death repeatedly for a long time, we didn't do much."
Silence echoed in the room. She knew they both messed up and now they had to play detective and figure out exactly what happened that December morning.
"Not us Natalie. Just you. The living you. We have to go to places that we haven't gone to. We have to go to the places where you had been. I think we can do this. I even think that we could have some time to spare, but you need to work with me."
"Okay, I'll go change."
"I have a better idea."
Natalie looked at Jesse expectantly and waited.
"I can make it so that we can be in a room without being seen. So, in other words-"
"You can make us invisible," Natalie finished.
"Pretty much."
Jesse pulled out the book from his pocket and turned to the chapter.

"To see beyond what you already know is to take the chance and reap what you sow. Invisible, Invincible, Untouchable is what you seek. Take the Shield and the Locket and link them as one. Together say Veritatem dies aperit. ("Time discloses the truth.") Your journey to enlightenment will begin anew. Great power comes at a great price. With this ability, time will run faster. So keep an eye on the clock and good luck.

"Time runs faster?" Jesse said and met Natalie's eyes. He saw worry there and he felt the exact same way. A price would have to be paid and in this case, time wasn't going to be on their side. "How much is left?" he asked. "We need to establish that before we even think about doing this."

"Because if it's not much, then we're not going to do it?"

"No," he said. "We're going to do it. It's the only to prove what happened to you, but we are going to be smart about this. I'm not going to make any mistakes and we can't afford to screw anything up."

He paused and looked at her. She needed reassurance and they both needed to be certain about this. "I just want us to be careful," he told her. "I don't want to risk wasting time with this." He paused and put the book in the breast pocket of his jacket. "We won't have control over it. So let's do this."

"Wait," Natalie said and touched his arm. He tried his best to not flinch, but given how this invisibility was going to work, they would have to be touching.

"As much as I have enjoyed wearing this dress, can we change?"

Jesse nodded and let out the breath he'd been holding when she let go of his arm. While she pulled off wearing the dress, he could tell the running around town in it would be awkward. He wasn't a fan of his suit either and wearing jeans and a shirt seemed like a better alternative.

"Okay. You take the bathroom and I'll change here."

They headed to the closet and picked out appropriate attire for their next mission. When he heard the click of the bathroom door shut, he stripped and pulled on a pair of blue jeans, a white t-shirt and added a black V-neck sweater. When the door opened, Natalie walked out wearing a pair of skinny jeans and a red, cashmere turtle neck sweater. She was pulling her hair up into a loose bun while perusing the closet for footwear. He too walked back to the closet and put on a pair of boots. He didn't know where they would end up going this time. The only thing he knew was that he had no intention of freezing. As he tied his boots up, he felt a tap on his shoulder. Natalie was holding a black pea coat out for him. He noticed that she was wearing a matching one and he looked at her, confused.

"We're matching?" he asked and took the coat from her.

"Well, I figure we'd look less conspicuous in black."

"Natalie," he said and pulled the coat on. "We're going to be invisible."

Natalie turned a shade of crimson and smiled. He pulled off the Shield from around his neck. Natalie unclipped the necklace around hers. They looked at each other and brought them together.

"They look like they have to connect," Jesse said as he examined both pieces. He looked up and saw that Natalie agreed. They raised the shield and the locket together. When he heard a click, a yellow glow appeared around them.

"Why do I feel like I am in 'Ghost'?" Jesse asked.

"Jesse, not now. Just say the words."

"Right. Are you ready?"

"Jesse!"

"Okay on three. One. Two. Three."

"*Veritatem dies aperit*," they said simultaneously.

The yellow glow around them faded and turned silver.

The necklaces separated. Jesse's medallion folded around Natalie's wrist and Natalie's locket wrapped around Jesse's. The silver light disappeared and the necklaces turned into silver bracelets. Inspecting the bracelet, Jesse saw the heart inside the shield where the swords once were.

"That's amazing," she uttered in disbelief.

"That's weird. There's only one sword."

"I think I have the other one."

Jesse and Natalie raised their bracelets, taking a closer look at their own and their matching one. Each sword rested behind the shield.

"I can still see you," Natalie told him.

"I think the point is for no one else to see us," he answered as he stared at his bracelet.

"Now, give me your hand."

Natalie placed her hand in his and closed her eyes.

"21 Club," she whispered.

Jesse felt the familiar pull and held onto Natalie. Memories flooded them again and they landed at the entrance of the restaurant.

"Let's see if this works."

Jesse walked over to a man and stood right in front of him. Waving his hand in front of his face, Jesse waited for a response. When he got none, he walked back to Natalie.

"They work. Now come with me."

Natalie obliged and followed. They sat down at the table and watched.

"What are we looking for? What does being here have to do with my death?"

"Everything you did that week ties into your death. I know it. It has to."

Just then, Natalie's family walked in. Jesse did his best to ignore the current conversation between Natalie's father and his own. They entered the dining area, heading toward the table, passing by the two without as much as a glance.

"So, what conspiracy is going on here?" Natalie asked.

"Fast forward a bit." Jess replied.

"How far?"

"Half-hour."

The room moved about them at a fast pace. Jesse waited for the moment he wanted Natalie to stop at. When Jesse saw Nick reach for Victoria's leg he told Natalie stop.

"Right there! Now rewind a few frames."

Shaking her head, she did.

"So," Jesse said. "How close were your sister and fiancé?"

"What?"

"The way he's looking at her. I've never seen him look that way at you."

For a moment, he could have sworn she was going to give him a matching black eye.

"I told you. They dated briefly."

Jesse looked back at the table and watched Nick and Victoria closely. Natalie, too, was staring at them.

"You knew something was going on between them," he said. "Didn't you?"

Natalie stared hard at him and stormed out of the restaurant. Jesse stood there dumbly as he watched her leave the restaurant.

"You better go after her," came a voice.

Jesse turned around and saw Joshua standing there.

"You can see me?"

"Of course I can see you," he added. "Now's not the time. Go after her."

He nodded at the Missionary and bolted out the doors.

West 52nd Street was littered with people, but once he saw Natalie, he ran to her.

"Natalie," he said as he ran in front of her. He could see tears pooling in her mismatched eyes.

"I'm-"

"Yes, I knew," she said.

Before he could say anything else, she raised her finger to his lips.

"I knew and I didn't do anything because I would have ended up losing everything," she admitted. "My job. My family. From the looks of it, I was destined to anyway."

"So, you would have been okay with your sister having an affair with your husband," he said. "Right in front of you?"

"Of course not, but I was in deep and I did…do love him."

Jesse sighed. He knew there was no point in prolonging this. She had her reasons and arguing over it would waste time. Which, in fact, was going faster.

"Ok," he said. "You win. So, this was Sunday. What were you doing Monday?"

He winced at the inconsideration of his own question.

"Lunch with Victoria," she said. "I needed to go over a few things with her for the wedding."

"Natalie-"

"Let's go."

Her cold hands reached for his. When his hazel eyes locked onto her mismatched ones, he saw her tears ready to fall.

Moments later, Jesse could feel his feet land soundly on the floor, clutching Natalie's hand. Instinct told him to open his eyes, fear told him to wait. He was feeling uneasy and unsure and he hated it. For the first time, he felt like he had a disadvantage. He was certain that Natalie would believe that Nick and Victoria had something going on and that the answer would be right there. Now, he wasn't so convinced.

"Jesse," Natalie spoke. "We're here. Open your eyes."

"Where exactly is here?"

"The Plaza."

Jesse followed Natalie to a room and instantly knew where he was.

"You had lunch at The Palm Court?"

"Have you met my sister? Nothing but the best for the

best."

"Speaking of your sister. There she is now. Where are you?"

Jesse made his way over to the brunette. She was on the phone and seemed nervous.

"I'll call you back. She's here."

Jesse whirled around and found Natalie making her way over. He watched as the living Natalie passed by him looking anything but happy.

"Really Tor? The Palm Court? Why couldn't we have gone some place closer to the publishing house?"

Jesse sat down at a nearby table.

"Nat, lunch is on me," she said.

"Don't you mean lunch is on Mom and Dad?"

Jesse grinned, while his Natalie, who had joined him at the table, seethed.

"Fine. Okay, enough is enough, I want to see the wedding dress. What kind of person, namely you, goes and buys a gown without anyone? Especially your maid of honour."

"I already told you-" Natalie started.

"No, Natalie. You said nothing. Nick is expecting you to walk down the aisle in a vision of white. Knowing you and your style, you will probably look like a zombie."

Jesse snapped up as he heard that. It irked him because the irony of the statement was true. He looked at Natalie, both Natalies, and watched their reactions. Natalie one, who was sitting with Victoria, brushed off the comment like water on a duck's back. Natalie two, who was sitting next to him, became restless. It was clear to him that she was growing agitated by this, but for him, something about this interaction didn't sit well with him.

"Alright, Sunday, Monday equal big busts. But I know that somehow, they are all connected. Let's see Tuesday."

Natalie shook her head and sighed. "You don't want to see the rest of the day? I mean you never know what you might find. Perhaps the second gunman on the grassy knoll?"

"Not funny. Just take us to Tuesday. What did you do that day?"

"I was writing my book."

"And?"

Jesse patiently waited as Natalie closed her eyes. When

she opened them, he could see her shaking her head in frustration. She couldn't remember and he was starting to worry.

"Mom wants to know if you are meeting us for lunch tomorrow?" she heard Victoria ask.

"Can't. Finishing my draft for my latest book and then I have meeting with Mr. Manning at three."

Jesse and Natalie looked at each other and smiled.

"Ding, ding, ding! We have a winner!"

"Guess she's not as useless as I thought," said Natalie. She reached for Jesse's hand and together they traveled to their next destination.

***

The smell of old books and ink consumed Jesse as they arrived.

"Where, pray tell, are we? Because my nostrils are protesting greatly."

When he didn't get a response, he turned to Natalie. There were tears there. He was hoping that the smell was the reason for her crying.

"You okay?"

"Fine," she said as she wiped her eyes.

"Why of all places would your meeting be here?" Jesse asked.

Jesse watched as nostalgia emerged from Natalie and he couldn't explain why he was so drawn to her that moment. He was admiring her as she walked around the stacks of books that filled the room. Her body language spoke volumes. Here was her home and it was where her books came to life. Where her stories were no longer just in her head and in her heart, but on paper, in a book, to be read.

"Guess I missed it," she admitted. "The meeting is upstairs."

"You know, if we're late-"

"Instant replay will be provided."

Natalie led the way out of the room and Jesse followed her.

They arrived at the entrance to the office and groaned when they saw that the door was closed.

"3:03," Jesse said in a scolding tone. "Reminiscing took too long."

"Jesse!" she yelled and grabbed his hand.

Rewinding backwards, Jesse looked at the clock on the wall and waited for the time to read 2:59pm. Jesse began to protest as it passed by, but Natalie appeared to know what she was doing. The clock turned to 2:55pm, and that's when Natalie stopped.

"If you're not five minutes early before a meeting, you are late."

Natalie made her way into the room quickly and Jesse ran after her. Seconds later, Natalie and Charles walked in.

"Drink?" Charles asked.

"No, thank you." Natalie replied.

Jesse walked over to the desk and sat on it. There was something about Charles Manning that he did not particularly like. The fact that he disliked his son only amplified his hatred more. He observed Charles carefully. Something about his demeanor toward Natalie bothered him. Even now, he could see that he was the authority figure and that he did not like successful women.

"Natalie, I know that after today that you are taking the rest of the week off. I want to know what your plans are after the wedding."

Jesse stood up and walked to Natalie.

"Guess this was his way telling you he was getting rid of the section," he said.

"I don't know why I didn't see it coming," she answered.

Jesse nodded in agreement and focused his attention back to the conversation.

"Well, I have completed the final draft for the book. So, I was thinking that a book tour would-"

"No, I mean, what are your plans writing wise? Do you plan to continue after you marry my son?"

Jesse was on the edge waiting for the answer.

"Well, I..."

He waited for the words, but a hand on his shoulder and spinning room told him that Natalie had had enough.

"Natalie, what the hell?" he said and looked at her.

"This is a waste," she replied with her hands on her hips. "Besides, he took a phone call and we know what happened.

He broke the news to me on Thursday. So let's go!"

"Natalie-" Jesse started.

"Jesse don't!"

"Okay. Fine. You win. Let's go to Wednesday."

"Jesse, we could be doing something different," she said.

"You said that you wanted me to show you what happened to you and I am still working on proving it. If I am wrong you won't have to see me again, ever. So, could you indulge me for a little while longer?"

Natalie hesitated and he watched as she looked at her watch and saw that they were down to 18 hours. 'Crap' he thought. When they started this they had 60 hours. 42 hours had just ticked off. Time was speeding up and he was no closer in proving to her, and to himself, what had happened to her.

"Wednesday it is," she said.

Jesse started to panic. He knew that she saw the time ticking down too. She seemed depressed and he couldn't explain it. Then he remembered reading one of the last chapters in the book regarding the Ward's soul. Within the last 24 hours of the person's time, they begin to lose faith and begin slipping toward Purgatory. He grabbed her hand gently. Her eyes haunted him and so did the last words of the chapter.

Tempus neminem manet. Time waits for no one.

Chapter 26:

Beyond What You've Seen

The cold ocean air filled Jesse's lungs. He listened to the sounds of the Atlantic's choppy waters. While Natalie seemed to relish their new setting, Jesse was freezing his butt off. Before he could protest, Natalie looked at him and smiled.

"Cold?"

Jesse gave her his patented 'are you kidding me look', but she disregarded him completely.

"Winter in the Hamptons isn't exactly my idea of fun. So, why are we here? Other than the fact that tomorrow is your rehearsal dinner."

Natalie sighed.

"Look over there," she said.

Jesse followed her eyes and saw that the living Natalie was there.

"When did she get here?" asked Jesse as he rubbed his hands together for warmth. "Well, I mean you? When did you get here?"

"I came here to contemplate a few things. One of those things was whether or not I wanted to get married."

Out of all things he expected Natalie to say, that wasn't one of them.

"Yes, Jesse, I had cold feet and no, I don't care if yours are freezing right now."

Jesse smiled at her response.

"You were right," she continued, "I had a feeling something was going on and chose to ignore it because losing everything wasn't an option."

"My pending marriage was turning into a business merger. That rehearsal dinner put so many things into perspective."

Natalie reached for his hand and Jesse obliged in giving his to her.

"Follow me."

After fifteen minutes of walking in the cold, Jesse could see the stables. They were back at Natalie's house. Following her, Jesse was drawn to her vulnerability. She was letting him in. She was now showing him a side that she hadn't before. That meant a great deal to him.

As she led him further into the stables, he saw the living her sitting on a stack of hay stroking what looked like a future thoroughbred.

"Hey Bullet. I miss you so much, but I'm always thinking of you and lots of children love reading about you."

Jesse turned and found Natalie staring and listening to her living form. Intrigued, he listened further.

"I don't know what to do," she sobbed. "I love him, but I don't know if I can marry him."

Jesse had a strong urge to comfort her. Instead, he forced himself to sit down. When he turned to look at his Natalie, he saw that she wasn't beside him any longer. He started to panic but thought better of it. He knew she couldn't have gotten far and continued to listen to past Natalie's conversation with her horse.

"Look at me," he heard her giggle as she wiped away her tears. "I am talking to a horse. I must be insane. The only thing that would freak me out more would be if you responded."

Jesse then watched as she fed the horse a carrot and left. He then took off to find his Natalie.

"It's amazing isn't it?" he said as he observed the twinkling stars above and then at her.

"What?"

"That one defining moment can change your life and make you gain perspective."

Jesse's eyes stared into Natalie's. He leaned towards her and was surprised to find her leaning towards him too. He could smell the vanilla shampoo from her hair and feel her cool, minty breath on his skin. She was so close and practically his. He could feel his eyelids closing shut on their own.

"Oscar!" came a voice.

The sound of the dog barking pulled them apart and Jesse found himself staring at a wide eyed Natalie.

"We have to hide," she whispered in panic.

Jesse grinned.

"We're invisible. Remember? No one can see us or hear us."

"Okay, so now what?" she asked. "Because in all honesty, we haven't found a thing."

Jesse sighed as Natalie turned her back to him. He was grasping at straws. Determined to prove his point more than ever, Jesse decided to use their lack of time to his advantage.

"Take us to the party. We still have time and I have no intention of wasting it. So, you can either pick another fight with me or-"

Before he knew it, he felt the familiar tug whisk them away. His arms were wrapped securely around her as she wrapped hers around him. With a soft thud, Jesse regretfully pulled away from Natalie.

"Looks like we're in the library," Jesse concluded.

"Thank you for the observation, Sherlock."

Before she could say anything else, the sound of footsteps approaching outside worried them.

"Closet," Natalie whispered as she dragged him in.

"Is this about the new book?" the other Natalie asked.

"Actually, it has something to do with it," replied Mr. Manning. "It will be your last."

This time, Jesse could see Natalie's reaction.

"You realize we're invisible. We can't be seen or heard."

"I'm well aware. Remember what I did to your eye?"

Jesse touched his shiner and grimaced. How could he forget?

"Do you really want me out there right now, invisible, in my frame of mind?"

"No. Not really."

Jesse focused his attention on the conversation at hand.

"We are dropping the children's section," he told her. "I just don't have the time to have one. Our best sellers are for older age groups. With only three authors on our billet, I just don't think it's worth it."

"But I thought that I was-"

"There you are!" Nick said as entered the room. "What's going on? Dad? Are you doing what I think you're doing?"

"You mean you knew?" Natalie demanded.

"Well, you seem to be making this a night I'll never forget!" she spat at both of them.

Jesse could see that Natalie was losing it not only out there, but right before him. He needed to bring her out of wherever the hell she was.

"Natalie," he whispered. When her eyes met his, he knew exactly what he needed and wanted to do. He wanted to finish what he started with her in the stables. Ever so gently, he pulled her closer to him and kissed her.

***

The kiss was soft and gentle, but slowly grew intense. Every cliché Natalie she had ever heard played in her head as his lips moved against hers. His hands had cupped her cheeks and she felt her own gripping his shoulders tightly. For a moment, she swore she heard him groan as his hands moved from her face to her waist. Natalie's body was molding into his and she ran her fingers thorough his hair. He pulled her closer and she could feel his heartbeat against her own. The need for oxygen outweighed her desire to continue their kiss and she pulled away, but left her arms wrapped around his neck. Her eyes were still closed and she felt his forehead resting against hers. Their lips hovered around one another and she could smell the cologne off his skin.

"So I'm expected to be some socialite wife!" they heard her shout.

Her eyes snapped open and she jumped out of his arms. Instantly she felt the loss of his body heat.

"Dad, would you excuse us?" Nick said.

"No! It was his idea, I want to hear his answer!" Natalie heard her past self say.

"Natalie, I don't have to explain myself to you," Charles said. "My son can provide for you. This is a business decision."

"Sweetheart," Nick said as he interrupted his father. "You always talk about how much you miss training horses. I thought that you would prefer to do that."

As Natalie heard the conversation unfold again, she looked at Nick and how blasé he seemed. Here was the man she was going to marry, the man she was going to spend the rest of her life with, and he didn't really know her or what she wanted. She began to shake in anger.

"I-" Natalie began.

"Nick! Natalie!" called a female voice. "Everyone is looking for you!"

"Victoria, not now!" Natalie yelled.

"Victoria, did you find-" Natalie's father started, but stopped. "What's going on?"

"Oh nothing!" Natalie said. "My future husband and father-in-law have decided that I should be subjected to living life as a 1950s housewife!"

"Drama queen much?" said Victoria.

Having heard enough, Natalie ran out of the room with Jesse hot on her heels. She was feeling many things in that moment. Anger was definitely one of them. Pain was another. But then she also felt confusion and passion over what had just happened between her and Jesse in that closet. She was worried that he wanted to talk about what had just taken place, but the last thing she wanted was to talk about it with him. It wasn't the time. 'Time' she said and looked at the watch. There were 12 hours left.

"Don't say it," she breathed. "I don't want to talk about what happened in that room."

Natalie hoped that he got the message that she wasn't just referring to the scene that unfolded. His nod indicated that he knew what she meant and she was grateful.

"Natalie?"

She wanted to avoid him, but given their current situation, she knew that was impossible.

"Natalie?" he whispered this time. "I need you to see something."

Holding out his hand to her, Natalie tentatively placed her hand in his and waited. She looked away from him and tried her best to the fight the memory off where his hands had been just moments before.

"Take us to when your dress was ruined."

Closing her eyes, she did what he asked and let that memory take over her.

"Stand right here and tell me what you see."

Natalie opened her eyes and saw that they were in her bedroom in the Hamptons.

"Nat?"

"What is it, Tor?"

"I'm sorry about before."

"Don't worry about it."

"So, where's the dress?"

"I have told you before, you will see it on my wedding day!"

"Fine, but what if it's hideous or something. You need to have a second opinion."

"Why? I have no doubts about the dress!"

"Natalie, as your maid of honour, don't you think I should see it. I promise not to say anything."

Natalie watched herself head to the closet, pulling out the dress. Turning to Victoria, she could see that she was sitting on the bed swirling the glass of wine.

"Here it is," Natalie said to her sister. "I take it you approve?" Natalie asked.

"Yes! My God Natalie, it's gorgeous! Sweetheart bodice, a beautiful brocade design! Oh and I love the wine-coloured trim. So Christmassy!"

"Oh and there's a shawl!" Natalie said as she walked back into the closet.

Natalie watched her sister carefully, waiting for the moment to happen.

"See the shawl goes-

Then it happened. Natalie helplessly watched as Victoria jumped in the air, turning around, spilling the wine all over her dress.

"No!" Natalie shouted as the wine hit the dress.

Natalie stopped the scene and walked over to the dress. Sitting down on the floor, she picked up the train and played with the hem of the gown.

"She did it on purpose," she said.

Natalie felt Jesse sitting beside her, pulling a piece of the dress into his hands.

"You know something," she began. "I think I always knew. I just didn't want to believe it. Guess I was a naïve idiot."

Natalie avoided his gaze and stood up.

"I think we should go."

"What about your fight with Nick?" Jesse asked.

"Just come with me."

Clasping her hand in his, Jesse and Natalie drifted away once again.

Chapter 27:
The Truth

Jesse knew where he was the instant he smelled the burning candles. They were back at St. Patrick's Cathedral, but somehow, it seemed different. Natalie let go of his hand, heading toward a pew near the front.

"Why are we back at the Sanctuary?"

"You know," she said, sitting down in a pew at the front, "before this place became a Sanctuary to me, to us, it was the place where I was supposed to get married."

"Yes, I knew that," he said and seated himself next to her. "So why did you come here?"

Natalie sighed and looked at the Gothic architecture that surrounded them. "I came here the day before my wedding. Want to know why?"

Jesse nodded silently and waited for her answer.

"Guidance," she said. "I came here looking for answers. I wanted to know if getting married was really what I wanted. I figured coming here was a little more practical than talking to a horse."

"Did you get an answer?"

Natalie's look of longing at the altar bothered him.

"No. Then again, maybe dying was a sign."

Not knowing what to say, Jesse remained quiet. Her death had weighed heavily on him since he returned from Purgatory. His chat with Sofia and Redmond had cleared up a lot of things and while his theory on what happened to her had been confirmed by both Sofia and Redmond, he had nothing concrete. He heeded Sofia's advice and they went back to the beginning.

"The beginning," Jesse muttered. Shaking his head, he tried to wrap his mind around what Sofia had meant by that. He wasn't going back to 21 Club again because that proved to be a waste of time. He leaned back against the pew and crossed his arms. He processed everything up until that point from the moment they landed to now. 'Landed' he thought. Then it hit him.

"The beginning!"

Sofia said to go back to the beginning. They were doing it all wrong.

"I'm an idiot," he said under his breath and he swore he heard Natalie chuckle. He ignored her and tried to work out the problem in his head to see if it made sense. He closed his eyes and thought back. The day they went to 21 Club wasn't their beginning. They had wasted the majority of their day because of their stupidity. Jesse stood up fast and exited the pew. Realizing that he had forgotten Natalie, he went back and gently pulled her along.

"Jesse, where are we going?" she asked as he pulled her gently out of the cathedral. He led her out the door and ran up to the Sanctuary. Jesse sat Natalie on the bed and paced the room.

"Natalie, where did we begin?"

Natalie glared at Jesse.

"Jesse, we are not going back to 21 Club-"

"That's not where we started. Natalie, how much time is left?"

"Jesse you're not-"

"The time, Natalie. How much?"

Natalie hesitated, Jesse was determined to get his answer. He needed to know and he needed to know now. Maybe there was a chance after all.

"The countdown clock says 3 hours and 43 minutes. The time clock says 9:48 PM Eastern Standard Time and the Date Clock reads December 16, 2005."

Jesse paced the floor making Natalie extremely nervous with his erratic behavior.

"Jesse?"

Looking at Natalie, he stopped his pacing and kneeled down beside her.

"Natalie, remember when we first got here, you know after we jumped into the portal?" Jesse asked hoping that she would and was relieved when Natalie nodded her head.

"Remember you ran and asked the guy for the time?"

Again she nodded her head. So far, so good, Jesse thought. Now for the tough one.

"Natalie, do you remember what time the man said?"

"Yes." Nodding her head once more and Jesse looked at

her expectantly.

"12:12 AM, December 10th 2005. I remembered because I made a wish."

"A wish?" he asked.

"You know. When the numbers are the same, you make a wish and hope it comes true."

If he weren't so agitated by their current predicament, Jesse would have found the whole thing cute. However, there was something about the time that bothered him.

'What did Redmond say?' Jesse closed his eyes and focused on the Keeper's parting words. "'You will be going back to the exact moment in time where Sofia felt you would find your answers.'"

Jesse's eyes jerked open and he directed his attention toward Natalie.

"Redmond said that Sofia would send us back to the exact moment in time where we would find the answers."

"And?" Natalie asked.

"Think about it. Where were we when we landed?"

Natalie rolled her eyes. Jesse pleaded with his own, hoping that she would humour him a little while longer.

"44th Street and 5th. Hmm, actually, we were near the publishing house."

That's when he knew he had his answer. His proof. His way to show her the truth. The smell from before when they had gone to see Natalie's meeting with Chuckie. He had smelt it when they first landed. Sofia had sent them to a certain moment in time. He sent them to the beginning. He sent them to the place where Natalie's life changed.

"Son of a bitch!" Jesse yelled. "All this time and the answer was right there!"

"Would you calm down and please explain!"

"How much time?"

Natalie moaned in frustration.

"I just told you-

"I know what you told me, just tell me again!"

Natalie looked down at the watch.

"3 hours and 20-

'Damn' he thought. Time was still counting down too fast and they were so close.

"Now, what time did we get here?"

"12:12am! And?"

"The time Natalie, the time doesn't make sense! You asked the man what the time was after we had been walking for a few minutes! Now think, what time did we really land?"

Jesse could see her racking her brain with the math.

"12:09am! The bus that went by was the 12:09. I would know because I would catch it sometimes instead of taking a cab when I worked late."

Everything made sense now. The time was a factor. Redmond flat out told Natalie that 'Time Knows No Boundaries'. It wasn't just some clever phrase, it meant so much more. The only thing confusing him now was the fact that Redmond had forgotten to give them the watch before they left.

"Why did Redmond give you watch after we were sent back? Why not before?"

Her perplexed expression did little to ease him. He changed their appearances after they went through the vortex. He gave Jesse the book later too. Redmond had said that he would have done it sooner, but both he and Natalie had wasted time.

"Jesse!"

"Hang on a second!" he muttered as he whipped out the guide book.

Jesse flipped through the pages to Chapter 3.

"Idiot!" he groaned. Jesse only read what the watch did. He never read the full chapter.

"What's wrong?" Natalie asked.

"I never read the whole chapter. I read only the beginning of it. I only read the part when it said what it could do."

"Get there faster, Jesse!" she said.

"The watch was given to you at that time because we wasted time. It was a lesson. We didn't value what we had because of our arguing. The watch is a symbol."

"Symbol?"

"Yes and I think our Keeper did it on purpose. Think of the irony, Natalie. We landed right near your work. Which leads me to believe-"

"The answer is in that building," Natalie finished for him.

"Yes. Now think, where did Nick go?"

Jesse calmly waited for her to remember. He wasn't going to force her, not now at least.

"Nick wanted to see me because he hadn't for a few days."

"He got a phone call at 11:30pm. From his father. There were papers for a client that needed to be signed."

Jesse knew where this was leading. He knew where they had to go and he knew what they needed to do now.

"We need to go to the publishing house!" she said.

Linking their hands, they waited for the pull, but it never came.

"Why aren't we moving?" Natalie asked out loud.

"Natalie, it's not working because you weren't physically there! Remember? We can only go where you actually are."

"I know! Why would Redmond do this to us?"

Jesse didn't have an answer to that. It was clear that Redmond wanted them to succeed. The issue Jesse was struggling with was why Redmond and the Son hadn't told them this. The wheels were spinning in Jesse's head. He failed to notice that Natalie too was trying to figure out a plan.

"Jesse! Grab my hand!" she said.

Looking at her confusedly, Jesse didn't understand what she was trying to do. Before he could say anything, Natalie reached for him and they went back through all her memories. Landing as they did before, Jesse was on top of Natalie.

"If you say déjà vu, I am going to give you a matching black eye!"

Jesse smiled and got off her quickly. Lending her a hand, he picked her up.

"Where are we and what time is it?" he said as he took in his surroundings.

"My apartment. 12:09am"

Not giving him a moment to respond, Natalie grabbed something off the table by door and flew down the stairs hailing a cab. Jesse chased her while trying to catch his breath.

"Again with the running!"

"Why aren't any cabs coming. I'm yelling for them!"

Jesse laughed.

"What is so funny?"

"Natalie, the bracelets. We're still invisible."

Pulling off the bracelets, the medallion and locket re-emerged.

"Now try yelling for a cab."

Within seconds a cab pulled up.

"Natalie, we can't pay for this! We don't have-"

Natalie whipped out a one-hundred dollar bill and jumped in the cab.

"I swiped it from my wallet," she said. "Now let's go!"

Not wasting any time, Jesse hopped in.

"5th Avenue and 44th Street! Manning Publishing and hurry!"

The cabbie stepped on the gas, making his way through the city.

***

Fifteen minutes later, Jesse and Natalie stood in front of Manning Publishing.

"It's 12:22am, Jesse."

We're late!" Jesse said as he kicked the newspaper stand. "It's impossible. We can't be at your apartment and make it here in time. And we can't go back because you aren't physically here!"

How did anyone expect them to solve this if couldn't get there without the living Natalie being there?

"What about the book? There has to be something in there?"

Jesse reached for the book in his jacket and swore.

"Damn! I left it in the Sanctuary," he said. "I threw it on the bed after I found out about the watch!"

"Why can't you just say 'Templum' and take us there?" she asked.

"I can..." he started.

"But?"

"Every time I say it, a piece of your soul fades. It didn't count the first time because that was a freebie. That's why I had to rely on you to take us places. The only other time I said it was when you passed out after watching your death."

Jesse tried to think of their possibilities. They could go back and use the watch again, but they would be cutting it close.

"The Causidicus coin!" she shouted as she pulled it out of her pocket.

Crap, Antonio to the rescue, he thought glumly.

"What? Natalie, no! The 24 hour deal-"

"It's doesn't have to be that one!"

Jesse had completely forgotten about the coin and hated the idea that Antonio would have to come to their rescue, but at this point, they needed help.

"Fine."

Natalie closed her fist around the coin. "I Want to Make a Deal." Counting to five, Natalie opened her palm and the coin was gone.

"Hello, Natalie. Jesse."

Jesse and Natalie turned around to find Antonio standing there.

"We need to make a deal. I really hope you have one because-"

Antonio raised his hand in agreement.

"Since I caused you to lose some time, I am willing to make a deal. Tell me what the problem is."

Jesse was ready to rip into him about Redmond and the watch, but Natalie's pleading eyes told him to let it go.

"We can't make it into the building in time because I am not physically here. So-"

"You can't get here on time because the living you wasn't here that night," Antonio said as he pointed to Natalie. "You need to be here, but you can't. I think I understand your dilemma."

Natalie simply nodded her head.

"Natalie, other than your life, what would you give up? What is precious enough to you that you are willing to part with? Something that means more to you than anything?"

The look of contemplation on Natalie's face captivated Jesse. He could see the turmoil she was going through. She loved so many things. So many people. Her heart was purer than anything he had ever known. Holding his breath, Jesse waited to hear her answer.

"My books. My stories. They are precious to me. To see a child's face light up when they read my stories is what I would give up."

Seeing that Jesse was about to protest, Antonio intervened.

"Most people would say a house, a car, friends, family. Rarely would someone give up something that brings joy to others. Natalie, I won't take that from you."

"But-"

"The fact that you would give that up leads me to believe that you are honest about things you care about and I will give you what you need." Antonio stepped away from the pair. *"Tempus Confuto."*

The moment Antonio said those words. Everything stopped. Cars were frozen. People stood still. Life was paused.

"I don't get it?" said Jesse.

"Just wait. *Revetere,"* Antonio replied.

The scene unfolded before Jesse and Natalie. Cars were going backwards, people were going backwards.

"Look at the watch," Antonio said with a slight smile on his face.

Jesse and Natalie did and saw the time going backwards as well. The countdown clock remained the same, but the actual time was rewinding.

"Antonio..." she started, but when she looked up, he was gone.

When the watch reached 12:09am, everything went back to normal.

"We might just make it!" she smiled at him.

Although Jesse was happy, he felt like he had let her down. Realizing that now wasn't the time to sulk, he snapped to and looked at the entrance to the building.

"One question, how do we get in?"

Natalie pulled out her key card and smiled smugly at him.

"When I grabbed the money, I also swiped my key card from my wallet. I knew we would need it."

Amazed by her quick thinking, Jesse bowed down to her and smiled back.

"Your life is waiting for you."

Before Natalie could swipe the key card Jesse placed his hand on the door.

"Ahem," he said as he dangled his medallion in front of her.

"Right!" Pulling the locket out of her coat. They said the phrase like before. The bracelets were back on their wrists.

"Now, we can storm the castle."

She smiled and ran upstairs. She could feel her heart racing in anticipation. The answer was here. It had to be.

"Nick's here," Natalie whispered.

The beating in her heart slowed as she neared her fiancé. Just seeing him there put her at ease.

"Nick," Charles said as entered the room.

"Dad," he greeted in return.

"Sign the papers and you can go. I have a meeting here shortly. What you do on your own time is fine."

Jesse and Natalie watched the interaction between father and son quietly.

"Done. This could have waited until Monday."

"Yes, it could have, but your mother has some ridiculous notion that working during the week of your wedding is not an option."

"I guess that's the difference between men and women." Nick replied as he walked out the door.

To say that Natalie was confused would have been anything but an understatement. This was the moment that changed the course of her life? Her fiancé leaving her that night to sign papers only to return? Natalie was confused, to say the least, because she knew for a fact that he didn't come back to her that night. The only question on her mind at that moment was 'where did he go?'

"I don't get it..." Jesse whispered.

Finally they could agree on something.

"Where are you?" Charles asked aloud as he poured himself a scotch.

"Don't get your knickers in a twist." Victoria said as she walked in. "I'm here. Had to make sure Nick didn't see me."

"Never mind that!" Charles interrupted.

Natalie looked at the two of them and could not fathom why they were together.

"I think it's time we finished our talk from earlier," Charles started.

"Talk?" Jesse mouthed to Natalie.

Natalie shrugged her shoulders and listened to the conversation.

"Seems to me like we want the same thing."

"Natalie, gone." Victoria stated.

"I used to think that she was the best thing for my son,

but since she became a bestselling author, she has become nothing but a nuisance."

Natalie stood there in shock as Charles uttered those words.

"My sister had him dangling by his balls since day one. I never thought they'd end up together."

"Stupidity on your part."

"Don't remind me. I didn't think they'd hit it off so well!"

"Well congratulations! They're getting married!"

Natalie grabbed Jesse's hand. She could hear him moan in displeasure, but she didn't care.

"So, we're putting our plan into action." Plan? What plan? Looking over at Jesse, she could see the wheels spinning in his head.

"It's not going to be easy," Charles said.

"I know," Victoria said in agreement. "An accident. On her wedding day no less. We both know my sister and your son will never see it coming. In the end we all win. I mend your son's broken heart. You keep your son and we make money off Natalie's books. Rumour has it authors make more money dead than alive."

Natalie closed her eyes and shook her head while her body shook with rage. The voice in her head begged her to wake up. It told her to move, to think, to do something. Natalie felt tears streaming down her face. This couldn't be happening. Her little sister, the one she took care of, loved and protected, wanted her dead because she was jealous of her career, of Nick, of her life?

"I think the less you know the better," she replied. "Let's just say it will involve a certain dress."

Natalie's eyes widened in horror. She knew her sister ruined her dress on purpose. Natalie could feel her head pound and her chest tighten. How could they do this to her? How could they hurt her so much that they would want her dead?

"You're not going to tell me more?"

"Charles, trust me. The man I've hired is a pro. She won't see it coming."

"Well, this calls for a toast," Charles said as he raised his glass to his lips. "To getting everything we ever wanted."

The truth hit Natalie like the car that killed her. She watched with tears in her eyes as the two drank to her demise. She helplessly saw them exit the office and collapsed to floor. Within seconds, Natalie felt the warmth of Jesse's arms, cradling her like a parent would a child.

"Natalie," he said. "I am so sorry. So very sorry."

In a matter of minutes, the people she loved and trusted had taken away her dignity and her pride, because they didn't want to deal with her anymore. Natalie had lost more than her life. They had taken her innocence, her love, her everything.

"Everything," she whispered.

Chapter 28:
Aftermath

Jesse had been holding Natalie in his arms since Victoria and Charles left. She was crying freely now. He could feel her shaking and asking why repeatedly. He had a feeling it was them, given the convenience of the dress being ruined and everything that had led up to that point. He was in shock that Nick had not been involved and for Natalie's sake, he was glad that he wasn't a part of it. He had been wrong about Nick and despised it.

Deciding that he needed to do something soon, he pulled himself away from Natalie and gently lifted her head so that his eyes could meet hers. What he saw worried him. She was detached from herself and he sure as hell wasn't going to allow them to get away with this.

"Natalie?" he whispered. "Come on, Princess, we need to stop them. We can't let them win!"

The hurt look in Natalie's eyes broke his heart. He wanted to go after them and hurt them as they had hurt her. "You knew didn't you?" she said barely above a whisper. "That's what you needed to show me. It's what you needed to prove."

Jesse winced as he heard the accusation in her words.

"That's exactly what I said to Sofia when I figured it out." Jesse answered and turned away from her. He closed his eyes and found the courage and the words to tell Natalie about what had happened while he was up in Purgatory and the mind blowing conversation he had had with Sofia.

A conversation that changed everything.

***

"Son of a bitch," he said and stared hard at Sofia. "Please tell me it's not that easy! It can't be," he said as he replayed Natalie's death in his head, something didn't add up. "If she had died when the car hit her, she wouldn't have gone to Purgatory. She would have been like me and given a second chance, or she would be tucked away safely behind the pearly gates. From what I know, Purgatory is for people who have unfinished business. At least I think that's what it means."

Jesse looked closely at Sofia. The expression on her face was palpable. A grim look of remorse appeared and for the first time, she was the one to look away from him.

"Natalie's death," he paused and watched as Sofia avoided his gaze. "It wasn't an accident was it? I mean, the only other option would be that her death was intentional."

It finally dawned on Jesse what had actually happened to Natalie. They had watched her death multiple times from every possible angle and yet, they overlooked one aspect. How it actually happened.

"Her life was taken away from her on purpose! She was murdered! That's it, isn't it? Someone wanted her gone and out of the way. But why?"

Jesse looked at Sofia hoping for some kind of answer, a sign, anything that would prove his theory. He needed to know the truth or else the same thing would happen to her again.

"Redmond knew didn't he?" he accused. Sofia's sombre look was telling and Jesse was livid. Both of them had known the truth all along. Of course they did. They were the powers that be. The ones who got to play 'God' with their lives. He was angry at them and he was even angrier for Natalie. He was now in an impossible position because they knew that he would have to be the one to tell her.

"So what do I do now? How do I explain to her that 'Hey, Natalie, someone tried to kill you, oh and by the way, they succeeded!' without her thinking that I am not joking? Not to mention that Redmond and Sofia knew about it!"

Jesse turned away from her in disgust. Running his fingers through his hair, he sighed. He was hating his long brown locks with a passion.

"Natalie's death breaks my heart," Sofia said. "Especially because someone else took her life away from her. You look at us as if we're monsters and we're not. Redmond and I could not say anything to her because in doing so we take away her chance of learning the truth on her own. When she learns what happened to her, things will be different. The decisions she makes will be different."

Jesse heard remorse in her voice and sat down on their chair once more.

"She won't believe me," he said as his voice cracked. "She just won't."

***

After he finished telling her his story, and conveniently leaving out the part where he admitted that he was in love with her, he turned back to face her and saw that she was rooted in the same spot.

"I wanted to tell you," he said. "I didn't know how. Natalie-"

"I'm better off dead," she interrupted.

Jesse heard her admission and was stunned. She was letting them win and he wasn't going to let her let them win. Jesse rushed toward her and placed his hands on her shoulders. He took note of her defeated form and decided it was time to knock some sense into her.

"We have spent six days, twenty-two hours and fifty-six minutes fighting for this! We fought each other, we fought Redmond and his crew. Well, at least I did!"

Natalie shrunk back from him and he realized that he was scaring her.

"Natalie, we know the truth," he said in a softer tone. "We know what happened. This is what you wanted."

"This is not what I wanted," she spoke.

Natalie shrugged his arms off her and sat down on the couch.

"Not what you wanted?" Jesse asked. "Where's the girl I met in Purgatory?"

"She's dead. You heard them. Plotting. Laughing. Drinking to my demise because they can't stand me or my accomplishments."

Jesse kneeled down on the floor and looked up at her. He tenderly grasped her hands in his.

"No, she's not," he said. "She's right here."

Natalie ripped her hands away from him and stood up,

nearly knocking Jesse over.

"She's gone!" she admitted. "They killed her!"

"So that's it. You're going to let them win? You're going to let them make you suffer while they go about living their lives? You can't-"

"Yes, I can! Why would I go back to a place where I'm hated? Why would I want to live knowing that they want me dead? I would have to look over my shoulder every day for the rest of my life. Jesse, that's no way to live."

Jesse got off the floor and shook his head in disappointment, he walked to the bookshelf and picked up one of Natalie's books. He opened the book gently and read the dedication.

"'To my mom and dad. Thank you for believing in me and letting me follow my dreams. This book is for you.'"

Jesse turned around and faced her. She was wiping the tears from her eyes and shaking her head.

"I can't let you do this," he said and threw the book across the room. "I can't let you lose."

"Too late for that."

Jesse walked over to her and shook his head.

"Could you put your parents through that again? The friends you left? The children who loved your stories?" He paused and turned away from her. "Could you do it to Nick?" he whispered. "Could you leave him again? But more importantly Natalie, could you do it to yourself? I mean, what was the point of using the Causidicus coin if you are not even going to do anything about it in the end. Knowing that you were so close, but chose to die because others didn't want you to live." Jesse paused and closed the distance between them. "Why should you suffer and let them live? If it were me..." he stopped.

"If it were you?" she said as she held her breath.

"If it were me, I would take that second chance and do something with it. I know what it's like to find out that the people you loved and trusted with your whole heart could take your life away from you like that. It may not be the same, but I know what it's like to be betrayed. I also know one other thing. To wait as long as you did for this chance and to not take it, well, it would be a waste. Think of all the people in Purgatory right now. At this moment they are waiting for their chance and some, some might not even come close," he said. "Don't take away the one thing you were lucky enough to get back. You get the dream wedding like you were supposed to have to the man that you love with all your heart."

Jesse looked at Natalie and could feel nothing but pain. He could feel his heart breaking. He was going to lose her and there was nothing he could do about it.

"You have to live the life you were meant to live."

As Jesse uttered those words, he knew that the decision was up to her. That his life was in her hands and there wasn't anything he could do for her anymore.

***

As Natalie listened to Jesse plead his case, she found herself feeling sorry for him. He was trying to help her and she could only think about the people who wronged her. Then she thought about Nick. It was obvious to her that Jesse thought he was somehow involved and for a moment, she thought so too. The look on his face spoke volumes and all she wanted was for the pain to stop.

"My Lord, The Jury of Twelve, Ms. Parker is asking for a second chance. I feel that she should not be permitted a second chance based on the fact that she has not been dead that long and that she has done nothing to prove to the courts why she should be given a second chance for redemption. As far as I am concerned, her death was legitimate. She belongs here and only here."

Natalie shook her head as Edward's voice resonated in her head. She didn't belong on her earth. She belonged in Purgatory, just as The Defender had said.

"Well, this calls for a toast. To Natalie, the bride she'll never become and to you Victoria, the daughter I always wanted,"

Natalie could then see Jesse wearing a black suit standing by her grave. She could see him placing a red rose on her coffin, shaking his head as he did. Then she heard his words resonate in her ears. She then saw Nick. He stood there with no emotion on his face. He looked torn and relieved at the same time.

"You have to live the life you were meant to live."

'What did that even mean?' she said to herself and repeated Jesse's words in her head. She was still trying to process everything that she had just witnessed. The venom in her sister's words and the pleasure that both Victoria and Charles had in wanting her gone made her sick to her stomach. How could her sister do this to her? They were close as sisters could be growing up and now her sister wanted her dead? What was the point? Her sister had always gotten what she wanted and now she had everything and then some. Natalie died because her sister had been jealous of her success, her fiancé, and life.

At that moment, she thought of every battle she and her sister had ever had. As the older sister she caved in and let her have her way. Apparently Natalie gone and out of the way was another win for her sister. If Victoria thought that she could play God with her life, her little sister was in for a rude awakening.

"Not this time!"

Jesse ran to her side immediately. Reaching out to him, Natalie grabbed him by the lapels and looked into his eyes. She ripped off her bracelet and tore Jesse's off too.

"They can't win," she declared. "She's not going to win this time!"

Wiping her eyes, Natalie took in a deep breath. She looked down at the watch and could see that they had less than one hour.

"Jesse, we have thirty minutes left. What do we need to do?"

***

"What do we need to do?" Jesse echoed. He reached for the Protector's book and remembered it wasn't there.

"I don't know. I don't have the book. Remember? I left it in the Sanctuary," He held his medallion in his hand.

"What?" she replied. "Help me!"

"Where's your locket?"

"There," she replied and pointed to the floor by the couch. He swiped it and handed it to her.

"Okay. It's okay. We'll just go back," he said, running for the door. "We'll grab a cab and go back!"

"Jesse! I only grabbed a hundred and paid it all to the cabbie!"

Jesse sighed and punched the door. All they needed to do was get to the Sanctuary. Running back over to Natalie, Jesse lifted her wrist and looked at the watch. Twenty-five minutes were staring him in the face. Time was going faster because of the bracelets. They needed to move fast.

"I guess we're going to have to run for it!" Jesse said and grabbed her hand in his.

"Jesse! It's twelve blocks! The snow is piled on the sidewalks and streets. It's cold and this is New York City! There are people everywhere! We won't-"

"Don't say we won't make it! Come on! Just run!"

Running down the stairs, Jesse and Natalie burst through the door ignoring the alarms going off. Hand in hand, they ran together, as fast as they could.

Jesse could feel his breathing becoming labored, but he ignored it. He ignored the pain beginning to build in his legs and focused his eyes on the road.

***

Leading them around hundreds people wandering about the streets of New York, Jesse began to push himself faster. Trudging through the snow and taking various shortcuts, Jesse turned to Natalie.

"Time!"

"Fifteen minutes!"

In the distance, Jesse could see the Cathedral and saw his motivation.

"We're almost there!" he yelled.

"I see it!" she answered back.

Maneuvering their way through the cars, Jesse reached the steps of the Cathedral. Natalie was seconds behind as they burst through the doors. Making a hard right, they made their way through the passage way and up the stairs leading to the door of the Sanctuary.

Jesse kicked the door open, collapsing on the floor in the process. His breathing was labored, but he was doing everything in his power to fight it off. Rising to his feet, Jesse found the book by the foot of the bed. Picking it up, he turned to see where Natalie was and found her leaning against the door breathing heavily.

"Got it," he told Natalie between breaths.

Natalie nodded and made her way to the bed.

"We have ten minutes," she said. "The clock is counting down even faster!"

Jesse flipped through the book, going to the last chapter. Natalie watched him helplessly hoping that he would find the answer.

"Got it! Chapter 20: A Life Renewed. Natalie, this is it!"

Natalie got up and made her way to Jesse.

"Well?"

"You have found your answers, you have followed the clues. Now, it is time to speak the truth. You began your journey long ago. It is time to live your life once more. Before this can begin, say these words aloud, your Protector is the one who can save you now."

Jesse looked at her expectantly and waited. This was up to her, she had to decide. All she needed to do was say the words.

Natalie nodded her head.

"Find the truth, Live the Life," said Jesse. "Invenit Veritas, Ago Vita. Seriously, sounds way better in Latin," he laughed. "Natalie, all you have to do is say those words."

Her hesitation worried him. That's when Jesse saw it. The fear, the worry, the doubt. Jesse gently grabbed her shoulders and stared into her mismatched eyes.

"You have to live the life you were meant to live."

Jesse swore he saw Natalie smile. Before he could say more, she held her fingers to his lips.

"Jesse, I need to do something."

"Now?" Jesse asked.

"Jesse, I really need to do this."

Sighing, Jesse waited for her to make a move.

"Give me your hands," she said.

Jesse raised his eyebrow at her. He hesitated for a moment and obliged her request. The familiar tug wrapped around them as they gracefully landed on a street corner.

Jesse looked around and waited.

"Here it goes."

He instantly knew where he was and started to panic.

"Natalie, please don't-"

Her soft hands covered his mouth.

"Just watch," she uttered.

Jesse did as he was instructed. He watched Natalie walk out of the dry cleaners one last time. Closing his eyes, he waited for the familiar sound of metal to make contact with flesh.

"*Invenit Veritas, Ago Vita!*"

Then everything went black.

Chapter 29:

Remember or Forget

Natalie could feel her body being pulled apart in every direction. Her head began to spin out of control, her vision was blurred by her own memories, and her heart pounded hard in her chest. She could hear Jesse yelling beside her, but could not make out the words. How was it possible to feel this much pain, to hurt this much, yet feel so alive at the same time? She felt like a child on a roller coaster. Unsure of the twists and turns that lay ahead, she let the pain take over. Was it like this last time? When she died, she saw grey. There was no life, no happiness, just loneliness and longing.

"Jesse!" she screamed.

Her cry fell on deaf ears. She didn't know what was happening to her. She and Jesse had figured it out. They knew what had happened to her. So why was she falling to the beyond? Hadn't she suffered enough?

"Natalie."

The voice was soft, soothing, and familiar.

"Who are you? And where am I?" she asked.

"I think we both know who I am, Natalie."

The voice captivated her attention as she felt a hand rest on her shoulder. Natalie turned on her heel to face the voice comforting her very soul.

"Hello, Natalie."

Shock rocked her core.

"Where are my manners? Allow me to introduce myself. I'm Death."

Death? The figure before her was Death? Of all things she had been told about Death, she never imagined this.

"But you look-"

"Like your grandfather?" Death answered. "Well, for you, this is what I look like. I am a comfort to you when I look like this."

Death as a comfort? Natalie knew what Death was and the person before her wasn't Death. It was her gramps. It was the man who taught her to ride a horse. The man who taught her about books, horseback riding and life. Why was Death embodying the man who understood her?

"I..." Natalie began but could not speak. She had experienced so much in the last few days, especially the final hours, and now she was with the person who put her through hell.

"I'm here to congratulate you, but now is not the time to get into all that. Now's the time for a decision to be made."

Natalie stared at Death with anger in her eyes.

"Where's Jesse?" she demanded.

The look Death gave her had been provoking. She desperately want to wrap her hands around his neck, taking away his life, just as he had taken hers.

"Alas, young Mr. Knight is currently with Redmond," he replied and produced a glass of water and handed it to her. "I believe they have an agreement that needed to be worked out. As for you." He paused, sighing in hesitation. "You have to deal with me."

"Not without him," she answered and pushed the glass of water away from him.

"This isn't about him," said Death. "It never has been. When he made it about him, it angered you. I'm the only one who can help you now. You have three choices, Natalie, and you only get this chance just once. Beyond that, the decision becomes final."

Natalie sat down on a chair, massaging her temples to ease the headache that was starting to formulate. Looking up, she took in her surroundings. She was in a library. One that resembled her grandfather's. The smell of old books and mahogany shelves filled her senses. The warmth of the fire taunted her as the embers from the flames flickered wildly. Maybe she was in hell. Beside her, resting on the table, she found a copy of Romeo and Juliet. Picking up the book she skimmed through the pages looking for something.

"'Come what sorrow can, it cannot countervail the exchange of joy that one short minute gives me in her sight. Do thou but close our hands with holy words, then love-devouring death do what he dare.'" Out of all of Shakespeare's quotes, that one always left her feeling haunted.

"I always come off looking like the villain," Death said. "Never mind. Natalie, you have little time here. I'm giving you three..."

"Jesse and I figured it out. We know how I died-"

"Yes, you did. Now is the time to make a decision. Would you at least hear me out?"

Natalie placed the book back and nodded.

"Try not to interrupt," he said while giving her a stern look. "Your first option is death-"

"But..."

Death gave Natalie a glare and resumed his speech.

"You can choose death and be here. At this moment, you're in your own version of paradise. Your own haven, your own world and can dream it up any way you like."

Choose death and remain here for eternity? She thought about that possibility carefully. It was an ideal place to be. Surrounded by her books and knowing that she would be safe and sound. She would be able to rest in peace to some extent, but she would always know that her sister would get to walk around freely and live. Maybe this would be her resting place one day in the future, but not today.

"Option two?" Natalie inquired.

"Option two, you go back and live your life."

Natalie waited for option three. She wasn't entirely sure what else she could possibly choose from. The choice was to live or to die and for Natalie, she wanted nothing more than to live again.

"Option three, Ms. Parker, is that you go back and really live your life."

"What's the-" Natalie began.

"Difference?" Death answered.

"Yes."

"Remembering. Forgetting," Death said.

"Remembering? Forgetting?" Natalie repeated.

"Sounds more difficult than it really is, however, that's life. Remembering would mean knowing what your sister and future father-in-law did to you. It would mean remembering all of this. Everything."

Natalie didn't know if she was hearing things. To remember her time in Purgatory and everything that preceded would be unbearable. Knowing that she would be surrounded by the very people who wanted her dead meant that she accepted it and at the moment, she preferred blissful ignorance over the harsh reality.

"Forgetting means that your time here never happened. That you could walk down that aisle and marry Nick. You'd be protected, of course, and live a long and happy life with your husband. It would also mean that you'd never know about this world or -"

"Jesse," she finished. "I would never know about Jesse."

Natalie became aware of the fact that blissful ignorance came at a cost. Could she really forget that two people she trusted wanted her dead? Could she just go back and live her life the way it should have been? The life she had wanted to live with Nick? Could she forget Jesse? From the moment she got her chance, she wanted to go back to way things were and up until a couple of hours ago, a part of her she still wanted that. Yet now, knowing the truth, she didn't know if she wanted to forget. Natalie didn't even know if she could.

"You're in love with him, aren't you?" Death asked.

"Of course I love Nick."

"That's not what I asked you and I know that you are far more intelligent than that. You know exactly to whom I am referring."

The sound of Natalie's heart beat echoed.

"You're in love with him?" Death repeated.

"I refuse to answer that!" she stated and walked over to one of the bookcases.

"Why? Because it's true? Because it would mean that Nick isn't your happily ever after? Jesse Knight is a lot of things and I know one thing for certain about him." Death paused and gently placed his hands on her shoulders and turned her around to face him. "He's in love with you too and you know it."

Shrugging his hands off, Natalie sat back down and reached for the copy of Romeo and Juliet once more.

"If he's in love with me, then why did he tell me to fight for my life and be with Nick?"

"What was he going to say, Natalie? 'Pick me? I'm the one you're supposed to be with.' Jesse has lived his life hiding behind his emotions. He's been hurt and alone. He feels unworthy of love and more so unworthy of your love."

Natalie blinked back the tears that were threatening to fall. This wasn't supposed to happen. She was meant to get back what she lost and she had no idea what that was any-more.

"How do I know what I am supposed to choose?" Natalie said, bewildered by her choices.

"I can't tell you that. I guess that's why people sometimes choose death. As of now Natalie, you have sixty seconds to choose. Sixty seconds and counting. If I were you, I'd think fast. When you decide, open that door over there. It will take you to wherever it is you've decided to go."

Death gently grabbed her hand and pulled her up off the chair. He guided her to the door and stood beside her.

"You ask me if I am in love with Jesse and proceed to tell me that he is in love with me and you're telling me that I have to make my decision now. What if I don't decide?"

Death hesitated. "If you don't decide, then you go back to Purgatory and become a lost soul. After everything you've been through to get here, going back would be a waste. Thirty seconds, Natalie."

Natalie's heart began to race. She didn't have the answer. She didn't know what to choose. Natalie wished she still had the Causidicus coin in her pocket. How she wanted another 24 hours!

"You have to live the life you were meant to live."

Natalie heard Jesse's voice once more. In her head she knew what she had to do. Her hands trembled as she reached the handle of the doors. Take a deep breath, Natalie opened them and met her destiny.

***

"Natalie!" Jesse screamed as he landed roughly on the floor. Opening his eyes, Jesse was greeted by bright white lights for the second time in seven days.

"I'm already dead!" he yelled.

"True, for now anyways," came a voice.

"Redmond?"

"Yes."

Jesse was in obvious pain. Despite the rough landing, he could feel his eyes burning and had had enough.

"Open your eyes," Redmond said.

Jesse slowly lifted his lids, letting his pupils return to normal.

"Where am I? No, I got a better one. Where's Natalie? Last thing I remember we went back to where she was hit by the car. I waited for the hit, but she yelled and I... Redmond, where is she?"

"She's fine."

"She's fine?" he confirmed. Redmond nodded in agreement.

"Jesse, you helped her. You solved her problem. I believe that was your one and only intention when all this began. You did your job and now it is time for me to honour our agreement."

Jesse stood there stunned. Words could not describe how he was feeling. At first he wanted to get his life back, but now, there was so much more to it. He needed, no, he wanted to see her. To see that she was okay and safe.

"Redmond, that's a load of crap! I know it and you know it."

"Jesse, you asked me to make sure that everything would be okay. That I would make things right and I have. You asked me if I was a man of my word and I am."

"A man of your word? Really? Then Mr. Man of Your Word, tell me what the hell happened."

"Sofia and I couldn't have made it easier on the two of you if we tried. The answer was there the whole time. Jesse, you and Natalie didn't listen to a word I said. "

Jesse lowered his head in defeat. Redmond was right and they both knew it. The man had literally handed him the answer on a silver plate and Jesse failed to pick up on it.

"When we last spoke, you knew that her death was in fact intentional. You needed to prove it and you did."

"And what if I didn't? Did you ever think about that?"

He couldn't help but think of what could have happened to her or to him if he hadn't made that realization when he did.

"I never set a Protector up for failure. You did a good job Jesse. You and Natalie grew up and gained perspective. Now, I'm going to hold up my end of the bargain and give you your life back..."

Jesse stared bleakly at the ground. Did he want his life

back? He thought. He shook his head. Of course he did, but what life was he going back to?

"That is what you want," Redmond asked. "Isn't it?"

Jesse looked up and sighed. He despised Redmond right now, but he was his only chance. If he were really honest with himself, he wasn't entirely sure of what he wanted. In the seven days that he had spent with one Natalie Parker, he changed. Looking back on his life, Jesse saw how pathetic he had become. He was everything Natalie had said and more. Now, he didn't think he could go back to a life that seemed so empty, so lonely, and so incomplete.

"I don't know anymore."

Jesse thought about it carefully. He wasn't the right person for this job. He wasn't a Protector. Everyone could see that, including Natalie.

"Send me back, Redmond. All of this will just have to a memory for me."

"Actually, you can't remember it at all," Redmond replied.

Jesse's head snapped up.

"What do you mean?"

"Jesse, I can't send you back to earth with all this knowledge about this world. It's not that we don't trust you. It's a matter of liability and your sanity."

Trust, liability and sanity. Jesse knew that he should be offended, but he didn't blame Redmond for it. It wasn't fair. He understood that it was his way of protecting a world from people who weren't part of it, but he was getting used to the idea. Not remembering all this felt like a piece of him would be gone and for some reason, he'd know that a part of him would be missing. The part that linked him to her.

Natalie. Could he really forget her? Could he forget helping her and everything that happened during the course of the seven days together? She would be going back to her life and he would be going back to his.

"Jesse. You have two choices."

"Redmond, if it's between life and death, you know which one I will choose."

"How about the choice between remembering and forgetting?" Redmond asked.

"I thought you said I was a liability," Jesse said.

"You are. But not if you're a Protector."

"I thought you said that that there was never a catch?"

Redmond laughed.

"It isn't a catch. I am a man of my word. Forgetting means living the life you were living before. Remembering means that you can have your life and the memories of your time with Natalie too. But only if you become a Protector. It's still your choice, Jesse. I am not going to force your hand."

Jesse became flustered by the options Redmond had presented him with. He could go back to his life and forget all this, forget everything, forget her or he could remember.

"What if she chooses him?"

"Him? You mean Nick?"

"Yes, Nick. I wanted so badly to believe he was behind this and I was wrong. He's the one for her and I now know that forgetting will make the pain go away."

"Jesse Knight giving into defeat? I don't believe it. You are in love with her and you're scared that she won't feel the same way."

The ground around him shook and a vortex opened before him. The deafening sound hit him in waves.

"What's happening?" Jesse shouted.

Redmond walked closer to him. The noise around them raged on as Jesse felt Redmond's hand touch his shoulder. Jesse focused his attention to Redmond and waited.

"You have sixty seconds. Sixty seconds to decide your fate. Sixty seconds to take a chance. Your time is almost up and you must decide."

"Just like that?"

"Just like that," Redmond repeated.

As Redmond walked away, Jesse felt more lost than ever.

"You have to live the life you were meant to live," Redmond said as he walked out of the room.

A wave of emotions hit Jesse all at once. Redmond had used the same words Jesse had said to Natalie. Even now that phrase was coming back to bite him in the ass.

"Thirty seconds."

A voice echoed into the room and Jesse knew he didn't have much time left. Two choices. Forgetting or Remembering. He didn't know what he wanted in life, much less what he needed.

"Natalie," he whispered.

Looking into the vortex, Jesse saw the images change. He was with Natalie. If he had made the choice to forget, he would never know her. Never be the person he believed he could be. He'd live as he did before. If he remembered, his life would change and the consequences of his choice would impact others. Their lives would be in his hands, just like Natalie's was. They would rely on him, trust him, and need him. But what did he need?

"Natalie."

"Ten, nine, eight..."

"You have to live the life you were meant to live," Jesse heard his own voice echo and he knew.

"Five, four, three..."

Taking a deep breath, Jesse jumped.

***

A young man in the distance watched a woman tightly clutch her wedding dress in her hands as she walked out of the dry cleaners. He could tell that she was carefully inspecting it to ensure that everything was perfect. He watched as she headed in the direction of a white limousine parked across the street. He stared in awe of her and saw her answer her ringing cell phone.

"Hello?" she said.

The man followed her and tried to listen to the conversation.

"Natalie, where are you?" he heard.

"I picked up the dress, I'm on my way."

Stepping onto the street, he watched as she made her way over to the limo. Out of the corner of his eye, he saw a car losing control heading right for her.

Without hesitation, the man ran across the street and pushed her out of the way. She screamed loudly in his ear as his body and hers hit the ground hard. He cradled her head between his chest and hands. Opening his eyes, he checked to see if she was okay. Her eyes remained shut and he could see that her breathing had become ragged.

"Excuse me," she said as she tried to catch her breath.

He watched as her eyes fluttered open and sighed when

he saw that she was indeed okay.

"Are you alright?" he asked.

Concerned blue eyes met confused brown ones.

"Hey, you two!" a voice shouted out. "Are you okay?"

Breaking their gaze from each other, the pair of eyes landed on a man on the sidewalk. They nodded their heads in agreement. The man turned his head to look at the car and could hear the sound of screeching tires echo as the car drove off. When his eyes locked on hers once more, hazel eyes met one green eye and one blue eye.

"You know. I feel like we have done this before. Kind of like-"

"Déjà vu?" she finished.

He smiled at her.

"Jesse," Natalie whispered and raised her hand to his face.

"Hi," he whispered back. "You remember me?" he smiled.

Jesse was having a hard time believing this was real. Yet, there she was in his arms, safe and protected and smiling back at him. Remembering was the right choice. Becoming a Protector was an even better one. There was a lot more that they would have to deal with, but with Natalie, he had a feeling that they could do it, as long as they were together.

Unable to resist her any longer, Jesse pulled Natalie closer and kissed her.

The familiar warmth and taste of her lips made his heart soar. Breaking the kiss, he groaned at the loss of contact. He rolled off her and stood up. Offering her his hand, he gently helped her up off the cold road.

"I think we better go," he said as he tucked a strand of her hair behind her ear.

"Me too."

Hand in hand, they walked down the street ignoring the people staring at them.

"Wait!" she said, turning him around to face her. "There's one thing I need to know."

Jesse gave Natalie a quizzical look and waited.

"What deal did you make with Redmond?"

Out of all the questions, she had to ask that one. He nervously ran his fingers through his hair and wished it was hers running through his hair instead.

"The deal was that if I helped you, I would get back to my old life. If I succeeded, I wouldn't have to become a Protector."

Before Natalie could protest, he took her hands in his.

"When I was up there staring into the vortex, Redmond gave me two options. Live my life as before or become a Protector."

"But if you didn't want to be one-"

"When living my old life meant that I couldn't remember you, I knew what I wanted. To live the life I was meant to live and that meant being a Protector so that I could be with you," Jesse paused. "Wow, that sounded corny."

"Not as corny as you think," Natalie said.

Jesse looked at her expectantly.

"I was given similar options, only Death gave me three choices. He offered me death. Which I didn't choose. To go back and live my life or to go back and really live my life."

Jesse was definitely confused.

"What, pray tell, is the difference between the second option and the third?"

Natalie smiled and gently wiped the cut on his face. It would scar and he had no doubt that it would look like exactly like the one he had before.

"That's going to scar," she affirmed.

"It's okay. Rumour has it chicks dig scars."

Natalie swatted at him, but he grabbed her hand and smiled.

"The difference, Natalie. What's the difference?"

"Right. One of those options meant that I wouldn't remember you and I don't think I could have ignored the fact that people wanted me dead," she told him.

"So, you chose to remember me?" Jesse asked.

"Looks like you did the same," she answered back.

"I chose to become a Protector."

"Yeah, you did. Mine."

Jesse grinned and took her hand in his once more. As they walked toward the limo, Jesse stopped in his tracks.

"Wait."

Natalie's look of confusion matched his own.

"What about Nick? Natalie, I can't break you two up. I know that I thought he was behind this, but he-" Natalie placed her fingers to his lips.

"I know. He wasn't ready to marry me and he still isn't. I don't love him like I..." she stopped.

"Like I?" he prodded

"Like I love you."

Jesse looked at her and tried to process what she had just said. It was one thing to hope that she felt that way about him. It was completely different to hear her say those words to him. He saw panic on her face and knew that he needed to reassure her.

"I love you too," he said and pulled her to him. "So much."

Jesse saw tears starting to stream down her face. She launched herself into his waiting arms and held onto him tightly. Jesse gently pressed his lips to her forehead and sighed. While this moment was amazing, he knew that they had to face reality.

"I think it's time we crash my wedding and let everyone know that I am alive," she said as she placed a kiss on his cheek. "I think a few of them will be disappointed."

After everything that had happened to her, to him, to them. Turning to her once more, Jesse lifted her chin so that their eyes would meet.

"Don't worry," said Jesse, "I'm right here." Natalie smiled.

Hand in hand they walked over to the limo and drove off. Natalie's wedding dress rested on the side of the road, ripped apart at the seams.

***

In the distance, a tall, dark figure watched carefully as the pair drove off. "Enjoy your happiness. For now."

Making his way to the dress, he reached for it and held it delicately in his hands, he looked up and watched as the limo rounded the corner. Shaking his head, he smiled, and left, taking the dress with him.

About the Author

Patricia Bandurka was born and raised in Mississauga, Ontario. She is a graduate from the University of Guelph-Humber where she earned a degree in Media Studies from the University of Guelph and a diploma in Public Relations from Humber College. She recently graduated from George Brown's post-graduate Sport & Event Marketing program. She is currently working at the Dixie Curling Club in Mississauga as the Curling Club Coordinator and has a passionate love for the game. This is her first novel and she is looking forward to continuing the next book in the series.

She would like to acknowledge the following people:

This book was an eight year process with countless revisions, edits, and above all else - commitment. First, I would like to give a special mention and thanks to Jody Aberdeen. I seriously would not have been able to complete this book without you. You have no idea how lucky I was to have been introduced to you and am quite appreciative of your time and efforts for making this crazy dream a reality. Though it took months before we got to sit down and meet, I am thankful that you took the time to read The Protector and made this book publishable. You know what I am talking about!

I would also like to extend a big thank you to John Sliz. Because of you, I get to hold this book in my hands and share it with everyone. I appreciate the time you put into this and lending an ear when I needed to vent my frustrations with the publishing process. You made it so much easier!

Next, I want to thank my 9th and 12th grade teacher Ms. Daniels. You gave me the chance to appreciate the English language and not take it for granted. Without question, my paper on tragic heroes was the inspiration for the character of Jesse Knight. But the real reason for this acknowledgement is to say that this is my way of trying to disturb the universe, I hope you will consider this a decent start.

This book would not be completed without a few other people. To Jennifer Boots, Taryn McElheran-Crowther, Matthew Lunardo, Laura Sliz, and Cassandra Chin. Thanks for taking the time to read this and giving me your honest opinions about the world I have created. You have no idea how much your reviews meant to me.

To Marisa Baratta, my fellow writer and one of my best friends. Only you know what it was like for me to write this. I wish you luck with your book and want you to know that I am grateful and thankful for you and our friendship.

I want to thank my family and friends. Your support and encouragement has made this possible. It's now something I am not just talking about anymore. It actually exists.

Dad, thank you for telling me that if I can speak English, then I can write it. Those words resonate with me to this day. I made sure that the vortex was quite obvious, so you can't miss it this time.

And finally, to my sister Stephanie, without you, there is no book. You were and are the reason this story exists. It's plain and simple. I will never forget that December day in 2006 and I am grateful that you are my sister because I could not have asked for a better one. To be honest, I can't imagine a world where you don't exist and never want to.

I hope you enjoy the world that I have imagined, but I've only just begun.

Here's to the next one!